Praise for *The Silent*

**WINNER OF THE BLOOD
CRIME DEBUT PRIZE**

'This murder mystery makes for compelling reading . . .
Cuthbert himself is a finely conceived and drawn character'
Allan Massie, *The Scotsman*

'The first in Allan Gaw's Dr Jack Cuthbert mysteries . . .
has a gritty historical edge'
Rosemary Goring, *The Herald*

'Heartbreaking and harrowing in equal measure.
Dr Jack Cuthbert is a brilliant, damaged genius you'll
want to follow to hell and back'
Pauline McLean, BBC Arts Correspondent

'The central character perfectly expresses the damage of both
the period and his environment, and the author's pathology
background was skilfully deployed'
Tariq Ashkanani

'Deliciously dark, vividly visceral, heartbreakingly harrowing'
Sharon Bairden

ONLINE REVIEWS

'There's a sense of doom, there's a complex and damaged
main character . . . vivid and well researched life of LGBT
people and the medical procedures'
Scrapping & Playing

'I couldn't put it down . . . Jack is a wonderful character'
Lyndas_bookreviews

'Excellently paced and full of tension'
BooksbyBindu.com

A Note on the Author

Allan Gaw studied medicine at Glasgow and trained as a pathologist. Having worked in the NHS and universities in the UK and the US, he took early retirement and now devotes his time to writing.

His non-fiction publications include textbooks and articles on topics as diverse as the thalidomide story, the medical challenges of space travel and the medico-legal consequences of the Hillsborough disaster. His debut poetry collection, *Love & Other Diseases*, was published in 2023 by Seahorse Publications.

The Moon's More Feeble Fire is the second novel in the Dr Jack Cuthbert series. You can read more about Allan and his work at his website: researchet.wordpress.com.

Also by Allan Gaw

FICTION
The Silent House of Sleep

NON-FICTION
Born in Scandal
Trial By Fire
On Moral Grounds (with M. H. Burns)
Testing the Waters
Tales From an Oxford Bench
The Business of Discovery
Our Speaker Today
Abstract Expressions

POETRY
Love & Other Diseases

THE MOON'S MORE FEEBLE FIRE

A DR JACK CUTHBERT MYSTERY

ALLAN GAW

Polygon

This revised paperback edition first published in Great Britain in 2025 by Polygon, an imprint of Birlinn Ltd. Previously published by SA Press in 2024.

Birlinn Ltd
West Newington House
10 Newington Road
Edinburgh
EH9 1QS

www.polygonbooks.co.uk

1

Copyright © Allan Gaw, 2025

The right of Allan Gaw to be identified as the author of this work has been asserted by him in accordance with the Copyright, Designs and Patents Act 1988.

All rights reserved.

This is a work of fiction. Names, characters, businesses, places, events and incidents are either the products of the author's imagination or used in a fictitious manner. Any resemblance to actual persons, living or dead, or actual events is purely coincidental.

The narrative takes place in 1930 and contains language and prevailing attitudes of the time which some readers may find offensive. The publishers wish to reassure that such instances are there for reasons of historical social context.

ISBN 978 1 84697 723 7
eBook ISBN 978 1 78885 802 1

British Library Cataloguing-in-Publication Data
A catalogue record for this book is available on request from the British Library.

Typeset by Initial Typesetting Services, Edinburgh

Printed and bound by CPI Group (UK) Ltd, Croydon CR0 4YY

For those who die without names

concipit illa preces et verba venefica dicit
ignotosque deos ignoto carmine adorat,
quo solet et niveae vultum confundere Lunae
et patrio capiti bibulas subtexere nubes.

Now she invokes the Daughters of the Night,
Does noxious Juices smear, and Charms recite;
Such as can veil the Moon's more feeble Fire,
Or shade the Golden Lustre of her Sire.

Ovid Metamorphoses Book XIV.
Trans. Samuel Garth, 1794

Chapter 1

London: 22 February 1930

The acid-yellow light of the advertising sign overhead shimmered in the gutter at her feet. She watched as the night wind caught the surface of the puddle and twisted the inverted words. When a car sped past, she stepped back to avoid the worst of the splash. Momentarily, the electric reflection was shattered. Cursing under her breath, she wiped stray drops of dirty water from her stockings.

It was after midnight, and she was too tired to call out after the driver. Instead, she straightened her clothes and repositioned herself under the gaslight at the corner of Gerrard and Wardour Street. Working girls like her were carefully spaced along the pavements, making sure they did not stray into each other's patch, and there were still people hurriedly coming and going from the private clubs, the lone men furtively seeking whatever Soho had to offer for sale that night. And being London, there were always cars, and noise and smoke – the stench of a night so sour that you could taste it.

She shivered. Her blouse was low cut and her coat too thin to offer any real warmth or protection against the rain. She had no umbrella, only a cloche hat that framed her face and red curly hair.

As each car drove by and slowed to turn the corner, she raised her painted eyebrows and forced a smile. And any man on his own who came within earshot would receive her whispered invitation. Three that night had already accepted, but she needed the same again if she was to pay her rent that week.

There was a sudden squeal of high-pitched laughter. A group of fashionably dressed men and women exploded onto the pavement from the nearby jazz club. Before the door swung closed behind them, a blast of heady music from within escaped. There were many like them – toffs who enjoyed a night of illicit pleasure in the city's underbelly. They would go home now with tales of how frightfully ghastly and yet simply thrilling it all was.

As they reeled towards her, she caught the eye of one of the men. She thought she recognised him and made it plain what she was selling. She could see there was interest in his eyes, despite the silken glamour of the young woman he had his arm around. The others in the group were oblivious to her as she stood in the gaslight, but she hoped he might be back soon for something he had never tried before. However, only a few yards on down Wardour Street, still laughing, they all disappeared into a taxi. It would whisk them back to their real world, to some smart apartment in Mayfair or Knightsbridge where they could gasp over more cocktails at how daring they had all been.

They were gone now, and she was alone again, waiting for some man with beer on his breath to slip five shillings into her hand so he could use her for a few minutes of pleasure. His, not hers.

Across the road, she saw one of the regular girls she knew well. She had some trade and was sweet-talking him into coming back to her room around the corner rather than the alleyway he was pulling her towards. She could not hear what was being said, but she could imagine. So often they wanted you up against a wall, but even here the girls had standards. Besides, they could always charge more for a bed.

She made no move to help because that was not the way on the street. You had to learn to handle your own trade. Nevertheless, she felt in her bag for the small knife she kept there. She had never used it in anger, but just knowing it was there had helped her stand night after night on that corner.

Across the road, the tussle suddenly turned to mirth. Whatever the girl had promised, the man had calmed himself, and now laughing was being led meekly away. It would not be long before he was scurrying home to wife and children, the girl back on the street waiting for the next punter.

The bars had long since closed for the night, but there was an illuminated clock above one of them. She tried not to look at it. Watching the minutes drag by just made the night even longer. Instead, she tried to think about happier times. But that was not so easy any more. It had been a long time since anything in her life might have been described as happy. No, better to think about the here and now, she decided. It could be worse. She could be working the docks. Or the ponces could be all over her. But she was too old for them. Those bullies with their cheap suits and quick fists knew the amount she could make in a night now was hardly worth their trouble.

She did have to wonder though: what would be next for her? How long could she keep on this game? She still had her figure, but her looks were fading fast. Lately, she could see the men eyeing her up and down and deciding more and more to move on to the younger ones up the street. She remembered starting out and how the old drabs would talk. Back then they had seemed ridiculous to her – old women trying to sell their bodies. But now she realised they had been no older then than she was now.

She closed her eyes, trying to rid herself of the thought, but was startled by a sudden chill. She turned away, trying to avoid the damp air that was blowing along the street. It was then that she saw some movement up ahead. A black car had slowed and stopped in the shadow beneath a broken street lamp. Someone was getting out. From this distance, he looked well-dressed, and she wondered for a moment if she had hooked that young toff after all. Perhaps, after taking his girlfriend home, he had come back to Soho to see what the place really had to offer.

But as he approached, she saw that she was wrong. It was not him, but whoever it was, was now coming in her direction. She broke her rule and glanced up at the clock. It was half-past midnight. When she looked back, the elegant figure in black evening dress was now beside her and whispering in her ear. This time there was no need for her to give her usual come-on. This one knew and understood the terms exactly and took the lead. She was surprised but not enough to show it, and she put her hand through the arm that was offered.

Together they walked in silence along the wet pavement of Gerrard Street. The illuminated sign above the café door advertised Real Italian Coffee. The irregular flashes of shocking pink light caught the sheen of a silk hatband and the detail of a silver topped cane. What had made this one choose her?

It was impossible in that light to see the door properly, but it was certainly not an entrance to anywhere respectable. The paint was peeling, and the woodwork so badly cracked that the gaslight in the hallway beyond was shining through the panels.

She pushed it open with her shoulder and led her trade into the narrow hallway and then by the hand up the creaking staircase to the first floor. There, the floorboards were covered in old newspapers, and three doors led off the landing. She unlocked the middle one, and there was nothing inside but darkness and the sour smell of men's sweat.

With a match, she reached up to light the gas mantle. The faint yellow light from the hissing pipe soon found its way into the corners of the room, revealing its squalor. Although she could see that this room was not what was expected, it was all she had to offer, and besides it was reflected in the price. If they wanted a Mayfair tart, they could go and pay for one.

She went to the door and slipped the key back into the lock but made sure, as she always did, that the door stayed ajar. It was the first rule of safety she had learned; after seeing the state of some of the girls on the street who had forgotten it, she was not about to do the same.

A black hat and a white scarf were removed and placed on the side table. A bow tie was loosened, tailcoat and waistcoat slowly unbuttoned. Now, in the dim light, she could see at last who she had brought up her stairs and at once knew what this one would want.

She turned away to ready herself, wordlessly removing her hat, unbuttoning her blouse and pulling up her skirt before lying on her back on the unmade bed. But as she did so, the trade, watching her intently, leant back on the door and closed it. With one gloved hand, the key was turned in the lock. Then, the other hand reached up and the gaslight was turned off.

Chapter 2

London: 23 February 1930

Simon Morgenthal had tears in his eyes. The canopy under which the wedding party stood was made from his grandfather's prayer shawl and was stretched above them, fixed to four brass poles adorned with flowers. This was the symbol of the newlyweds' first home, and now as the ceremony was nearing its end, Simon looked up at it and felt a stronger connection with his family and its past than ever before.

The shawl had been brought to London in a suitcase more than sixty years before by a young immigrant seeking a new life in a new country. He had died, tragically lost at sea, when Simon was just a boy, but not before he had taught his grandson the lessons of a very different life. Now, it had only seemed fitting that the kind old man's most prized possession should play such a key part in the next chapter of his family's story.

In that moment of stillness, Simon was suddenly confused by his feelings. There was joy, of course, at standing there beside such a beautiful bride. But there was also sadness at his grandfather's absence. And there was fear. Not only were the eyes of 200 guests on him, but now he sensed that he was standing under the watchful gaze of his grandfather too. Could he ever measure up to that man? Would he ever leave behind as much as his grandfather had? Sarah saw it all in her husband's face. She reached over to touch his arm so she could bring him back because there was one last rite still to observe.

A wine glass had been placed in a cotton bag and now lay at the young man's feet. Startled by her touch, Simon looked at his bride, and then nervously at his parents who were standing by his side, and then at his new in-laws who were also huddled under the canopy. All were smiling and urging him on. Finally, he glanced at the rabbi, who was used to dealing with the nerves of young grooms. He merely nodded at the bag and raised an impatient eyebrow.

With a sudden movement, Simon stamped hard on the bag, shattering the glass, and a loud cheer swept like a wave around the room. All Simon and Sarah's Jewish friends and relatives cried, '*Mazel tov!*' And one or two of the many non-Jews present joined them in the traditional shout of congratulations.

Amongst them was Jack Cuthbert, who had been savouring every moment of his first Jewish wedding. He had of course studied the details of the ceremony beforehand from a book, but as the rich symbolism of it all was played out before him, he found it so much more beautiful and romantic than he had imagined.

He watched now as his assistant pathologist at St Thomas's was warmly embraced by his parents and in-laws and then as the young man took his new wife in his arms to kiss her. There were tears and laughter and an overwhelming feeling that this was a new beginning.

Cuthbert had not expected to feel as he did when he watched them under that canopy, and he could not help but smile and cheer along with the other guests. However, at the back of his mind, and all the time pressing to the front, was a much darker emotion. This, he knew, would never be for him. He would never experience this kind of joy, of being enveloped, of being raised, of being swathed in love not just by one person but by their whole family. Simon, he thought, was such a fortunate young man, and in that brief moment he envied him.

A wedding, however, was no place for deadly sins, and Cuthbert quickly put such thoughts aside. He moved with the others from the gold-leafed room where the ceremony had been held through to the adjoining grand ballroom for the reception.

Soon the new Dr and Mrs Morgenthal would be standing in a line-up to greet their guests. The ballroom was resplendent in its polished finery. Large mirrors framed in blue marble reached from the floor to the ceiling, while crystal candelabras vied with the central chandelier to see which could add the most sparkle to the space.

Flowers were everywhere, on every table and in every buttonhole. The mirrors reflected the guests as they milled around, sipping the expensive champagne and enjoying the canapés. All the while, a string quartet played on a dais at the far end of the room. The music was light and just loud enough to be heard over the buzz of a hundred conversations.

As neither the Morgenthals nor the Fieldings were especially orthodox families, they had opted to have both the ceremony and the reception at the Dorchester Hotel. The religious formalities over, the couple now had to attend to their much more onerous social obligations.

Jack Cuthbert stood watching it all at the edge of the reception, oblivious to the appraisal of several guests. Three of Sarah's female cousins were huddled together in conversation, and they had decided that the immaculately dressed man must be one of the groom's relations. Simon's maternal aunt, on the other hand, thought his angular good looks must belong to the bride's side.

Cuthbert could claim neither affiliation and stood alone because he knew no one there other than the groom. He was a broad-shouldered man, taller than everyone else in the room, and in his tailored black morning suit he cut a striking figure as he sipped on the one champagne flute that he was allowing himself. This was not his natural milieu. He was not from this world or even this city, but he knew it was the duty of a gentleman to be at ease in any setting.

Cuthbert tuned into snippets of conversation as the guests mingled and floated past him.

'I mean, isn't Sarah's dress just divine? But I think I might die if I had to wear those shoes. I mean, they are so last season.'

'Well, I said Hugo would never come, not with his back playing up. Poor man is a martyr to his lumbago. Do you know, he even has to get his man to help him put on his socks and shoes?'

'Was it very bloody, darling? I mean how could you possibly manage with just the one maid for the whole weekend. It's simply intolerable to think what's expected of one these days.'

'Rebecca's hat is rather awful, isn't it? I don't think I've seen an uglier one since the last thing she wore. She does have a rare talent for picking them!'

As the laughter trailed by him, he realised he was studying them as he would a crime scene. He was looking for the smallest of clues and focusing in on the apparently insignificant, in the eager hope that it would help him understand what was going on. But in this room, there was too much for him, and he gave up trying. He decided instead to enjoy the gentle Haydn being played.

Simon's Aunt Rachel had kept an eye on Cuthbert from across the room, noting his stillness. She saw the faintest of smiles creep across his face as he studied the bright young people around him. But she could bear it no longer and resolved to go over and introduce herself. As she approached, she noticed the mirror-like gloss on his black shoes and as he turned to her, the arresting blue of his eyes. Cuthbert's manners were as impeccable as his bearing, and she was immediately charmed by his accent.

'Irish?'

'Scottish, madam, but it couldn't matter less. What a beautiful day and, might I say, what a lovely couple.'

As Cuthbert looked over at Sarah, who was greeting some short, overweight man she had clearly never met before, and Simon, still wearing his fixed smile, he found himself looking at the young man rather than the bride. Of course, she was beautiful; everyone said as much. But it was the tall, handsome young man who drew Cuthbert's eye.

He had worked with Simon Morgenthal for almost two years and had grown accustomed to his presence. The young doctor was dark and wore his masculinity lightly, and Cuthbert knew that he had matured even in the short time he had known him.

Sarah was fair, fresh and dressed in ivory silk that flowed from her shoulders to the floor, clinging to her figure as it went. The veil was lace and tied close around her head into a bonnet with flowers and silk ribbons before it cascaded over the dress and swept around her hem. She wore her mother's pearls and the diamond ring that had once belonged to Simon's grandmother. She almost looked happy, but Cuthbert could see she was tiring with the task and trying to hide her fatigue behind a smile.

He took the smallest of sips of champagne as he watched them and said, 'She looks radiant, don't you think?'

'Yes, Simon is a very lucky young man. But, of course, every bride looks her best on her wedding day. If she can't be radiant then, when can she be?'

Aunt Rachel was making shorter work of her champagne than Cuthbert and was glancing around for the waiter.

Cuthbert made use of his height and immediately reached over and took a crystal flute from a passing tray and handed it to her.

'How kind of you, Dr Cuthbert. I do find it helps one get through these affairs.'

'Surely not too great a hardship? There are worse ways to spend an afternoon, I should think.'

'Indeed. So you work with our Simon. I do hope you keep him busy. He's very keen, I'm sure, but he always had a habit of getting distracted.'

'He's a pleasure to work with and a great credit to his family, madam.'

'You do say all the right things, don't you, doctor? Now, what's a man like you doing here unaccompanied? Don't tell me there isn't someone special in your life because I simply won't believe you.'

Cuthbert had become adept at fielding such questions over the years. There was no one now and there never had been – at least no one who had returned his affections. He put his hand over his heart and bowed his head just enough to emphasise the point.

'Alas, we are not all as fortunate as young Simon.'

'Well, in that case, let me introduce you to my daughter, Naomi. Come along, young man, and indulge me.'

'With pleasure, madam.'

Cuthbert took a longer sip of his wine and allowed himself to be led like a prize bull across the room. He was introduced to a shy woman not much younger than himself, and he chatted and smiled and did everything that was expected of a gentleman. He made those around him feel special, while feeling nothing at all himself.

Finally released from the clutches of Aunt Rachel and her long-suffering daughter, Cuthbert eased himself back across the room to stand beside one of the mirrors in the corner. From there he was able to survey the throng of beautiful people in all their finery. The women sparkled, but to his eyes, it was the men who shone. While he was lost in the view, a voice said in his ear, 'I don't know why we're here.'

'I'm sorry?'

The man beside him was about ten years his junior, and he smiled at Cuthbert with his eyes as much as his lips. His handshake was firm and strong, and Cuthbert reciprocated with equal force.

'Maxton-Forbes. How do you do? You must be the doctor they're all talking about. I was just saying, I'm not sure why we were invited. Don't know a soul if truth be told.'

As he leaned in to make himself heard above the din, Cuthbert could smell smoke on his breath and expensive cologne on his skin. The man was almost a head shorter than Cuthbert and held on to his arm as he spoke.

'Jack Cuthbert. How do you do? I, on the other hand, know exactly why I'm here, but I'm afraid the only person I know is the groom.'

'I think my mother may have been a godparent.'

'Do Jews have godparents, Mr Maxton-Forbes?'

'Do you know, I'm not sure. But it was something like that. We don't share the happy couple's faith, just their taste in champagne. More fizz, old chap?'

Before Cuthbert could decline, he found the half-empty glass in his hand replaced with a fresh one. As the man turned his back to the doctor, to look across the room, Cuthbert studied the taut muscles of his tanned neck and the sharp razor line of his haircut, and he found his eyes slowly following the contour of his back, his thighs and the bulge of his calves through his trousers. As Cuthbert did so, he was conscious of his breathing as he had been so many times before; he swallowed the feeling quietly.

'Ah, there she is. Darling, do come and meet someone.'

Maxton-Forbes was waving across the room at a young woman in lavender silk who appeared to be gliding towards them through the crowd.

'Celia, darling, I want you to meet Dr Cuthbert, who I think may know even fewer people here than us. I've decided we should join forces. Safety in numbers and all that.'

'Dr Cuthbert, Celia Maxton-Forbes. And this fool is my husband. How do you do?'

She extended her gloved hand and Cuthbert took it and held it as he looked into her violet eyes. She was by far the most striking woman in the room; even Cuthbert could see that. Still holding his hand, she pulled him gently towards her so that she might be heard. This time it was an expensive scent of floral femininity that enveloped Cuthbert.

'Tell me, doctor, what do you make of all this?'

'I'm sorry. I'm not sure what you mean.'

'All this glamour. There's enough money in this room to feed all the unemployed in the East End. Look at the clothes, the jewels. That vase of flowers alone must have cost more than a week's wages for some impoverished soul. Don't you find it ever so slightly obscene?'

'It's a wedding, Mrs Maxton-Forbes – wouldn't you be disappointed if the guests didn't wear their best?'

'You must think me a terrible socialist, doctor. It's just that I have such an uncomfortable relationship with privilege. Most of the men here, my husband included, have never done a hard day's work in their lives. And I think it rather shows, don't you? They're soft. Of course, I don't include you in that generalisation, Dr Cuthbert.'

She was playing with one of her large diamond stud earrings as she was speaking, and Cuthbert wondered if she felt a genuine sense of guilt over her obvious wealth, or whether it was simply a nod to the fashion of the day – concern for the masses.

'But I've become such a bore. Do forgive me. Now, tell me all about your world, Dr Cuthbert. It must be so much more interesting than this one.'

'I'm afraid my world is not really a suitable subject for refined conversation.'

'Don't worry about me – I'm much stronger than I look.'

Cuthbert had no doubt about that, and so proceeded to talk of the general nature of his work without detailing any of the specifics. He explained his role as one of Scotland Yard's pathologists and how his job was to provide the detectives with whom he worked all the factual evidence that could be gleaned from the crime scene and from the victim.

She hung on his every word, urging him to tell her more and to explain anything she did not quite understand. She was interested in a way that most people with whom Cuthbert spoke about his work only feigned out of politeness.

As he was telling her about his department at St Thomas's Hospital and the kind of work he did there, they were interrupted. Her husband joined them after speaking to another small group of guests. He seemed a little agitated, and Cuthbert noted he was perspiring just above his stiff collar. He whispered something in her ear, and she delved in her lavender clutch bag to take out a small leather case and handed it to him. He nodded to Cuthbert and disappeared.

'Oh, don't mind Charlie. He has a little health problem. He'll be as right as rain in a moment. What were we saying? Oh, yes, you were telling me about how you can tell if someone's bumped their head before or after they've died.'

Cuthbert was flattered by her interest and relieved to have someone to talk to, if only to save him from any more aunts with unattached daughters. He politely turned the conversation to her and discovered that she and Charlie Maxton-Forbes lived in Mayfair, and they had been married for almost two years.

'I wish I had something exciting to say about my life before I was married, but the truth is it's a rather stifling existence for a young girl in this kind of society. Boarding school, finishing school and then coming out.

'After a season, or perhaps two if she's spared, it's off up the aisle without any real thought for what might be going on between her ears. If, indeed, anything is going on, that is. We might have the vote now, Dr Cuthbert, but I don't think they expect us to know what to do with it. And they might be right.

'Take the young ladies here, for example. Over there, in the lemon satin, that's Georgina Semple, and I know for a fact that she's next for the chop. I'm sorry, I mean the next one of us to get married. And if you were to speak with her, which I hope you won't have the misfortune to do, you would find that she doesn't have a single thought in her head that hasn't been put there by *Tatler*.

'And over there, in the chartreuse crêpe de chine, is Ruth Lieberman. She's another one for a canopy, and the lucky young man is over there chasing the champagne waiter. That's going to end badly – she has nothing but small talk, and he can't see past the end of a glass. Made for each other, I suppose; they don't have an original idea between them. But you think I'm being harsh, Dr Cuthbert. I can see it in your eyes. I suppose I am, but the featherbrains in this room deserve it. Now, where on earth is that husband of mine? Oh, here he comes.'

Maxton-Forbes strolled over and kissed his wife's neck with a little more passion than seemed appropriate for the setting. As he did so, he slipped the small leather case back into her hand and then smiled broadly at Cuthbert, showing the dimples in his cheeks. He was relaxed now, almost dreamy in his expression, and Cuthbert knew exactly what his 'little health problem' was.

Cuthbert still badly wanted to look at him. He moved back just a little so he could drink him in more discreetly. Celia Maxton-Forbes did the same, but so she could watch Cuthbert, and she enjoyed catching the momentary flash of hunger in the doctor's eyes as he surveyed her husband.

She had seen that look before and knew exactly what she was dealing with. She thought for a moment that it might be interesting. There were times when she knew Charlie would do anything she asked. But perhaps not here, not now.

The married couple had now done their duty on the reception line, and the wedding lunch was about to be served. Cuthbert had studied the seating plan when he arrived, but on looking again he now found he had been moved and would be spending more time with Aunt Rachel and her daughter. He looked around and saw the Maxton-Forbeses move off in the direction of their table, and Celia glanced back over her shoulder to make sure he was still watching them.

The lunch was light and just kosher enough to satisfy the rabbi. The conversation was never in danger of failing at Cuthbert's table, not with Aunt Rachel who was now on a mission. She questioned him about his family, his schooling and his war. She moved on to his profession, his friends, his likes and dislikes and even his favourite colour. And, of course, she landed finally at her destination: what did he think of her darling Naomi?

Cuthbert, however, was a man who valued his privacy and had learned to be very good at saying a lot in these sorts of interrogations without revealing anything. After the dessert, Naomi, who was seated on Cuthbert's right, turned to whisper in his ear, 'I'm so very sorry, Dr Cuthbert.' He smiled and assured her that it had been nothing but a pleasure.

As the speeches started, Cuthbert searched the room again for the Maxton-Forbes couple and found them three tables away. Charlie looked relaxed and was keeping himself that way with even more wine. Celia, however, was barely touching her drink, and sat straight-backed in the chair with the kind of poise that had been expensively taught. She glanced in his direction, and he immediately looked away and tried to focus on what was being so wittily said by Simon's best man.

Cuthbert had been unsure about coming to the wedding and, if he was honest with himself, was far from certain that the marriage was a good idea at all. Indeed, only a few months ago, the wedding had looked as if it might not go ahead, such were the cross words that were exchanged between Simon and Sarah one afternoon in the park.

*

The couple had been engaged for almost a year, and in that time, Simon Morgenthal had been finding his feet working with Cuthbert in the mortuary and forensic laboratory at St Thomas's Hospital. He started as a fresh-faced new graduate, yet had already grown accustomed to the wickedness that was on the streets of London.

He had also decided, largely because of working alongside Cuthbert, that he wanted this to be his life's work, and he strove every day to emulate his mentor. As his outlook matured, the beautiful fiancée who had so captivated him began to appear as if she inhabited a different world. It was a world for a time that Simon had shared. After all, he had been born into it too.

Now, however, the life course that had been plotted so carefully for him had lost its appeal, and he found he had quite different aspirations. When he had shared this realisation with Sarah, she was understandably taken aback and angry that she would no longer be the wife of a Harley Street society doctor.

She did love the boy, and he still doted on her, but both were aware that a new, uneasy alliance had developed between them. She felt Simon's distance and started to worry that she might be losing him altogether. Perhaps it was just the natural course of their relationship, but Sarah made the conscious decision to yield to his advances. She wanted him to feel that they were meant for each other. The rest she could sort out after they were married.

One late November day, when her parents were in the country, she sent the maid and the cook home early, saying she was going out for the evening and that they should do the same. Simon came round, as he did most evenings, and only realised he was alone with her when she led him to her bedroom.

Although he had been pressing her for greater intimacy for months, he was surprised as she started to loosen his tie and then kissed him passionately. She did not know exactly what to expect, although her mother in preparation for her daughter's wedding night had talked to her in polite euphemisms.

She unpeeled Simon from his clothes with interest and delight, but when she saw him completely naked she was startled. She was an only child and, having no brothers, she was completely unaware of what lay beneath the fig leaves on the statues in the Victoria and Albert Museum. She closed her eyes, as her mother had urged her to do, only to open them again as she found his body beautiful and what he did with it all rather wonderful.

As they made the gentlest of loves, she realised he knew more about her body than she did herself and concluded he had either been with other women or had read a lot of books. Having invited him into her bed, she felt she had earned the right afterwards to ask, but all she received for her pains was a dismissive remark.

'My darling, a gentleman never discusses such things.'

*

Now, with the speeches over, she smoothed the ivory silk of her dress and wondered if she could feel the beginnings of the swelling in her stomach that no one else could yet see. Indeed, she hadn't even told her new husband, unsure of how he might react. But there was plenty of time for that, she thought. Plenty of time for her to let him know just how he should think – about that and about all the other things she needed him to change his mind on.

She looked around the room and saw one of her more delicate problems rising from his table. Cuthbert was just beginning to take his leave of the aunt and her daughter when a bellboy approached; the doctor bent down to allow him to whisper in his ear.

'Please forgive me, ladies, but I have an urgent phone call to take in the foyer.'

Cuthbert strode across the room, trailing the gaze of several young women as he went. The call, as he expected, was from Scotland Yard. He quickly went back to the reception to find Simon and Sarah to make his apologies.

'What is it, Dr Cuthbert? Do you need me?'

'Simon, my lad, this is your wedding day, so please don't be so daft. It's a body, like all the others. I think I can handle this one on my own. Mrs Morgenthal, it's been such a lovely day, and I wish you every happiness for the future. Now, I really must find your parents to thank them for inviting me.'

'Oh, there's no need for that, Dr Cuthbert. They know how busy you are, and I'll explain. But you can kiss the bride before you go, can't you?'

Cuthbert politely took her hand and raised it to his lips, but as he did so she pulled him to her and kissed him on the mouth. She tasted of champagne and cigarettes, and he thought she looked at him as if she suddenly knew everything about him – as if everything he was had been betrayed by that kiss.

Of course, she thought nothing of the sort and had already moved away to chat with another guest. With his pocket handkerchief, he discreetly wiped her lipstick from his mouth and made for the door. He collected his hat and coat and took a taxi to his home in Gordon Square to change. He could hardly attend the scene of a murder wearing a morning suit.

In truth, he was relieved to have an excuse to leave the gathering. Cuthbert had never been a social animal. He rarely ventured out in the evenings and would spend his hours in his study. He had to read so much to keep abreast of developments in his own specialist field, that for pleasure he would escape into the past and into a different language.

His favourite poets lived almost two millennia ago and wrote their exquisite verse in Latin. He read and re-read the ancient works of Ovid and Virgil, and he kept Catullus by his bed. Ever since he had been a small boy growing up in his grandfather's house in Edinburgh, he had been surrounded by books. And when he first started to learn Latin at school, he was immediately enthralled by the voices that still spoke to him from a lost world.

As he mastered the language, he began to cherish it. The rhythm and metre, the shape of their verses – all that and more drew him in. In those ancient poets' words, he found meaning and some understanding of love and loss. He used their poetry to relax, but he also used it to soothe his soul.

And it was often a troubled soul.

By any measure he was a successful man. People admired him and often envied him – his looks, his intelligence, his position – but none knew what was going on behind those eyes. His inner thoughts were often tainted with melancholy, and recently he had become aware of the emptiness in his life. He had never had many true friends and had learned to appreciate his own company, but now he felt increasingly alone. Perhaps it was the passing of time and the inevitable dwindling of a hope that it would one day change. Perhaps he was just now beginning to realise that this is the way it would always be for a man like him.

Chapter 3

London: 23 February 1930

The uniformed constable on the door recognised Cuthbert as soon as he arrived and saluted him before permitting him access to the premises. The battered door on Gerrard Street led into a narrow, damp hallway and a bare stairway to the rooms above the café on the ground floor.

Detective Sergeant Baker was already in the room on the first floor, and he greeted Cuthbert with a warm smile. 'Here we are again, sir.'

'Indeed, sergeant. Good afternoon to you. Tell me, what do we have this time?'

'A female found dead late this morning by one of the other women working here. We only know her by the street name she used, "Dutch Edie", and not a great deal more, I'm afraid. There's no sign of forced entry or anything that would suggest a struggle, but then again, look around you. It's not exactly the Ritz, is it? So I'm not sure we'd know if anything untoward went on.'

'I think we can be certain that a lot of untoward things have gone on in this room, sergeant, but I take your point.'

The room was a single bedroom, sparsely furnished, with peeling wallpaper. A window looked out onto the street; a broken quarter pane had been replaced by folded cardboard. The rest of the glass was thick with grime. The curtains were heavy and tattered, and Cuthbert suspected they were rarely, if ever, opened. But they were today.

'Did you open the curtains, sergeant?'

Baker knew that Cuthbert was a stickler for preserving the integrity of any crime scene. No other police pathologist was as demanding in this respect, and it was a source of great annoyance to his colleagues. But Baker also knew that he had broken Cuthbert's golden rule.

'I'm sorry, sir, but I had to. The meter had run out, and it was the only way we could see. Nothing else has been touched, I assure you, sir.'

Cuthbert said nothing, but his frown was enough for Baker to realise it was a bad start. Lying on the bed was the body of a woman. It was difficult to judge her age, but she was not a young girl as many of the prostitutes in the area were.

She was lying on her back, her legs spread, with her skirt and underclothes pushed up around her waist. The top of her blouse was ripped exposing her right breast. Cuthbert noticed a mark on the breast close to the nipple and took a closer look without touching the body at this stage.

There were two opposing crescent-shaped bruises, in broken lines that Cuthbert recognised as probable bite marks. He looked over the body but found no others. The face of the corpse was suffused, and the eyes were open and bloodshot.

Although the bed was dishevelled and stained, there were, as Baker had said, no obvious signs of a struggle. Cuthbert opened the wooden case he had brought with him, which everyone else but him referred to as 'the murder bag'. He took out a pair of rubber gloves and put them on. From his own briefcase he took a white coat and donned that too. He made a further careful survey of the corpse, writing in his black notebook as he went. By now, Baker had seen the pathologist at work on many occasions, and he was well used to his ways. In particular, he knew they would both be there for some time.

Cuthbert took the temperature of the body and that of the room and asked for a series of photographs to be taken of the corpse before it was moved. He made a quick calculation in his head based on the assumption that a body indoors at this ambient temperature was likely to cool by around one and a half degrees per hour after death. The rectal temperature of the corpse was 77.5 degrees Fahrenheit, and he concluded that the woman had died roughly fourteen hours earlier, at around midnight.

He checked the level of stiffness in the muscles of the face and the limbs, and the complete rigidity of the arms and legs confirmed his estimated time of death. Baker knew that few other pathologists would spend as much time on a prostitute killing, but he also knew that, if challenged, Cuthbert would say what he always said in such a setting – that she was someone's daughter.

After gleaning all he could from the surface examination of the body, Cuthbert turned to the rest of the room. There was little to see, except a cheap, dusty side table and a pillow on the floor beside the bed. He took a closer look at the pillowslip and noted there were coloured marks on one side that might have been make-up. He asked Baker to remove the pillowslip and place it as evidence in one of the large brown paper bags he had brought in his case.

As he was looking closely at the face of the corpse to see if there was any matching make-up, he noted a number of hairs on the bed around the body. The corpse had what appeared to be dyed red hair, and there were a number of long strands that matched the colour.

There were also a number of small, dark, curly hairs, probably of different shades, that Cuthbert collected with his forceps and bagged, even though he suspected they were simply some of the material left behind from a night of trade. There were also some longer, straighter dark hairs that did not match those of the corpse. Again, Cuthbert carefully gathered these, placed them in separate evidence envelopes and labelled them.

When he looked a little closer at the side table, what he had taken to be dust appeared to be a white powder, rather like icing sugar. From his case he took a fine brush and swept as much as he could into a small glass jar. He sealed it with a screw cap and recorded the details both in his notes and on the label of the jar itself.

'I think we've learned all we can here, sergeant. Let's get her back to the mortuary at St Thomas's so that I can take a proper look.'

*

The police took the rest of the day to transfer the body. It was a low priority for them. The woman had died in a rented room in a building that housed a number of fairly low-end prostitutes and it was unlikely that there would be relatives clamouring for answers in this case.

One of the women, Anne Brown — at least that was the name she had given the sergeant — had found the body. She was unable to tell him much because she said she knew so little about Dutch. She had knocked her up that morning to see if she wanted a cup of tea, but when she got no reply, she just thought she must be sleeping it off. The night before had been a busy one for many of them. She tried again later and when she still got no answer, she went in and found her.

'And when exactly was that, miss?'

'Must have been gone twelve. And she never sleeps in that late, no matter how much trade she's had.'

'Was there anything unusual about last night? Did you hear anything from her room around midnight?'

'Well, I was a bit busy myself, sir. And as for hearing anything – just the usual, if you take my meaning.'

'Do you know what her real name was?'

'She was always Dutch Edie as long as I can remember. Don't think she was Dutch though – more like East Ham if you ask me. The punters like it, see, bit exotic. Feel they're getting more for their money. Lots of the girls say they're foreign; if you put on a good accent, you can add a shilling a time.'

'And her age?'

She was one of the old-timers – here when I started and that wasn't yesterday. We've had a few run-ins, but not too bad. The coppers round here know us, and we know them. And as long as we give 'em a little palm oil regular like, they leave us alone. But you'll know all about that, won't you, dearie?'

Sergeant Baker knew only too well the reputation that his colleagues had in C Division. Their whole approach to prostitution was not any attempt to eradicate it, but rather to contain it and prevent it from getting out of hand. They knew they could never get rid of it completely, even if they had the manpower, which they did not.

Instead, they had to do just enough to make sure the beaks saw sufficient numbers of girls coming before them in court, and the politicians were untroubled by their constituents about soliciting on their doorsteps. Such an approach inevitably led to a live-and-let-live attitude on the streets, which in turn could almost become complicity. And that was only a small step away from corruption.

There were bent coppers, and Baker knew they were everywhere in the force, but those working vice in the West End had the worst reputation of all. That said, they were still his fellow officers, so he closed his notebook before he was forced to write down anything else.

*

The next day, unusually, Cuthbert was the first to arrive at his office. He checked the mortuary and found that the body had been delivered from Gerrard Street and lay on one of his slabs, covered in a white sheet. It would be a good couple of hours before the morning mail would find its way from the hospital sorting office, so he decided to make a start. Just as he was changing into his white dissection coat, the door opened and in walked Simon Morgenthal.

'So sorry I'm late, Dr Cuthbert.'

'What are you doing here? Do you not have more pressing matters to attend to?'

The young doctor's cheeks flushed. He had already endured all the jokes about new grooms from his friends the night before but was unprepared to hear them from his mentor.

'It was a late night, sir, and I left Sarah sleeping in, so I decided it would be fine to come to work.'

'Tiring, I'm sure, for all concerned, but you had no need to come in this morning. Why don't you get back to your bride and surprise her by still being at home when she wakes up?'

'Really, Dr Cuthbert, I would rather be here working. And besides, you have a post mortem to perform. It will be so much quicker with another pair of hands.'

Cuthbert looked at Morgenthal's hands and nodded without committing himself.

When Cuthbert removed the sheet covering the body, Dutch Edie was still arranged as she had been in the room. The rigor mortis had not yet subsided, and she lay, her knees bent and her thighs wide, probably as her last client had left her. Morgenthal cut off the clothing and placed each item in a separate evidence bag according to Cuthbert's protocol and put them aside for later study. The woman now lay naked on their slab and looked very small. Cuthbert checked again to see if there were any other bite marks, but the only one was on her breast.

'What do you make of this, Dr Morgenthal?'

Cuthbert spoke in the stern, rather distant manner he adopted when he remembered that Simon was there to be taught as much as to assist. Here, he thought, was an opportunity to get that obligation out of the way for the morning.

'Approximately semi-circular marks that would be consistent with a bite, sir.'

'Human?'

'The size and orientation would certainly fit with that, but it's impossible to be certain, sir.'

'Ante mortem or post mortem?'

'The associated bruising would strongly suggest that this was inflicted before death.'

'I agree.' And that was the end of the tutorial. Simon could stand down and Cuthbert could get on with the work that fascinated him: the unravelling of a puzzle.

'Make sure we have a few good photographs of the bite mark, Simon. She could have received it from any one of a dozen clients the day she died, but maybe it was our killer.'

'So you think this was a murder, Dr Cuthbert? Couldn't she just have died of natural causes or perhaps even taken her own life?'

Cuthbert looked at his assistant long and hard before he spoke. The young man had learned many things during his tutelage, but it appeared common sense was not amongst them.

'Simon, take a look at the body and tell me what you see.'

The assistant systematically surveyed the corpse and offered the kind of commentary that he knew Cuthbert expected.

'This is the body of a Caucasian woman in her mid to late thirties. She is poorly nourished and bears the stretch marks consistent with previous pregnancies. In addition to an obvious fresh bite mark on her right breast, she has a number of bruises on her arms and neck which appear to be three to seven days old. There are no defensive wounds on her hands or arms and no ligature marks on her neck.'

'What about her face, her eyes?'

'Her face is discoloured and there are obvious petechiae in both conjunctivae.'

'And what do those tiny pinpoint haemorrhages usually mean, Dr Morgenthal?'

'That she was asphyxiated, sir.'

'And do you think that she did all that to herself or that it happened naturally?'

'No, sir, it's clearly a murder. I missed the obvious, didn't I?'

'Perhaps you just have other things on your mind, this morning. Shall we prep for the dissection?'

As Simon laid out the surgical instruments that they would need to examine the internal organs, Cuthbert took a last detailed look at the surface of the body. He noted again everything that he had previously documented, and then he saw it.

On the inside surface of the right elbow there was a small red dot with a slight flare around it. He had to force the arm straight to see it clearly, but it was unmistakable. In the crook of her elbow was the mark left by a hypodermic needle.

No needles were found at the scene and none were expected. These were the rooms of Soho prostitutes who would be lucky if they could charge five shillings a time. They would have enough money on occasion to drink themselves into oblivion, but buying drugs to inject was quite a different matter. Suddenly, Cuthbert thought this case had become very interesting indeed.

The examination of the internal organs confirmed the early suspicions of asphyxia. The tell-tale pinpoint haemorrhages that Morgenthal had seen in the victim's eyes were also to be found on her lungs, suggesting that she had been strangled or suffocated. The absence of any ligature marks around the neck and the fact that her larynx was undamaged favoured suffocation.

The possibility of a drug overdose was not discounted by Cuthbert, and he especially looked for signs that she may have aspirated and choked on her own vomit as so many addicts did. But again, they drew a blank there; her airways were clear.

Surprisingly, there were few internal signs of chronic alcohol consumption, which Cuthbert noted as unusual in a woman such as this. He did find further evidence of past pregnancies. The cervix was consistent with at least one previous delivery. Instead of a small, round opening it was slit-like, and the cervix itself was thicker and bulkier than that in a woman who had never given birth to a child. For them to examine the cervix, Morgenthal had to wipe away the pool of semen in her vagina.

'I expect that might have been left by the killer, sir.'

'I'm afraid, Simon, that this is probably the seed of several different men. She might have had as many as ten clients that night. This woman inhabited a very different world from you or me.'

Morgenthal grimaced and shook his head and muttered something about her being a foreigner and what could you expect. But Cuthbert was having none of it.

'Dr Morgenthal, I expect you to leave such small-minded opinions at the door when you come into my department. Vice has always been linked to other people in this country, especially to foreigners, and I would prefer not to hear such a distorted view of it all. We think, if it is obscene, then it must have come here from elsewhere.

'Take syphilis – in England they still call it the French

disease. Do you know what they call it in France? The English disease. Nobody, I'm pleased to say, however, has ever seen fit to call it the Scottish disease. Now, make use of that extra pair of hands you promised me and clear up here while I write the report.'

*

At Scotland Yard, Sergeant Baker knocked on his D.C.I.'s office door. James Mowbray had only been a detective chief inspector for eighteen months, but during that time he had successfully concluded one of the most high-profile murder cases the Yard had seen in some years. Because of his age – he was only 32 – his appointment had been controversial, but his performance had more than justified it. The brass upstairs at Scotland Yard were certainly taking notice and realised they were dealing with a man who might rise all the way to the top. Today, however, there were more mundane matters to be dealt with.

'Anything to get excited about, Baker?'

'Dr Cuthbert did seem to take an interest, sir.'

'Thought this would have been one for his junior. Why did the great Scot show up?'

Mowbray had found a working relationship with Cuthbert. He was a pragmatist and did whatever was needed to get the work done, and that included opening up his duty room to the pathologist from St Thomas's.

He had recognised almost as soon as he met him that the pathologist had a remarkable mind, but he also found him to be arrogant, dour and, at times, insufferable. For the most part, Mowbray could overlook all that; perhaps because he knew he could be exactly the same. They came from different worlds, but over a glass of single malt he found he could talk to Cuthbert, and he couldn't talk to many.

'I believe Dr Morgenthal was getting wed, sir, so Dr Cuthbert did the scene on his own.'

'I bet that took a while. Did you slip out for a shave halfway through, sergeant?'

'He was meticulous, sir – as usual.'

'Better get him in, I suppose. Why don't you ask him to come over and deliver his report in person? I think that chair in the duty room still has his name on it.'

Baker made the call and got the board ready. At the far end of the duty room, Mowbray liked to use a pinboard as a visual summary of the case he was working on. Some of the detective constables saw it as a piece of nonsense designed to attract attention.

They called him the Pie behind his back and thought he was trying to show off his modern credentials. He was young for the job, and he was intent on using his youth to show that he wasn't stuck in the old ruts of investigation. Nonetheless, Mowbray found his case board much more than a symbol of his new way of doing things: he found it really worked.

Baker pinned a post mortem photograph of Dutch Edie's face on the board and beside it a sheet of paper listing the few key points that were known so far. He hoped after Dr Cuthbert's visit to have much more to add.

*

It was a cold day, but a bright one, and Cuthbert decided to walk over Westminster Bridge and along the Embankment to Scotland Yard. He had been in the building many times, yet he still found he had to speak slowly to the desk constable at reception.

His Edinburgh accent had undoubtedly mellowed since he had arrived in London several years before, but obviously not enough to make himself understood to the bemused young man.

Once he had managed to sign in, he quickly took the stairs two at a time and arrived at the duty room on the third floor, fresh and with his breath unlaboured. The desk constable there looked up to see the imposing Scot towering over him, and without saying a word directed him through to join Mowbray's team assembling around the board.

'Ah, good to see you, Dr Cuthbert. On time as always, I see.'

'I think you'll find I am three minutes early, chief inspector. Being on time is being late.'

'Well, doctor, we appreciate you taking the time to deliver your report in person. Perhaps we should get started and that way you can leave three minutes early too.'

Mowbray was, as ever, unimpressed by anyone who took his good nature for granted. He didn't like being contradicted in front of his staff and in his own duty room at that, and he wasn't about to let even Cuthbert away with it. The pathologist, for his part, was just as unimpressed by the petty sensibilities of other men and moved on immediately to the reason he was there.

He stood in front of Mowbray's board and described his findings. He focused on the fact that Dutch Edie had died from asphyxiation, most probably with a pillow over her face. He highlighted the bite mark but added that there were other facts that suggested a more complex picture. Until that point, Mowbray had been silent, but now he looked up and asked for more detail.

'Chief inspector, the victim had a single hypodermic needle mark on her arm. However, she was clearly not a drug addict. For one thing she wouldn't have the money for drugs, and there were no other needle marks on her body, or any paraphernalia related to drug use found in her belongings. So what might be the explanation? Was she experimenting with drugs for the first time? Was she perhaps injected by someone else? We do not yet know, but what is clear is that this is not a straightforward murder of a prostitute by one of her clients.'

'All because of one needle mark, doctor? I think we're going to need more than that, don't you? When you have it, do let us know. In the meantime, don't let us keep you. I wouldn't want you to be merely on time for your next appointment.'

Cuthbert scowled as Mowbray turned and walked back to his office, but he knew the chief inspector was right. If he was going to make the case for a premeditated murder over a client who had got out of hand, he was going to have to give Mowbray and his team more. He went back to the mortuary to find Simon.

*

'Given the needle mark on the victim's arm, I think it might be profitable to spend some time analysing the white powder I collected at the scene. It could, of course, be some form of cosmetic, perhaps even a simple stomach remedy that was spilled from a glass on the bedside table, but it might be more. Do you think you could take that on, Dr Morgenthal, while I take another look at that bite mark?'

Simon knew it was not a request but a polite instruction, and he quickly agreed to get the necessary analyses done that day. He assembled the various pieces of apparatus and chemicals he needed and retrieved the material itself from the evidence bag.

He took the sealed glass jar that Cuthbert had used to collect the white powder at the crime scene, and he first checked its label. His mentor's handwriting was small and neat and always very clear. The date, time and location of collection were noted, and Simon carefully transcribed these into a new page in his laboratory notebook.

He had three tests to perform that would tell him if various drugs were present or not in the sample. Working at the bench, he began by carefully mixing small amounts of sulphuric acid with different salts in order to prepare the fresh reagents he would require for the tests.

The first was called the Marquis test. For this he would need a mixture of the acid and formaldehyde. In a small, dimpled enamel dish, he sprinkled a minute amount of the powder into one of the wells on to which he then dripped a single drop of the clear reagent. He had to concentrate and control the tremor in his hand as he did so because he was anxious to do a good job. In a few seconds, the colour changed in the dish, and Simon consulted his notes on the test to interpret what he was seeing. The mixture had taken on a deep, purple-red colour, and this was a positive reaction for opioid drugs such as morphine and heroin.

He repeated the procedure with two different reagents. The next was the Lieberman test, which required a reagent mixed from the acid and potassium nitrite, and this time the colour formed was a very dark yellow. Simon checked his notes. Morphine gave a black colour with this test and the stimulant cocaine a bright yellow one. Putting this result together with that from the previous test which had suggested the presence of opioids, he concluded that he was most probably dealing with a mixture of different drugs.

Finally, he tried another colour test using the Mandelin reagent mixed from the acid and an ammonium salt. This formed a muddy brown colour. Simon repeated the test and observed the initial colour reactions. When he dripped the reagent into the well on the dish, he noticed some immediate deep orange colour, which would have been consistent with cocaine, and red brown and dark grey flecks that very quickly merged into the same dark muddy colour as before.

He knew that in this test morphine gave a dark grey colour and heroin a red brown, and his confidence was growing that the powder was indeed a composite of three different drugs so popular with addicts: heroin, morphine and cocaine.

Although these colour tests were highly suggestive of the presence of the drugs in the powder, he knew Cuthbert would need more convincing. Morgenthal knew he had to perform further tests.

His next approach was to perform one of the newer analytical techniques. He had read about this test and had watched Cuthbert carry it out only once, but now he had to run it himself.

He read up on the method before performing it. This test involved dissolving very small amounts of the powder in different solvents and allowing the components to recrystallise as they dried on a small glass microscope slide. Using the microscope on a low power, he could then examine the colour, shape and orientation of the crystals that were formed. Depending on the solvent used, each drug would have a distinctive set of characteristics, almost as unique as a fingerprint.

As he was using this as a confirmatory test, he confined himself to searching specifically for the two narcotics and the stimulant that the colour tests had suggested. He first dissolved a tiny sample of the powder in a gold bromide solution and noted the resultant crystals to be a pale pink or orange, arranged in a feather-like pattern. This was just what he expected to see if there was morphine present.

He repeated the test using two further solvents. With a gold chloride solution, he could see colourless rosettes of fine needle-like crystals down the lens, and these were unmistakably heroin. Lastly, with a platinum chloride solution he saw the very distinctive pale yellow, square and diamond-shaped crystal plates characteristic of cocaine.

He wrote up all these findings in his laboratory report, as he knew Cuthbert would want to see not just the results but every detail of the step-by-step procedures that had been used to obtain them. Only if Cuthbert was satisfied with the quality of the methods used, would he be satisfied with the quality of the results obtained.

'So there were drugs in the room – white drugs.'

'White drugs, sir?'

'That's what the addicts call the modern refined preparations of morphine, heroin and cocaine. They're the medical preparations we use in practice, and they can be readily and accurately dosed, as opposed to their raw counterparts, the brown drugs of opium and hashish. But I still can't believe our victim would have got them for herself. Someone else, probably her last client, must have brought them in, and he may even have been the one to inject her with them.'

'Why do that and then put a pillow over her face? It doesn't make sense to me, Dr Cuthbert. Surely if he wanted to kill her, he could just have done it with an overdose.'

'I have to concede, Simon, that is a serious flaw in my argument. I'm just not sure what else this woman can tell us about how she died. Cover her up, Simon, and we'll think again tomorrow. Perhaps some daylight might help.'

Chapter 4

Paris: 17 January 1908

The two women lifted their skirts to avoid the thick, grey slush on the pavement. A chilling wind blew about them, and the younger of the two shivered in her thin coat as they walked quickly along the Boulevard de Clichy.

'Now, when we get there, Claudette, I want you to smile. You have such a beautiful smile, little one, and it will help you get in. Everything depends on you being accepted.'

It was late morning, but the sun had hardly risen in the sky. A meagre light was all there was to reveal this part of Paris coming to life. Other districts in the city had been awake for hours, but here in Pigalle they lived at night and slept during the day.

The women walked past the cafés, which were open and serving their reviving cups of black coffee, and the bars, which had only closed a few hours before. Outside the cabaret, three cleaning women were tipping out pails of steaming water to wash away the stench and detritus of the night.

Claudette looked up at the towering red windmill that stood above the entrance and at the vivid posters advertising the shows, but she was hurried along by the older woman.

They turned the corner, walked along Rue de Bruxelles and stopped in the street outside number 10. Claudette looked up at the gaudy number plate above the door. The other houses in the street bore the usual small blue-and-white Parisian house numbers, but not this one. She did not know much, but she knew what that meant – everyone did.

The large house was shuttered even during the faint winter daylight and earned its name as one of the *maisons closes* in Pigalle. Although the others were smarter and frequented by the better classes, this was the one Jeanne and Claudette were looking for.

The street was quiet that morning, but at nightfall in the arrondissement there would be *filles publiques* standing beneath every gaslight. However, the girls who worked in the tolerated brothels of the *maisons closes* at least did not have to take their clients against the hard brick walls of the side streets.

These houses offered some protection, but the work was no less exhausting and no less degrading. The high black door on to the street was opened by a maid and they were shown into a small side room off the tiled hallway.

'Jeanne, my dear, how good to see you. How long has it been? Three years? I think you know you still owe me money, my dear. I hope you're here to pay up. You remember Georges, don't you? He's still very handy with that razor—'

'Madame Souquet! It's so good to see you again, and please don't think I've forgotten my debts. There's no need for Georges to know I'm here. No need at all. We can talk, can't we? Come to some understanding. As you can see, I have brought someone to meet you, madame. This is my daughter, Claudette. She has been so looking forward to coming to see the famous Madame Souquet.'

Jeanne Martin pushed her 14-year-old daughter into the light so that madame could see just how fresh and lovely she was. The brothel owner now knew exactly how her old employee expected to pay her debts.

'She is a pretty one, right enough. How old?'

'Sweet sixteen, madame, and never been touched.'

'Really? That does make her interesting. But she does know what's what, I hope. I don't have the time to hand-hold a new one.'

'Oh, no need for that. Claudette has a wise old head on young shoulders. She understands exactly what is required.'

The madame circled around the young girl as if appraising a heifer and then grasped her chin.

'Show me your teeth, dear. Good, all there and still white.' She surprised the girl by cupping one of her breasts and squeezing it. 'Yes, I could work with this one, and I think I have a very valued client who might enjoy having her first. But don't think that will be enough, Jeanne. You owe me two hundred francs plus interest, and the girl will have to work for a good while to clear that.'

'I know, I know, madame. But if you could see your way to accepting her work as a payment in kind, I would be most obliged. Things have not been going too well of late, and you know how it is.'

'No, how is it, Jeanne? How is it when you walk out of a good job in a fine house, running after the coat-tails of some man? How is it when you abandon the person who has looked after you and always made sure you were safe and clean? How is it when you run away without paying your dues?'

'I'm sorry, madame. I've said I'm sorry a hundred times, and I don't know what else to say. It was a terrible thing to do to you, after everything you did for me. But I'm here to make amends as best I can. Please, madame, please take Claudette.'

The madame looked the young girl over again and sighed. 'I suppose we'll get something out of her. Leave her here and we'll see. But you mind me, if she turns out to be a cry-baby, she'll find herself out on the street, or worse – I'll let Georges have her.'

'No need to talk like that, madame. She's a good girl. She'll do as she's bid.'

She turned to her daughter, who had said not a word during the whole transaction, and looked at her. She took her in her arms and held her and could feel her shoulders starting to shake. As she did, she whispered in her ear that she must never cry in this house. Then, so as madame could hear, she told her to be good and to make sure she minded what she was told.

Without waiting for the girl to respond or even say goodbye, her mother turned and left, and Claudette heard the street door close. Outside in the cold, Jeanne Martin held on to the wall of the house and clamped a hand to her mouth, holding in the scream she wanted to unleash.

She knew exactly what would happen to Claudette that night and every night from then on. She knew that she would never be allowed to leave the house and would be a virtual prisoner of the madame. She knew that her virginity would be sold for a premium and then her youth would ensure that she would work the upper floors with their smarter clients.

But in time she would end up on the ground floor with the sailors and the labourers queuing up outside her room with their numbered tickets – fifty, sixty, sometimes even seventy in one night. And she knew that no matter how many times her daughter would endure the weight of those drunken, filthy men, her debt would never be paid. That's the way the *maisons closes* worked.

*

Claudette never saw the first shoots of the early spring, but she did learn quickly, both to do the job and to hate everything about it. Madame Souquet smiled as she studied her ledgers and saw how much the young girl was bringing in, but she made sure she never revealed her pleasure. Better if all the girls thought she was doing them a favour keeping them under her roof. The madame, however, always had an eye for business, and when the opportunity arose to make an even quicker profit from Claudette, she seized upon it.

Georges, whom she kept in order to exert pressure on her girls whenever it was needed, could occasionally surprise her with an idea. Just over a month after Claudette had started work, Georges told his employer about a man he had met in a bar one night on the Rue Puget.

'They're looking for young girls, madame, and they need to be French. They want them for London,' he said. 'Apparently, they like a little piece of Paris over there and are willing to pay more for it. And here's the trick. They buy the girl and get her married to an Englishman over here, she gets a British passport as a result, and then they ship her over and work her in London. Because she's British, she can't get deported back here.'

'And what are they offering?'

'For a good one, he says they'll pay five hundred francs.'

Madame Souquet did some calculations in her head. She factored in that as business was slowing a little, she had one too many girls at the moment and therefore one too many mouths to feed. She had been planning to throw Marie out, but if she could sell Claudette, she would solve her problem and make a tidy profit at the same time.

'How does this all work, Georges? And don't tell me you'll be organising it.'

'No, madame. I'll just collect the money for you. They bring over some man they've paid for, and he marries her and then we never see him again. Once she's got the marriage certificate, she can apply for her passport. They pay up, take the girl, and then we never see her again either.'

'And what makes you think they'll pay?'

Georges took his razor from his pocket and caressed the blade with his forefinger. 'They all pay up, madame. You don't have to worry about that.'

Madame Souquet gave Georges the go-ahead and within a week there was a short, red-headed man who smelt of cheap cognac standing in the foyer. He had no French, but the madame spoke enough English to be understood. She watched him as he eyed the pictures on her walls and the inlaid tiles on her floor that spelled out *Maison Souquet*.

'Please do not get too comfortable, monsieur. This is a business transaction. The girl you will marry is Claudette. If you harm her, I will have your balls cut off – slowly. Clear?'

The Englishman was in no doubt that Madame Souquet was serious, and he was equally sure that she would probably not delegate the task. He had never met a woman with angrier eyes, and he nodded.

'Do I get to meet the young lady?'

'You will meet her at the town hall where you will be married. Once you have the papers, you give them to my assistant, Georges, and then you leave.'

'Can't I see her beforehand?'

'No one sees my girls without paying. If you have the money and you would like to spend it, I'm sure we can accommodate you. If not, we will see you tomorrow morning at ten o'clock precisely.'

The madame could see he would not be a paying customer and had him ushered from her house. As he left, he spat on the step and slurred some obscenity that she did not understand. Perhaps she should have a word with Georges anyway.

Claudette had been told nothing about the plans and found

herself roused early the next morning by the madame herself, who told her to hurry as she had an appointment to keep. Claudette had not left the *maison close* during the day since she arrived and was too frightened to ask what was happening. She remembered her mother's words and fought back the tears, then dutifully washed and dressed before presenting herself in the foyer.

Madame Souquet ordered Georges to escort the girl the short walk to the town hall and to make sure she returned untouched by the Englishman. As she turned to look at Claudette, she could see she was confused; only then did she explain that it was her wedding day.

'And remember, *ma cherie*, when they ask your age, you are eighteen. And don't worry about the man you are marrying. It's just business.'

Georges took the girl by the arm. He rushed her along, almost dragging her, and they arrived five minutes later on Rue Jean-Baptiste Pigalle.

'These are your papers. They're fakes, of course, but your name is Claudette Martin and you're eighteen and you're an orphan. You have a letter from madame who is listed as your guardian, giving you permission to marry. Say nothing unless they ask you. And try to look as if you're happy. It's your wedding day. I'll be waiting here and he's waiting inside for you.'

She looked at this rough, stocky man, and although she was just as frightened of him and his threats as all the other girls at the *maison*, she now found herself reluctant to leave his side. She also realised she had no idea what her new husband looked like, so how was she to know him?

Georges saw her confusion and pulled her arm from his. 'He's the short one with red hair who can't speak French.'

Twenty minutes later, the couple emerged into the courtyard. Georges stamped out his cigarette and quickly approached them.

'Have you got the papers?' he asked in French. Claudette nodded and pointed to the Englishman's jacket pocket. He simply looked at Georges and said in words that no one understood that he didn't know what the man was saying and now that he was married, he wanted his dues. Georges seized him, ripped the papers from his inside pocket and pulled the girl away.

'Wait up. What about me? I'm the husband. I should get my rights. That's the law, ain't it?'

Georges did not understand his words but he could read his eyes. He knew exactly what the ugly little drunk wanted. He took Claudette by the wrist and placed her behind him. Squaring up against the Englishman, he leant into his face and said the only words he knew in his language: 'Fuck off!' As he did so, he drew his razor in one swift move across the cheek of the Englishman. They left him bent over, squealing and clutching his face.

Georges ushered the girl quickly back to the *maison*, and when they arrived, Claudette actually felt some relief as the street door closed. The place was a prison, but it was safer than the streets outside.

The next morning, Georges took Claudette on the long walk to the British Embassy from the streets of Pigalle. She gazed in awe at the finery of the buildings and shops on Rue du Faubourg Saint-Honoré, but her chaperone hurried her along. He left her to enter the Embassy on her own. This time he waited for over an hour for her to emerge, but she nodded when he asked if everything was arranged.

Her British passport was issued eight days later, and that night she was told she was going to London. This time she was unable to control the tears, and she fell at the madame's feet and begged her not to send her away.

'Now, now, none of that, little one. It's only business. You will have someone new to look after you, and London is such a bright place for a young Parisienne. You will be so exotic, *ma cherie*. The clients will flock to you. Georges will take you to the station, where you'll meet the man you are to work for. I doubt he will be as kind and understanding as your madame, but then few are.'

She prised the girl's fingers from her skirts and left her on the floor, dishevelled and sobbing.

The man they met at Gare du Nord was tall, gaunt and humourless. He was more interested in Claudette's papers than the girl herself. He gave her only a cursory glance but seemed to be satisfied that she was the one that had been negotiated for. He had some French and said something to Georges that Claudette did not hear, but it made the minder cackle with laughter.

The Englishman handed Georges a thick envelope, and the Frenchman proceeded to count the notes while they stood on the platform for the boat train to Boulogne. He knew he could not hand over to his madame anything short of the agreed price.

He nodded, and the Englishman took Claudette roughly by the arm and put her on the train. She opened the carriage window and looked out only to see the broad back of her minder walking away. She never saw him, or Paris, again.

*

The streets of London were different, and she understood almost nothing of what was said. However, the men and what they wanted to do to her were exactly the same.

Bill, as she came to know the ponce who would work her, was just as menacing as Georges but relied on his fists rather than any razor. She soon bore the bruises he gave her if he thought she was slacking, and she would stay on the streets rather than go home to him in the rooms they rented in Soho. He never slept with her even though they shared a bed in one room and used the other for her trade. He collected all the money she earned but was never satisfied.

The other street girls, seeing how young she was, would try to speak to her, but not understanding their words or their intentions, she shied away from them and became increasingly isolated. She had no regular pitch, for such spots had to be earned or more usually fought over. Instead, she plied her trade around the streets in Soho, picking up men wherever she could.

One evening in the early summer, she was out after dark doing what she always did, strolling between streetlights and lingering in shop doorways and in the entrances to alleyways.

The plain-clothes constable walked along Wardour Street past the churchyard keeping to the shadows and avoiding the puddles of gaslight. His collar was up, and his hat pulled low.

On the corner of Old Compton Street, he saw the girl under the street lamp. This one looked like the others, but she was younger than the rest. He slowed as he approached, and she smiled and whispered something in a soft, plaintive voice. He could not make out the words but knew exactly what was being asked. He had to hear her plainly, though, and she had to approach him, so he paused to allow her to come over and she obliged. She even took his arm as she whispered again her terms.

'That's a good accent, right enough. Probably the best I've heard, but it makes no difference, darling, 'cause you're nicked. And don't go scratching me now, unless you want a thick lip.'

He twisted her wrists and led her around the corner to the waiting police van. With the help of a waiting constable, he threw her in the back along with three other women the team had picked up earlier that night.

Claudette spent the night in the cells at Vine Street Station and was brought before the magistrate the next morning. Their appearances were perfunctory, and the other two, older women were each given a twenty-shilling fine. Claudette, however, caught the attention of the elderly magistrate.

'I am well aware, miss, that we have double standards as regards prostitution in this city. Conduct by a *fille de joie* such as yourself in Cadogan Square, which would let her see the inside of a police cell, might well be passed over in the Stepney Docks or even the streets of Soho. Nonetheless, I feel compelled to make an example of you. You are a young woman and I do not feel you are wholly lost to this life of degradation. With the correct instruction, and if given the opportunity to reflect on your crimes, I sincerely hope you might put this way of life behind you and begin anew. As such, I sentence you to twenty-eight days in Holloway.'

Claudette Martin stood alone and frightened in the dock, and of course understood not one word of what the magistrate had said. If she had known how to work the system, she would have exaggerated her age because the old men sitting on the benches tended to hand down fines to the older women, whom they thought beyond redemption. It was only with the young ones that they hoped to exert any influence.

She was removed from the dock by the female orderlies and all but thrown down the stairs from the courtroom, before being taken across London to the women's prison. Four weeks later she was back on the streets of Soho after receiving a beating from her ponce for losing a month's earnings.

The heat of the London summer made it easier to stand on the streets, but the shorter nights meant the cover of darkness was harder to come by. Claudette had known she was pregnant when she was in prison and knew that it would earn her another beating or worse from her bully. She was almost beginning to show and had to adjust her clothes to make sure it didn't affect her trade.

She also knew she was going to need help when her time came. When one of the other street girls smiled and said hello to her one evening, she smiled back for the first time and spoke. The other girl was probably in her twenties and was surprised to hear Claudette speak.

'My, you really do sound French, luvvie. Is that where you're from?'

Claudette was still struggling with her English but was now able to understand enough to nod and tell the girl her name.

'Ooh, that is a nice name. Mine's Ethel. Been on the game long?'

Claudette was able to show with her fingers that she had been working for the last six months, but the way she stroked her belly as she tried to make herself understood made the other girl realise the situation the young French girl was in.

'You in the family way? I think you are. Don't worry. We can get old Meg to have a look. Follow me, luvvie, and I'll get you sorted.'

Claudette did not understand the words but could see the kindness in the other girl's eyes and knew she had no choice but to take whatever help might be offered. She knew she could not cope with whatever lay ahead on her own. The other girl took Claudette up a stair just off Greek Street and knocked on a door.

'Meg! You in? Need a quick word.'

The door was opened by a plump woman in her fifties who was smoking a cigarette. Claudette peered around Ethel to see what they had come to. Meg invited them both in and quickly assessed the situation.

She spoke to Claudette in soft, soothing tones as she examined her before turning to Ethel. 'Looks like she's five months gone. And she's big. I think the poor cow might be having twins.' Ethel asked about getting rid of them, only to be hushed by Meg, who just shook her head and said, 'Bit late for that, dear.'

After some false starts, they managed to find out who Claudette's ponce was, and both women rolled their eyes at his name. Bill Thompson was notorious. They quietly conferred and concluded that she would most likely be beaten so badly that she would not only lose the babies but also her life.

'And I'm not having that on this patch,' said Meg. 'She'll be able to keep working for a while. Some of 'em will even pay more to have her pregnant. But in the winter, she's going to need help.'

Meg again spoke softly to Claudette and thought she had managed to make her understand that she must get away from her bully and come back to her when her time was due.

That night Claudette worked the street as usual, and all the time she was thinking of how she could escape from Bill. She had no money and nowhere to run even if she did. She couldn't go back to Paris, for Georges and his razor would doubtless find her wherever she hid. Her only hope was to find somewhere where Bill couldn't reach her – and where was safer than prison?

The next night and the one after that, she walked around the Soho streets not looking for trade but searching for any policemen. On one corner she saw a uniformed constable chatting to a man in ordinary clothes. She could see that they knew each other and realised they were both policemen. When the plain-clothes constable walked away, she followed him and gave him his easiest arrest of the night.

She was back in Holloway the next afternoon and safe for another month. The prison was grim and frightening, but nowhere near as bad as the streets she worked every night.

While in her cell, she lay awake at night trying to make some sort of plan. She knew she could not go back to her room, but she still needed somewhere to stay and to give birth. She gave no thought to what would happen to her afterwards; all her focus was on securing a safe place for her babies.

On her release, she was surprised to find Ethel waiting for her outside the prison gate. Everyone on the street knew that Bill was waiting for his little French girl because he had told them all what he planned to do to her. He was bent on teaching Claudette a lesson. But it was early morning and Ethel knew that he would still be lying in his bed drunk from the night before. This was their chance to make the girl disappear.

'You all right, dear? Bugger of a place. Seen the inside of it too many times myself. You need to come with me now, d'you understand? You need to see Meg again and she'll sort you out.'

Claudette was relieved to see Ethel and clung to her arm. She found it hard to follow what was being said to her, but she could read the friendly concern on Ethel's face and managed to make out something about 'Meg'.

She recalled the older woman's kindness and gentle touch and went willingly with Ethel. When they arrived at the rooms on Greek Street, Ethel left Claudette with Meg and went back to her own lodgings.

'You'll be staying here now, dear. That man will not get his hands on you while you're under my roof,' soothed Meg. 'And when your time comes, you'll have the babies here.'

Claudette knew the risks this woman was taking and could not understand what would make her care for someone she hardly knew. In her broken English, she thanked her and asked her why.

'Because you're one of us, my love, and one day you can pay me back by helping some other poor girl that needs it. We have to stick together. No man is ever going to help us. Now, settle in, dear, and I'll put the word about that you've run away back to France. That'll get him looking in all the wrong places.'

*

As it turned out, Bill's drunken rage proved his undoing. When he learned that his Claudette had skipped the country and was on her way back to Paris, he used his fists in the wrong pub.

He was better at hitting women, but the man he chose to punch that night did not cower and weep and plead. He stabbed him in the throat and then carried on drinking his ale.

When Claudette heard, she allowed herself a rare moment of joy. She was almost due, and everything was uncomfortable about the small room on Greek Street, but she was safe and soon she would be a mother.

Meg helped as best she could, but Claudette's labour, when it came, was long and difficult. The boy was born first and ten minutes later the girl. Both looked healthy and, although she was exhausted, Claudette held them and suckled them. Meg watched her fall in love with the infants and knew the longer she spent with them, the harder it would be.

She offered to take them away, but the young girl would not let go of their tiny bodies. Meg knew what had to happen. 'It's best if you do this yourself, dear. That way you'll know it's done right, and you can say your goodbyes.'

When she managed to get up and get dressed, Claudette steeled herself for the inevitable. Her months in Pigalle had taught her how to bury her emotions, but nothing could stop her tears now.

She wrapped the twins warmly and then walked out with them in the early hours and placed the two small bundles huddled together in the doorway of the pawnbroker's on Old

Compton Street. All the girls said the elderly Pole who ran the shop was a kind gentleman who would never harm the children. As she swaddled them in her shawl, she placed a trinket inside and pressed her face into theirs to smell them and feel the last of their warmth.

The small brother and his sister did not cry but slept in peace with their cheeks touching. Claudette was overwhelmed with sadness but knew she could not keep her children. She had no money, no home and would have to work the streets just to get enough to eat herself. She stroked their tiny heads and kissed them one last time before whispering, '*Pardonnez-moi, mes petits.*'

Early the next morning, Marek Jankowski was met with two squealing newborn babies on his doorstep, and he immediately took them into the warmth of his shop and summoned help. The police constable, who was a new father himself, knew they were hungry and arranged to take them directly to the Foundling Hospital.

'Will they take them in, officer?'

'I'll do my best, sir. They'll at least get fed and baptised. More than that, I can't promise.'

Chapter 5

London: 3 March 1930

The following week, the call came in while Cuthbert and Morgenthal were performing the post mortem examination on a small child who had died after a fall from a fifth-floor tenement window in Elephant and Castle. The boy was three years old and lay white and still on the adult slab.

Simon was only too happy to leave the tiny remnant of the toddler's body to answer the phone in Cuthbert's office.

'It's the Yard, sir. They say they have another possible prostitute murder in Soho.'

'Take the details, will you, Simon? Perhaps you would be kind enough to deal with that one while I finish up here.'

'They say they think it's like the last one, sir.'

Cuthbert stopped his examination of the child's fatal head injuries and turned to his assistant. 'In that case, tell them we'll both be attending.'

*

On Greek Street at the back of the Palace Theatre in Soho, there was a huddle of people around the entrance to number 26, spilling out from the pavement and onto the road. As

Morgenthal and Cuthbert walked from where their taxi had been forced to drop them at the corner of Shaftesbury Avenue, they could see a young uniformed constable holding back three women. The officer saw Cuthbert approaching and immediately apologised.

'Terribly sorry about this, sir. I'll get you inside in just a moment.' Turning his attention back to the women, who were shouting all at once, he raised his voice. 'Enough, ladies! This is a crime scene and there is no admittance. I don't care who you are, who you know or what you want up them stairs, there's no one getting in. Right, make way for these gentlemen – they're with the police. Move aside!'

Cuthbert politely but firmly pushed his way through the throng, and Morgenthal followed suit. When they were through the door, the young man asked what all the commotion was about.

'Some of them probably live here, and all of them certainly work here. Everything they have, including any money they made last night, is probably in these rooms. And if you'd worked as hard for it as they have, you'd be doing everything you could to keep it safe too.'

'But the building is cordoned off, and it's only the police officers who are here. Anything valuable is surely as safe as houses.'

'I'm not sure those ladies would share your confidence in the honesty of our boys in blue, especially not in a brothel. Now, shall we see what we've got?'

They climbed the stairs to the second floor. The room was not unlike the last one Cuthbert had visited. It was just as small and perhaps even dirtier. The damp was making the paper peel from the walls, and the floorboards were gritty underfoot and sticky in places. The room smelt of unwashed linen and men's sweat. This time the curtains remained closed, and Morgenthal could only just make out the figure of a woman lying on her back on the bed.

Cuthbert checked the curtains carefully before drawing them back and flooding the room with the grey afternoon light of early spring. The dreadful scene became all too obvious.

The dark-haired woman was positioned in the same pose as the last victim, legs spread with her genitals fully on display. The bed, though dirty, was not disturbed, and Cuthbert could see she had not been able to put up any fight for her life. He asked Morgenthal to perform the usual temperature checks to help ascertain the time of death, while he changed into his white coat and took the rubber gloves from his bag.

'Tell me what we're looking at, Dr Morgenthal.'

Morgenthal recognised the change in tone and expression in Cuthbert's voice and knew he was being tested again. He took a breath and surveyed the scene and, remembering the order in which his mentor liked to have things reported, he proceeded.

'The is the body of a Caucasian woman who looks to be in her late thirties or perhaps early forties. She appears to be lying in a position that would be consistent with sexual intercourse.'

Morgenthal scoured the surface of the woman's body without touching her or her clothes. Still painfully aware of the errors he had made last time, he checked her neck for ligatures or their marks and her eyes for any sign of suffocation.

'She has extensive petechiae in the conjunctivae of both eyes, and the suffusion of the skin on her face and neck would suggest death by asphyxiation, sir.'

'Anything else, Simon?'

'And there are semi-circular red marks on the right shoulder, sir, that would be consistent with a bite mark. It could be human, and it certainly looks similar to the last case.'

'Yes, that's what I thought too. Does she have any needle marks on her arms?'

The woman's dress had been ripped to expose the shoulder, but her sleeves were rolled down and the skin in the crooks of her elbows was not initially visible. Simon carefully rolled up each sleeve and found the tell-tale red puncture wound in the right arm.

Cuthbert looked around to see what else he could learn. Like all these rooms, it was not designed for living in; it was a workroom, where a woman could sell the only thing she had worth buying.

There was a wash bowl and jug, a soiled rag and towel, and on the solitary wooden chair, a pillow from the bed. Cuthbert looked to see if it might be the murder weapon, and it did bear stains from the woman's rouge and marks that might have been saliva and nasal secretions. As Morgenthal was bagging the pillow slip at Cuthbert's request, Sergeant Baker arrived.

'My apologies, Dr Cuthbert. I would have been here earlier, sir, but it's getting rather rowdy down in the street, and P.C. Cummings needed a hand. Do you and Dr Morgenthal have everything you need for the time being?'

'Don't trouble yourself, sergeant, we're fine. We're almost done here.'

Baker's sudden expression of surprise made Cuthbert smile.

'I know, it's a red-letter day when I finish a crime scene in under the hour. But I'm afraid we've seen all this before, sergeant. Take a look, and you'll see what I mean. Same story as Gerrard Street, right down to the bite mark. No white drugs left behind this time that I can see, but a hypodermic has definitely been used on her.'

'Is it the same man, do you think, doctor?'

'We can never be sure at this stage, but if I were a betting man, which as a good Presbyterian I am not, I'd give you very good odds, sergeant. Dr Morgenthal will be writing up the report on this one, and after he's performed the post mortem examination, we'll let you know. Perhaps Chief Inspector Mowbray will be a little more interested now that we have a second victim.'

Baker had no doubt of that. This was going to be a much more important case than the killing of some anonymous tart in a grimy room in Soho. This was the kind of case that reached the headlines of even the quality papers, and made them recycle all the hyperbole they had first used just over forty years before with the Whitechapel murders. The kind of case that made the brass on the top floor of Scotland Yard ask questions. And if Mowbray got asked questions, he would only be asking them of his detective sergeant in turn.

Baker knew he needed to do everything by the book on this one, for the scrutiny was likely to be intense. He started on the witness statements downstairs. The three women who had been anxious to get into the building were still on the pavement outside.

'Which one of you ladies found the body?'

'Me. Gladys Watson's the name. It was horrible, so it was. I've seen a lot in my time, but that takes the biscuit, that does. God almighty, it don't bear thinking about. Just makes yer blood run cold, don't it, Floss?'

The woman looked to be about the same age as the victim and was clearly of the same profession. She was painfully thin, her clothes were shabby, and her face was thickly made up.

She shuddered as she spoke and wrapped her arms tight about her to banish the cold and the memory of what she had seen that morning. She could not provide a name for the murdered woman, but one of the other women told Baker that her first name had been Jeanette; no one knew her last name.

'She were lovely, just lovely. Liked a drink, but always had time for you, you know. It's a rough game, this is, and you need all the help you can get. She taught me a thing or two,

I can tell you, and it saved me more than once. And if you was short on the subs for the Fine Club, she'd always help you, wouldn't she, Ada?'

'That she would. Proper friend, she was, and it's not right what's happened to her, not one bit. No one deserves that, especially not Jeanette.'

'The Fine Club?'

'You should know all about that, dearie. After all, you lot are the reason we need to save up. Forty bob, that's what the fine is for us now, and who's got that sitting doing nothing in their purse? I'll tell you, nobody round here. So we all chip in two bob a week to the club, and it pays the fine when one of us gets nicked, see.'

Baker asked the three of them about the previous night and whether they had heard or seen anything out of the ordinary. Although they occupied adjacent rooms in the building, it was soon clear that they had all spent more time on the street than in their rooms, from about nine o'clock in the evening till four o'clock in the morning.

'It was just a normal Sunday night. I had five short times, and, Ada, what about you, love?'

'Six.'

'Me an' all. Trade was a bit slow, but it was a chilly night. That always affects things, don't it?'

'You're right there, Floss. Enough to freeze the balls off a brass monkey.'

'Well, it didn't have that effect on any of my lot last night. All present and correct.'

The women doubled up with fits of laughter and coughing. Baker had been around these sorts of women ever since he joined the force, but he still found their attitude surprising. Their work was hard and often degrading, but they found some humour in it, perhaps even dignity, as well as a sense of camaraderie. They were in effect competing with each other for business on the same street, but he had often found they would help each other out in the oddest of ways.

He remembered, as a young constable, asking one woman why she didn't give it up, only to be given an ear bashing.

'Why should I give it up? For what? So I can be a skivvy. Would that suit you better? Not on your life, sonny. My mother was a skivvy before she got married. And I'd sooner walk the streets till I dropped than have to go through what my poor old mum did.'

He learned from that point on never to question their choice of profession, if indeed it had been any real choice at all. He knew that for most of them it was the only way they could survive. Some worked in menial jobs, but their wages were so meagre that they occasionally worked the streets to make ends meet.

He recalled another woman he had arrested for soliciting who had told him she was a tailoress in the East End and earned twenty-five shillings a week. 'And the rent for my room is fifteen bob. That don't leave much to go with, sir. What else can I do but go with some on a Saturday night?'

Others had no prospect of any other kind of job from their earliest years, and with no family and no other support, they had found their way onto the streets just to be able to eat.

Like all police officers on the beat in Soho, he had also been propositioned many times, and when he was a young constable fresh out of the box he hadn't even heard of some of the things they were offering to do for him. He knew some of his colleagues had taken advantage of the working girls on their beat, but he had never once been tempted.

Many were young things, but none of them had any life in their eyes. They looked the part from a distance, but as soon as he got up close, he found he was looking at someone who had no light on inside. None of their forced smiles and come-ons had ever had the slightest effect on him. In fact, he found them almost devoid of sexuality and often wondered what the men who used them were thinking.

Once the three women had caught their breath, Baker asked if any of them had seen anyone out of the ordinary on the street the previous night, or anything unusual.

'A few regulars is all. And there's always some young bucks coming for a gawp. Usually they're too frightened to have a go, but we're good teachers, aren't we, girls?'

'And there's the chancers that don't know what they want, or if they do, they think they can sweet-talk you into getting it for nothing.'

'That's right. There were a couple of them last night, but we soon sent 'em packing. But nothing else really.'

'Tell me, do any of the girls around here use white drugs? The kind that you inject with a needle.'

'Drugs? Gin and fags, yes, but I've never heard of anybody doing anything like that. Ada, you ever come across anyone injecting drugs?'

'Can't say I have.'

'What about the punters? Any of them into that sort of thing?'

'They usually all stink of drink, but I can't say I've ever seen any of 'em messing about with drugs.'

Baker asked the three women more questions, but they were unable to give him anything else of use, and as expected, he learned little more from the other people in the building and in the neighbouring shops and bars. A few of them knew of Jeanette – 'yeah, the old one that worked the south end of Greek Street' – but no one knew any more. And no one even knew her last name.

As he was leaving, he went back to the three women who

were still waiting to re-enter the building. In light of what had now happened twice, he urged them to take extra care.

'Hark at him, Floss – says I've to watch out for a man wanting to stick a needle in me! I've had more than a needle stuck in me, dearie. And what about you, my lovely? Fancy a short time? Always on the house for a handsome young copper – you know that.'

Again, the women folded into each other, bent double with laughter. Baker smiled and thanked them for their time, then stammered something about having a murderer to find. He told the uniformed constable on the door to go easy on them and to allow them all back in as soon as the body was moved.

Just as he was walking back to his car, there was a commotion behind him. Someone was shouting 'Cooee!' to attract P.C. Cummings. The young constable looked up to see who was making the noise. At an open second-floor window of the building opposite there was a movement. Through a hole in the net curtain one of the prostitutes pushed her breast out, one large nipple rouged scarlet, and shouted, 'How'd you like a taste of this, darling?'

'Put it away, you daft cow!' shouted a woman from an adjacent window. 'Do you want to get us all knocked off?'

*

Back in the duty room the next morning, Baker added a second post mortem photograph to the pinboard. Jeanette X now joined Dutch Edie. He shook his head and wondered if, they were going to need a second board.

While he was pondering this question, work was beginning in the pathology department across the river. Morgenthal was by now used to taking the lead on post mortem examinations. At first, he had been hesitant and worried that he would slip up in front of his mentor. But after months of performing at least one examination each day on his own, he was gaining in confidence. And Cuthbert recognised that his assistant had indeed become sufficiently competent to be left to work alone.

Morgenthal approached the examination of Jeanette X in the same way he approached all the bodies – the highly formulaic procedure that had been drummed into him by Cuthbert, who in turn had learned it from his former professor in Edinburgh, Harvey Littlejohn.

He would go through his mental checklist, making sure he completed each task in order so as not to miss anything, however small and apparently insignificant, and he took extensive notes as he worked because, again, that was Cuthbert's way.

The woman's clothing was first carefully removed, bagged and labelled for later detailed examination; the surface of the body, back and front, was studied and photographed. Special attention was paid to the fingernails, the presence of any marks, abrasions or puncture wounds, and, of course, a careful study was made of the eyes and the mucous membranes. Only when every quarter-inch of the body had been examined could an internal examination commence.

Morgenthal knew that other pathologists might complete a post mortem examination in under two hours, but he had never seen Cuthbert spend fewer than four examining the body of a murder victim, and much of that was spent performing the detailed surface surveillance of the corpse to detect any clues.

The internal examination would begin with a long incision down the length of the body from the neck to the pubis. The organs would be removed one by one, weighed and examined with the naked eye before being carefully opened and dissected. Small tissue samples might also be taken at this stage to be examined under the more powerful eye of the microscope.

The only other incision that was generally required was the coronal incision around the back of the head from ear to ear. This allowed access to the skull which had to be opened to extract the brain.

Once examined, Cuthbert had taught his assistant to be rigorous in returning all the organs to the body. Although at work his mentor appeared to be detached, almost unemotional, the pathologist also had a profound respect for the bodies in his charge, and he expected everyone who worked with him to feel the same.

*

'I have my report for you, Dr Cuthbert. Would you like me to leave it on your desk, or shall I give you a summary now?'

'Why don't we do this? Let me try and guess what your findings are before you tell me. So, let's see, she is a poorly nourished Caucasian female, approximately forty years old, with evidence of numerous contusions, healed scratches and evidence of old fractures. She has an ante mortem human bite mark on her right shoulder and a single hypodermic needle mark in her right antecubital fossa. She has conjunctival and oral petechiae, which, together with right-sided ventricular engorgement and further pinpoint haemorrhaging over the surfaces of the lungs and liver, are consistent with death from asphyxia. Estimated time of death approximately two o'clock yesterday morning. Conclusion?'

'Thank you for leaving me something to tell you, Dr Cuthbert. My conclusion is that she met her death at the hands of a person or persons as yet unknown. In other words, sir, she was murdered.'

'Excellent. I think you should let Sergeant Baker know immediately. I'm sure he'll be delighted to share the news with his charming superior.'

'Don't you want to tell the chief inspector yourself, sir?'

'No, it was your work, Simon. You're the one who should let them know.'

'Oh, there was one other thing, sir. It's probably of no importance, but I thought it a little unusual given the age of the victim. She had bilateral lens opacities.'

'Cataracts?'

'It looks like that, sir.'

When Baker took the pathology report to the chief inspector, he wasn't sure how he would react. It certainly looked as if they were now dealing with a killer who had struck twice using exactly the same method, and that complicated things.

He thought the Pie might be excited at the possibilities of another high-profile case to get stuck into. But he also knew that it meant admitting that Cuthbert might have been right when he had said there was more to the Dutch Edie murder than appeared at first sight.

Mowbray had dismissed the pathologist out of hand, and Baker knew he didn't like having to backtrack and admit he might be wrong. The sergeant knocked on the glass pane in the door and went in.

'They're almost identical, sir.'

'And what's Cuthbert saying to it?'

'It wasn't him who performed the examination or wrote the report, sir. It was his assistant, Dr Morgenthal.'

'Hmm. Was it really, now?'

Mowbray stood up and went to his window. From his office he could look out to the Thames, across the wide brown river to the South Bank and over County Hall's roof to the dark, smoky mass of Waterloo Station.

He stood with his hands in his trouser pockets, thinking. The day was overcast, but a streak of blue over to the west where the clouds were parting allowed a shaft of pale sunlight to fall through.

The chief inspector was as arrogant as Cuthbert and could be just as difficult, but he was also far from foolish. As he watched a coal barge chug up the river, he was computing the various possibilities in his head, and he came down on the side of picking up the phone there and then and calling Cuthbert.

'Dr Cuthbert? Sorry to disturb you. I wanted to thank Dr Morgenthal for his report – it was most illuminating. It looks as if you were right, and I was wrong. We are clearly dealing with something less run of the mill here. I hope I can get your thoughts on the case. I have a gut feeling that this one is going to take all the heads we can put together to sort out. Might you be able to attend our case conference tomorrow morning here at the Yard?'

'Of course. It would be a pleasure, chief inspector. Allow me some time to brush up on Dr Morgenthal's report and I'll be with you. What time do you want me?'

'Any time you like.'

From the laboratory, Morgenthal watched Cuthbert on the phone in his office. Although he could not hear what was being said, he saw a smile spread across his mentor's face as he hung up. Cuthbert donned his white coat and joined his assistant in the laboratory. He was still smiling when he approached the bench, and the young man had to ask what was amusing him so much.

'Oh, nothing much, Simon. A small victory. And in this life, we must learn to appreciate the little things.'

Chapter 6

London: 22 March 1930

As it was a Saturday, Madame Smith served Cuthbert his lunch before she left for her afternoon and evening off. His housekeeper's cooking was heavily influenced by her continental upbringing, and although she had never been called upon to work in the kitchen of her own middle-class home, she had learned quickly when she came to England during the war.

She placed the dish on the table before him and waited for him to ask what it was. He never did so with any kind of admonishment. He was much too polite for that, but nevertheless he often looked perplexed by what she presented.

'Before you ask, monsieur, it is *boulet à la liégeoise*. Meatballs in a very special sauce.'

'Delicious.'

This was what he said no matter what she laid before him, such were his manners. Just occasionally, she thought it might be a little less English if he were to throw the plate of unfamiliar food across the room in disgust, but she knew such a thing could never happen in this house – especially as her employer would regularly remind her he was not English.

She waited as he took a small bite and saw the relief on his face as he found he enjoyed the flavour.

'Truly delicious, madame. Tell me, do you have anything interesting planned for your free time today?'

'I have some shopping to do and then I am visiting some friends.'

Cuthbert knew nothing of her social life, in part because she shared so little of that with him. He valued his own privacy and always respected that of others, and he never pried. He ate for only a few moments before pausing, and she saw that he was a little distracted. Normally, he ate heartily, but this lunchtime he lingered over the meal.

'Are your thoughts somewhere else, monsieur? Perhaps with a case?'

'There are always many cases, madame, but there are two at the moment that I think are connected, and it is a cause for concern.'

'For you, or for your colleagues in the police?'

'Both, I think. Two women, both killed in Soho, and I think it might be the same murderer. But I shouldn't say such things. You don't need to hear about that world.'

'Because I have led such a sheltered life, monsieur? I assume they were *filles publiques*, or you wouldn't find the matter so delicate.'

'Yes, madame, they were. But that doesn't make their murders any less important.'

'I know that, monsieur. I would expect no less of you.'

'I feel some of the others forget that they're human beings, and because of how they earned their living, they are somehow less deserving of our efforts. But I am perplexed by it all. Why does a woman do such things?'

'For an educated man, you ask the strangest of questions.'

'You think it is a stupid question?'

'No question is stupid, only the people who ask them.'

'Madame, if ever I have an overinflated view of my abilities, I know I can always count on you to provide the pin.'

'That is perhaps one of the reasons you pay me. You ask why women sell themselves. The answer is simple: because of men. Prostitutes are made by men, for men. Men use women for sex; women use sex for men – to get them, to feed them, to control them. Do you think those little girls playing with their dolls say, I'd like to be a prostitute when I grow up? No little girl dreams of that, monsieur. They have it decided for them.'

Cuthbert saw her cheeks colour as she spoke and heard the anger in her voice. He took a mouthful of meatball and chewed it slowly to give himself a moment to respond.

'I always thought of it as an act of desperation. Young women who are poor or hungry turning to the only option open to them to get money. The way you describe it sounds even more sinister and controlling than it already is.'

Madame Smith had recovered her composure. Wishing to give nothing further away, she simply nodded.

'I'm sure my thoughts on the matter are not as sophisticated as they might be, and you should think nothing of what I say. Now, I have laid out a cold supper for you in the kitchen as always and I may be late coming home, so please do not concern yourself about me.'

She left him to his lunch and the silence of the dining room. Later he heard her leaving through the front door, but he was already asleep when she opened it again that night.

*

The next morning, the third prostitute was found in a basement room on the corner of Dean Street and Romilly Street in Soho, only a few hundred yards from the previous victims. Cuthbert went through his usual procedures and was struck by the similarities.

Again, the woman looked to be older than the average street girl in the area, and everything about the scene was as before. There was the bite mark – this time on the woman's left leg – and there was the single hypodermic needle mark. Again, it looked as if he was dealing with a case of asphyxiation by smothering, and that was confirmed when he got the body onto the mortuary slab back in the pathology department at St Thomas's.

'It's the same story again, Dr Cuthbert. I don't understand. Why is it still happening? If they know there is someone out there doing this to them, why don't the prostitutes stop going with anyone who looks suspicious.'

'Have you ever walked through Soho at midnight, Simon? Because if you had, I think you would realise that every man these women take to their rooms looks suspicious. With every transaction, they take their lives in their hands. They're alone and vulnerable in the dark with a stranger.

'Even the men that run them aren't around to help when it gets rough. And you've seen their bodies on the mortuary slabs. Every one of them is covered in old bruises and scratches, and many of them bear evidence of multiple healed fractures. And that's even before we consider all the other diseases they run the risk of catching. These women aren't safe, and what they do must be terrifying. They deal with the kind of fear every night that you and I, as men, can only imagine. I doubt if one more frightening story is going to make any difference.'

Morgenthal looked at the corpse on the slab that Cuthbert had sewn up after replacing her internal organs. She was thin and discoloured. There was still rouge on her cheeks and her short hair was dyed black. The fingers of her right hand were stained yellow. She looked small and utterly beyond any help.

Cuthbert took a fresh white sheet and carefully shrouded her body taking one last look at her face before he covered that too.

'These women deserve some justice, Simon. No matter who they were or what they did for a living, they were still human beings. But someone who is still at large doesn't agree with that; he's treating them worse than animals, and we need to stop him.'

*

The case conference the following Tuesday in the Yard's duty room was a sober affair. The third post mortem photograph was pinned to the board by Sergeant Baker, alongside the other two, and he summarised what was known so far.

'This is French Renée – real name unknown – probably aged between thirty-five and forty and found two days ago in a basement room at 19 Romilly Street. She was killed at some time between the hours of eleven o'clock on Saturday night and two o'clock on Sunday morning. The same method was used, and all the characteristics appear to match our other two victims. In particular, please note, we again have the single injection mark on the arm.'

Mowbray stood up and looked squarely at the photos of the three mottled faces on the board and sighed. He knew that every photo on this board beyond the first was a sign of his failure. He also knew that the more this case grew, the greater the pressure would be on him and his team to come up with an arrest. But this was the underbelly of the city where, by cover of night, money changed hands and bodies were sold. No one was talking, but someone must know something.

'I need ideas. I'm not going to jump down anyone's throat for airing a stupid thought. So speak up. Any suggestion at this point might be of use.'

Despite this invitation, the three detective constables in the front row started looking at their boots to avoid Mowbray's gaze, and it was left to Sergeant Baker to get the ball rolling.

'It must be a punter, mustn't it, sir? Somebody who's working his way around the area, maybe even somebody who's been around for a while but now wants to make it all a bit more exciting for himself. Someone who's become more violent with the girls and is now taking it too far. Why don't we ask them about anybody who's into something deviant?'

'Are you suggesting, sergeant, that any man who goes with these women isn't already a deviant? I think there's a good case to be made that every one of these men is capable of this sort of thing.'

Cuthbert wasn't at all sure he agreed with Mowbray's analysis, but he also wasn't sure he wanted to explain why he thought that. Instead, he offered an alternative line of thought.

'Chief inspector, I agree with Sergeant Baker that our killer is most likely to have been a client of all three women. How else would he have gained access to their rooms? Remember, there were no signs of a forced entry or even a struggle at any of the scenes. Let's imagine for a moment what might have happened.

'He meets the women in the street, they solicit him in the usual way, and whatever he says and however he looks, he doesn't arouse any more suspicion than usual. He's just another punter. The women take him up to their rooms just as they have with several others that same night. Maybe they have sex first, but at some point in the proceedings, he offers them drugs.

'We know none of these women were drug addicts because they had no other needle marks on them, so it prompts the question: what makes them agree to this? Does he pay extra? Does he force them? We don't know. And nor do we know why he does it. He certainly doesn't need to offer expensive white drugs to get sex. He's already paid for that on his way up the stairs, and it's considerably cheaper than the drugs.

'We know they were all bitten before they died. This would have been very painful if the women were conscious. But, remember, no screams were heard, and the beds were not even disturbed, so I would conjecture that the mutilation occurred while the woman was insensible from the drugs.

'What I'm getting at, chief inspector, is that the drugs are at the centre of all this. The average punter in Soho is not a white-drug user – a drinker, yes – but they don't inject drugs there. This was someone out of their natural habitat, perhaps someone from a different social class entirely.

'So, although I agree with the sergeant, I think we should be looking for a very unusual client, and we should think about getting at them through the drugs, if such a thing is possible. Compared to the number of men in this city who are visiting prostitutes, there certainly cannot be that many white-drug users. Surely many of them must already be known to your colleagues, one way or another.'

Mowbray and the other detectives, who by now had all turned to look at Cuthbert, digested his thoughts and nodded. 'All right,' said Mowbray, 'I need to speak with Grant.'

*

Mowbray always thought the short, narrow street tucked away behind Piccadilly was an unlikely place to find what they claimed had been the busiest police station in the world at one time.

Now, almost a hundred years old, Vine Street Station was a battered four-storey brick affair with heavy bars on its ground-floor windows that opened directly on to the street. The only clues that it was a police station at all were the blue lantern hanging above the entrance and the uniformed constable manning the entrance.

Along with Marlborough Street, this was home to C Division, which took care of St James's and included both Soho and Mayfair in its reach. As such, it was hardly surprising that this was the station that dealt with most of the city's drug and prostitution cases.

Mowbray had come to see Chief Inspector Bob Grant. Although his opposite number was a well-known figure and somewhat of a legend at the Met, Mowbray was not in the mood to be starstruck.

Now in his late fifties, Grant had seen it all and liked to tell everyone about it at length. Although the Met had no official drugs team, Grant was acknowledged internally as having specialist knowledge. In fact, recently he had been described in one trial report in the *Daily Express* as 'the special officer in charge of investigations relating to drug traffic'.

Grant had worked the streets of this part of London his entire career, and it was said that he knew every addict in London by sight and every dodgy doctor by name. He had even assembled a small group of young constables at the station who had become known as the 'Clubs Office'. They had developed an intimate knowledge of the West End night clubs – largely, so it was said, by spending a lot of their time in them. Whether this time was spent officially or unofficially was open to question, as were the alleged kickbacks the team took from the club owners.

Mowbray had little time for such gossip; he needed information, and this was the quickest way to get it.

'Well, if it's not the Pie himself. Come in, Jim, and sit yourself down.'

'Bob, good to see you again. What's it been, five years?'

'The last time we met, you were still a sergeant, my lad. What do you need? You said something on the blower about some tarts and dope.'

Mowbray took a seat and placed his hat on Grant's desk. He glanced around the office, quickly evaluating it from a fellow chief inspector's perspective. It was bigger than Mowbray's but rather shabbier, and the Yard certainly had better views. In contrast to Mowbray's view of the river and the south bank, Grant's window looked out onto a brick wall.

Mowbray proceeded to press Grant for what turned out to be an invaluable seminar on the contemporary London drug scene. All he needed to keep the chief inspector talking was to massage his ego. Grant liked to be acknowledged as the fount of all knowledge when it came to his own specialist area.

'This case we're working over at the Yard – it looks as if we're dealing with a drugs connection. Thought I might pick your considerable brain on the matter. Where are we with white drugs in the city, Bob?'

'That's a good one. Where are we, indeed? It all goes back to that fucking useless Dangerous Drugs Act from ten years ago. That meant white drugs could only be legally obtained using a prescription from a medical practitioner. It's supposed to keep them off the streets, and it does in part, but it doesn't prevent them getting into the hands of those that can afford them – especially those in the flash clubs in the West End.

'There are doctors and there are *doctors*, Jim, and some of them will do anything for money. As well as forged prescriptions, we have to deal with an almost unlimited supply to known addicts or, and here's the rub, to anyone who claims to be one. These doctors aren't treating their patients, they're just pandering to them, and they're doing it because they're rich. They're not sick; they're upper-class medicalised addicts.

'To my mind, many of the doctors are doing little more than selling the prescriptions to anyone who has the cash. I'm sure there are some quacks who think they're doing the odd patient a favour, but the ones we're interested in are the irresponsible ones who know they're doing wrong. The ones who don't ask too many questions, other than "How will sir be paying?"

'They're supposed to get second opinions before deciding

someone's an addict, but that doesn't happen. In fact, they hardly look at the patients twice, and they write up prescriptions for huge amounts at a time. They even post the stuff out to them. Do you know, we've even got one in the West End who sends the drugs regularly up to a nob in Glasgow? There's a lot of money to be made, I can tell you. In my view they're little more than street dealers.'

'So what can you do?'

'Do? Here's what I *can't* do: I can't nick them for giving white drugs to an addict; I can't nick them for selling them to the buggers; I can't nick them for getting them to bring their pals around to their office so they can sell them to those buggers too; I can't nick them for running a mail-order business; and I can't even nick the bloody addicts for using or even injecting themselves in public.

'What *can* I do? I can nick a doctor, if he doesn't keep adequate records of his dangerous drugs, or if he doesn't prescribe them, and I quote, "so far as necessary for the practice of his profession". You try getting that to stick with the beaks. What does "necessary" mean, for fuck's sake? And you'd think they might police themselves. Isn't that what their General Medical Council is for? But how many doctors do you think they've struck off for dishing out the dope? I don't have to tell you – the polite word for them is "unenthusiastic". The whole thing is just a web of gentlemen's agreements.'

'You're well-versed in it, then.'

'Well-versed! I could set it to bloody music and sing it to you, lad. All the good it would do. They tie your hands behind your back and expect you to clean the streets at the same time.

'Do you know how many men I've got to police the drug scene in the West End of London? No, you don't – nobody does – because the answer is none. Not one bloody copper assigned specifically to tackle this problem, and we've still got the brass breathing down our necks because they've got the councillors breathing down theirs and all the time the press is having a field day.

'Any public sympathy we had has reached rock bottom. Because they don't trust us, and because the magistrates won't support us, the arrest rates in vice have fallen by two thirds in the last two years. Think about what that means for the streets.'

'And I don't suppose what happened to your predecessor here helped.'

'You mean Logue? Yeah, that was a real feather in all our caps. Sent down for taking bribes from the tarts. The stupid bastard got eighteen months' hard labour and a fine.'

'I heard it was about two thousand quid . . .'

'I mean, you only need to walk down Jermyn Street any night and you'll see lots of girls looking for business and young coppers watching and waiting. It's hardly surprising that some of the lads get a bit too friendly with the regulars on their beat. They're only flesh and blood like the rest of us. But, having them queue up in the street to give you backhanders, that was going a bit too far.

'That's just what you needed to see in the papers, eh?'

'And now, to top it all, the brass have just told me I can't even use plain-clothes officers. It has to be uniforms from now on doing all the warning and the arresting. Well, fuck that for a game of soldiers! What we do in the dark needn't concern them upstairs.'

'But what about the addicts?'

'Well, they start off on the booze then graduate to pick-me-ups they can buy at the chemist. They use them as hangover cures, and of course that gives them their first taste of it because those little tonics are laced with morphine and cocaine.

'Doesn't take them long to want more, and that's when they start snorting and injecting the hard stuff. And as the regulations change, they adapt and twist the system to get just what they want out of it. If you ask me, they're all sub-human, a race apart, and along with all the other ones – the alcoholics, the perverts and failed suicides – they should all be tossed in the clink and the key thrown away.'

As always with his chats with Grant, Mowbray was beginning to regret asking the question. He knew the man could talk for England when he got started and liked to use any opportunity to vent his frustration at a system that he couldn't change but was forced to work in.

However, Mowbray did sympathise with Grant's predicament and knew he had to acknowledge it before he could ask for his help. So he looked sympathetic, nodded a lot and enjoyed his tea.

'It's nothing short of a scandal, right enough, Bob. And I don't want to add to that workload, but I was hoping you could lend an ear.'

He quickly acquainted him with the facts of the case.

'We now have three street girls in Soho, all smothered, but with single needle marks in the arm. At one of the scenes, we have some white drugs but little else to go on. What's the likelihood that they're starting to experiment with injecting drugs? I'd have thought gin was their limit.'

'If they've only one needle mark apiece, they're not addicts. That much is certain. And by far the majority of the white-drug users in London are not in that class. I'm not saying some of them aren't tarts, but they're definitely what you might call the smart set.'

'That's what Cuthbert said.'

'Cuthbert?'

'Our pathologist from Tommy's. You'd like him, Bob; he's never heard any of your stories. Fresh meat for you.'

'Enough of your lip, lad. This is my office, remember. No,

looks to me you might have one of my gentleman addicts slumming it with the girls down on Old Compton Street.'

'That's one possibility, but the tarts are all on the wrong side of thirty. Not exactly what you'd call in their prime. They're cheap and used. I'd have thought if he was going slumming, he'd at least be looking for a pretty young thing.'

'But they're addicts, Jim. No saying what's going on in their brains. They're addled with the stuff. What's the word on the street? Are any of the girls talking? If it is someone from the Mayfair or Chelsea set, they'd likely stick out like a sore thumb down there. You see them in the clubs, but they don't tend to go up the stairs with the girls.'

'No, we're getting nothing from that direction. I've got plain clothes on the street at night, but you know how it is; the girls clock them the minute they turn up and nothing gets said or done while they're watching.'

'And how do you think I can help?'

'Do you have details of your known addicts? Names, addresses and such like?'

'We have an Addicts' Index which we've been compiling since about 1920, but I have to tell you before you ask, our figures are inaccurate. They're based on what we know about prescriptions being filled at chemist shops throughout the city, and it doesn't include any white drugs directly dispensed by a quack. And as for names and addresses, we have a lot of Smiths, and very few of the real double-barrelled ones. But you said he's smothering them. What's the deal with the injections then?'

'Well, that's what we're wondering too. Could be part of some sex game, I suppose. Getting them high before having them. And whatever he's up to, he's leaving them in quite a state. Here, take a look at some of these pictures . . .'

'Hmm. And you say you've got three all the same?'

'That's it, and nowhere to go with them. Which is why I'm here. I need some way into this, and it seemed that the most promising lead might be the drugs angle. Whoever was in that room with them had access to white drugs and needles and knew how to use them. So that pretty much means somebody on your books. Can we share notes on this one, Bob?'

They parted with an agreement that Sergeant Baker could work with his opposite number at Vine Street and have full access to the Addicts' Index. Mowbray knew that it might all be futile, but he needed something to say when he was asked about progress. And interdepartmental collaboration certainly sounded like it was something.

As he was going, Mowbray asked Grant if he thought they should be looking for a bigger fish. 'Do you think there's somebody behind all this, Bob? You know, somebody trying to silence the girls?'

'Jim, my lad, leave the idea of some organised criminal underworld to the newspaper headlines, and all those evil masterminds to the cheap detective novels. It's just poor working-class lasses trying to eke out a living for the most part, selling all they've got. It's the men that run them, but they're just small-time pimps. Bullies who only know how to use their fists on women. They're scum right enough, but they're not crime lords. Believe me, there's no such thing in Soho.'

Chapter 7

London: 12 December 1922

Lizzie Compton was summoned by the matron, and she knew this was the day. The day before had been her fourteenth birthday, and although it was barely marked by the staff and children at the Foundling Hospital, Lizzie realised what it meant.

She walked from the girls' rooms in the east wing, past the refectory and climbed the broad oak staircase to the office. Lizzie was physically mature for her age and if it were not for the childish brown serge uniform with scarlet trim and the white apron and bonnet she was required to wear, she might easily have been taken for a young woman of 16 or 17. She knocked and waited and was invited to enter.

Her recent years at the hospital had been turbulent, and she had visited the matron's office many times to be chastised for her behaviour. She felt older than the other girls and always wanted more than them.

The hospital had been a safe haven from the streets as she was growing up, but all too soon it had become stifling. She knew she had been brought there just after she was born and abandoned on Old Compton Street. That was where she got her name because that was the policy of the orphanage. Like the other foundlings, she was baptised quickly in case she should succumb to any of the myriad childhood illnesses and was then farmed out to be wet-nursed.

Those early years at the house in Surrey were the beginnings of her memory. She remembered playing on the grass and rolling fallen green apples under the tree. And there was the woman who kept her warm and fed. When she thought of her, she had to close her eyes tightly to see her face clearly, for Lizzie had not seen her foster mother again since the day she was returned to the hospital as a 4-year-old.

The thing she remembered most clearly about that day was the woman cutting off one of her dark ringlets and tying it with a small ribbon, before putting it away in a box as a keepsake.

Lizzie had been frightened that day, crying and clinging to her foster mother. But then the woman had left her behind, her head was shaved and her clothes removed. She was put into a rough serge uniform and a name tag was hung about her neck. She remembered sitting sobbing with all the other little girls – and that was almost ten years ago.

Life at the hospital quickly shifted from being new and strange to monotonous and routine. The young ones would rise with the bell at six o'clock and after saying prayers go with the others in their dormitory to the lavatories to get washed. Then it was back to their beds where they would dress in the brown uniforms.

Lizzie never starved but nor did she ever truly enjoy the food. All the children's meals were taken in the large refectory with its long tables and benches and were prefaced by a solemn grace. Breakfast was always the same – bread, butter, milk, and sometimes treacle or dripping – but most days they would have some form of meat for supper, and potatoes were almost ubiquitous. There were few treats and even fewer surprises.

School for the girls started with religious instruction, and most days included arithmetic and letters. They were taught to read the bible and write letters of gratitude, and in later years they were prepared for the world most of them would inhabit – domestic service. Lizzie had spent much of the last two years learning to scrub and sew and cook.

Now, as she turned the brass handle and pushed open the matron's door, she knew it would likely be for the last time.

'Well, Lizzie Compton, here we are again. I'm pleased to say that this time your visit does not cause me the usual heartache but should be a welcome one for us both. I know you are far from happy here and cannot wait to escape from us. I, for my part, look forward to the peace and quiet you might leave behind. Tomorrow, you will be leaving us, Lizzie. Here, take this letter and keep it safe, because it's your future. I have secured a position for you in a household as a scullery maid. You are to report to a Mrs Brompton at the address on the envelope. She is the housekeeper there and will set you your duties. It's a menial job, I'm afraid, but it will give you a roof over your head and food on the table.'

Lizzie took the envelope and turned to leave the office, but the matron stopped her. She took a small wooden box from her desk drawer, opened it and removed a cloth bag.

'This is for you, child. It was found with you. It's not much, but it belongs to you.'

Lizzie took the tarnished metal necklace and looked at the small pendant initial 'C'. As she stroked it in her hands, she asked the question she had never dared ask before.

'Who was my mother?'

The matron sighed, as she did whenever she was asked this, and wished she could give these wretched children back their life stories.

'I'm afraid I don't know, child. All we do know is that she worked in Soho. She was a young girl herself when she gave birth to you, and we think she wasn't English. The man who found you thought he'd heard about a French girl who was in a difficult situation. And as you can see from that little trinket, perhaps her initial was "C".'

'In Soho, matron? What did she do there? What was her job?'

'It was no job for any respectable woman, I'm afraid.'

Lizzie dropped her eyes and held tightly onto the necklace, for she knew what that meant.

'And there is one more thing you should know. You were not alone when you were found. Lizzie, you have a brother. His name is Robert Compton, and he is your twin. I believe he was sent to St Pancras because we had no space for another male child at the time and it was thought better to keep you apart.'

The matron said it in this way to emphasise that it had not been her idea, but Lizzie stared at her with hatred, nevertheless.

'Why did no one tell me? Where is he now? How can I find him?'

'I wish I could help you, but the truth is I don't know where he is. I don't know if he went back to St Pancras after he was weaned, and I don't know if he grew up there. I don't even know if he's working now or even still in London. A lot of the orphan boys find work on the ships, so I'm afraid he could be anywhere in the world now.'

Lizzie's anger turned to despair. She had always thought she was alone, and now to be given a brother only to have him snatched away in the same breath was too much to bear.

The matron rose from her chair and came to Lizzie to put her arm about the girl's shoulders, but Lizzie shrugged off her embrace and looked at her with disdain.

'Thank you, matron, for everything you and the staff here have done for me. I will never forget you.'

She left the office without closing the door and went back to the dormitory. She changed into the second-hand clothes that had been left on her bed. Nothing fitted well, but she was glad to be rid of the drab uniform she had lived in all those years. She had a small bag in which she placed her few belongings along with the letter and the necklace. Then she took the letter out, tore it in half and left it on the bed.

Lizzie Compton passed through the gates of the Foundling Hospital without considering if anyone would be sad to see her go: she knew the answer. As she walked through the cold afternoon air, she wondered where she should go. She did not know the streets of London, and after walking in circles for over an hour she went into a small café to get some respite from the chill. She had a few coppers and bought a tea and a currant bun, which she knew she could make last for a while.

As she sat holding the warm cup in both hands, she caught the attention of a young man at one of the other tables. Despite her shabby, ill-fitting clothes, he could see she was beautiful. Her short dark hair framed a fresh face and eyes that sparkled with youth.

He came over to her table and asked if he might join her. She was unused to this kind of courtesy from anyone, least of all the older boys in the orphanage. She blushed and said nothing, but she was glad not to be alone.

'Can I buy you another tea? That one must be stone cold by now.'

She smiled by way of thanks. They sat together, drinking from the fresh pot that was brought over by the waitress, and he told her he was Walter Bradshaw, he was 23 and he thought she was the loveliest thing he'd ever seen.

She looked at him in disbelief for she knew she was anything but lovely. She was awkward, and wilful, and moody, and all the other things they had called her at the orphanage, but she certainly wasn't lovely. Lovely was something that young ladies were, and she was just a girl.

'If I knew your name, we could actually have a conversation. It's all a bit one-sided, don't you think?'

'Lizzie.'

'Good. So what are you doing with yourself today, Lizzie?

'I need to find my brother.'

'Don't worry – I can help you with that. Two pairs of eyes are better than one when you're looking for someone, aren't they? Where is he?'

'I don't know.'

'What's his name and what does he look like?'

'His name is Robert, and I don't know what he looks like because I've never met him. At least, not that I can remember.'

'Well, this is sounding like a real monkey puzzle, Lizzie. It's going to take some planning. Where are you staying?'

'Nowhere. Not yet anyway.'

'Why don't you come back to my place? It's not far, and there's a spare bed you can have if you want. And then tomorrow we can go looking. How does that sound?'

Lizzie searched his face for any ill-intent and found only the warmest of smiles. He was the first man she had met other than the governors and the gardeners at the orphanage, and the first one even close to her age. She smiled and said yes, that sounded good. He paid for the tea, and he gave her his arm to hold as they walked towards Stepney and his rooms.

It was early evening by the time they reached Commercial Road, and he took her up to the third floor of the building where he stayed, overlooking the Regent's Canal.

'It's not much to look at, but it's only temporary, you understand. I've got big plans.'

When he lit the gas mantle, Lizzie could see how dingy the room was. And there was only one bed. Through the window she could hear the cranes at work in the dockyards, and she could smell the damp in the walls. How could anyone sleep in such a place?

The orphanage had lacked many things, but it had always been clean and aired and was set in large grounds. She had grown up in a London surrounded by trees and had never imagined there was squalor like this. She turned to leave and reached for the door. He took her wrist and held her tight, then he turned the key in the lock.

'That's not very friendly, Lizzie. I buy you tea and bring you back to my room and you haven't even given me a little kiss. Well, that's not the way it works, sweetheart, not the way it works at all.'

She started to speak, but he hit her so hard across her mouth that he cut her lip and she tasted blood.

'Now, don't make me do that again, Lizzie. I just need you to be friendly, so get on the bed unless you want to feel my fists next time.'

She was crying in fear now as much as from the blow, and she did as he wanted. That night he raped her three times, and in the morning, she lay on the bed shaking beside him as he snored. She looked at the blood mixed with his semen drying on her thighs, and she had no idea how to get away.

She eased herself out from under the weight of his arm without waking him. The key to the door was in the pocket of his jacket hanging over the chair, and she stared at it for a long time before making a move. She visualised the movement she would have to make to reach for the key, put it in the lock, turn it and get out of the room.

She looked at anything that was in the way, and she saw the clothes he had ripped from her body lying in a pile beside the chair. She knew she needed whatever she could pick up in the same single movement of her escape. She could not see her shoes, so she knew she would have to go barefoot, and her bag was by the window on the other side of the bed, so she would have to leave that behind too. Then she remembered the locket and knew she could not leave without it.

She slipped from the bed and tiptoed around the end to get the bag. He moved in his sleep and turned over, and she froze, not breathing. When he started snoring again, she moved slowly towards his jacket, fumbled in the pocket and pulled out the key. She scooped up her clothes and reached for the door. The creak of the floorboard beneath her foot filled the room and his hands were at her throat before she could put the key in the lock.

'Going somewhere, sweetheart? We've not finished here yet.'

He hit her again, this time with his fist, and her right eye smarted. She cowered into a ball at his feet and he kicked her in the ribs.

'Get back on the bed, and I'll show you how much I love you.'

*

The next day, while she was curled up in the bed, half asleep, there was a knock at the door. Walter was at the door inviting another man in. She pulled the sheet up around her and heard them laughing. Walter told the other man he would be just down the hall and left the room.

The stranger looked at her and started unbuckling his belt. After he left her, another one came who was even rougher than the first. Both men stank of drink and groped her with their unwashed hands before forcing themselves on her.

As the second one left, she saw him give Walter a silver coin. He tossed it up in the air and caught it on the back of his hand and grinned at Lizzie.

'Big plans, sweetheart, big plans. The lads like you. We'll need to get you tarted up a bit, but you should make good money.' He saw the look on her face and watched as she started to sob. 'Now don't give me that act. All you have to do is lie on your back. I'm the one that has to do all the work. Now get yourself washed because you look a right mess. Tonight you're doing the Stepney Docks. You're a shilling a time, mind, and don't take anything less. Bring it all back here or you'll make me angry again.'

At the end of the next night, she could barely climb the stairs to the room in the run-down building. There was a large wooden sign outside that offered 'Singles and Doubles'. The singles went to the vagrants and meths drinkers, the doubles to the prostitutes who had enough money to rent a work bed for the night. Walter was not going to waste money on that though: he had taken a single.

She came in as quietly as she could, hoping he would be asleep, but he just said through the dark, 'How much?'

She handed over the eight shillings she had earned, and without warning he slapped her so hard that she reeled back across the room.

'Need to do better than that, Lizzie. What's the matter with you? Do you think I'm giving you a roof over your head just so you can skive? Better be twice that tomorrow night. And get cleaned up – you stink.'

*

The weeks that followed were the same. By night she had to walk the streets down by the West Quay selling herself to sailors and stevedores. She'd take them up alleyways where they would take her on the coal sacks. By day, Walter would have his friends visit her in the dirty room.

She was young and her reputation soon spread: trade was easy. Lizzie soon learned that the closer she walked to the dockside, the rougher the trade was. These were drunken sailors who cared nothing for her and would hurt her as they took their turns. If she walked out along Limehouse Causeway to the small Chinatown, there would still be sailors, but they were mostly Asian, and they had the sweet smell of burnt opium on their breaths and were gentler.

As she walked beneath the gaslights, she saw other girls but kept away from them. She began to wonder if one of them might be her mother. Perhaps she had been only her age when she got pregnant – that would mean she would only be about 28 now and probably still working.

She scrutinised the faces under the streetlights and tried to imagine if any of the older girls looked like her. And then there would be a tug of her arm and a coin would be pressed into her hand, and she would be dragged into the dark.

One night, as a sailor was unbuttoning his flies, she noticed a knife hanging from his belt. As he took what he had paid for, she gritted her teeth and tried to keep her balance against the wall. Her hand brushed against the knife in its leather sheath, and without thinking what she was doing, she reached around to unclip it from his belt.

He knew nothing of what was happening, and when he was finished, he called out a few guttural words in a language she did not understand and stumbled off into the dark. Lizzie held the knife tightly and ran off in the opposite direction before the sailor saw that it was missing. She hid between two of the warehouses and waited for the night to end.

Not long before dawn, she went back to the lodgings on Commercial Road. She only had six shillings to show for her work but had already decided that tonight she was keeping them for herself.

She walked over to where Walter lay snoring, avoiding the empty bottles strewn on the floor, bent over and slit his throat in a single stroke. He convulsed and stared at her, choking on his blood, then he reached out to her, but she took a single step back and was out of his reach for ever.

In a few minutes his blood was already congealing on the bed and on the floorboards. In silence, Lizzie stood, mesmerised, watching the life drain from his eyes. Watching him die, she felt nothing. She thought she would feel better, cleaner, safer, but there was only emptiness. She sat at the table by the window and ate what little food there was in the room – a hunk of two-day old bread and some cheese. She must have fallen asleep where she sat because when she woke it was already growing dark.

She knew where Walter kept the money, and she prised open the box with the blade and counted the coins she had earned. It was nearly twenty-five pounds, and she took it all.

Then she stripped off her clothes, threw them on top of Walter and washed herself as best she could with the cold water from the ewer. She rinsed the knife clean. She put on one of Walter's shirts and the only other dress she had and then rubbed the clotted blood from her shoes. Looking under the bed, she found the bag she had brought from the orphanage and checked her mother's necklace was still there – she knew it was probably too cheap for him to pawn, but she needed to make sure.

She put the knife and the money in the bag and took a last look at the dead man sprawled on the bed. He had killed her just as surely as if he had slit her throat, but she had to keep on living. As she walked out the room, she felt an intense sense of freedom. It was fleeting but it came with the realisation that for the very first time in her life she was in control of her own fate.

She already knew what she would do. In those few weeks working the Stepney Docks, she had learned a lot about men and what they wanted – what she needed to do to please them. But she was no longer going to sell herself so cheaply.

Men, even the animals that passed for men in the docklands, called her beautiful, so perhaps she was, and now she intended to use it. She had to change, and she had to become someone or something else.

Clutching her bag tightly, she walked along Commercial Road and past the corner of Butcher Row where a Salvation Army captain was gathering a crowd. He stood on a box and spoke in a loud voice whose deep timbre made his words seem weightier than they were. In this part of East London, there was really only one topic for his oratory, and he put everything he had into it.

'"Why is she a prostitute?" they ask, and I ask in return, "Do we ask why another girl is in domestic service or a waitress or a shop girl?" Do any of these young women choose their profession or do they find themselves the victims of circumstance and necessity? Or is it in their very essence? Some believe that these women are mentally weak and that is why they become sexual delinquents, but not I, nor any right-thinking Christian. These women need our help, not our admonishment.'

One stevedore from the back of the crowd shouted, 'They'll take all the help you can give 'em, but it'll cost you a shilling just like the rest of us.'

The laughter in the crowd was pierced by an old woman, who raised her bony finger and pointed accusingly at the speaker. 'You don't know what you're talking about. Those whores are just lazy and deceitful, doing their work on their backs. They should try working for a living. I scrub floors all day and I can't afford to eat the way they do. Kippers for breakfast some of 'em have! We don't have that, do we, girls? Every fancy breakfast is just the price of another fuck!'

The crowd laughed and berated the woman for her language at the same time, but another woman shouted out in their defence. 'I think those girls are doing a bloody good public service. As long as my old man is poking one of 'em, it keeps him off me!'

The onlookers roared, and the speaker on his soap box knew he was in serious danger of losing any headway he had made. He picked up the pace and as he saw the crowd starting to break up, he called on his lieutenants to start the singing.

Lizzie walked on, hearing the strains of 'All Have Need of God's Salvation' strike up, thinking that none of them knew what they were talking about. Although it was almost dusk, there was still some light in the sky above the dark outline of the roofs in the west, but the coming darkness held no terrors for her any more.

No man would ever control her again and any who tried would taste their own blood just as Walter had. He had made her what she was and had determined what she would become. He had sculpted her and brought her to life as a whore.

Now she would take possession of that creation and redefine it. Her pace quickened, and she held her head high as she left Stepney and the docks behind. There was a sudden lightness to her step, and she began to think about her future. She had no idea where she was going, but the thought filled her with exhilaration rather than fear.

Chapter 8

London: 3 April 1930

On the Thursday afternoon, Cuthbert had to give a lecture to the final-year law students at University College London. He had been approached four years earlier by one of the lecturers there who was seeking to diversify the syllabus a little. The academic thought a talk on modern forensic techniques might be just the thing to spice up criminal law, which he had described as 'a little on the dry side of arid'. Cuthbert had agreed as he was keen at the time to make as many professional connections as he could in the capital. Because it was so well received by the students, it had now become an annual fixture.

It was a pleasant day, so he chose to walk the couple of miles from the hospital. As he did not take lunch, he could afford to take a leisurely route, and being early, he decided to take a turn around Russell Square.

The spring flowers were out in force, and he was reminded why it was one of his favourite parks. There were much larger affairs in the city, and he was sure the locals would not even class this one as a park, but he thought it was perfect.

He took the perimeter path past the clumps of daffodils, checked on his favourite trees and sat for a few moments on his preferred bench on the north side of the square. Just as he was getting up, he heard his name being called.

'I say, it's Dr Cuthbert, isn't it? I'm sure you won't remember me at all. Charlie Maxton-Forbes – we met at the Morgenthal wedding.'

Cuthbert nodded acknowledgement and shook his hand firmly. He was reminded of just how easy Maxton-Forbes was on the eye. The young man was in his mid twenties, cleanshaven with a sharp jaw and a smile that could melt ice. A single-breasted bright blue suit with a tight-waisted jacket accentuated his shoulders, and Cuthbert was surprised to see he was wearing brown leather shoes in the city.

The pathologist, who was wearing his usual highly polished black leather boots and an altogether more conservative suit, put it down to youthful rebellion but was forced to admit that the young man did carry it all off very effectively.

'Small world isn't it, Cuthbert? It was a good bash, even if we didn't know anyone. I felt like a gate-crasher, though. I do hope I wasn't. I think *Tatler* called it the "Wedding of the Decade", which is pushing it a bit, don't you think? I mean it was only in February, so I think they might be a little premature in their judgement, but, hey-ho, what do I know?'

Cuthbert smiled.

'Now, you must come for dinner, old chap. I think Celia was quite smitten with you, and of course I shall be insanely jealous, but I know she will be so cross if she knows I bumped into you and didn't invite you round. Next Wednesday, seven o'clock – bit of a soirée, don't you know – here's my card. Do say you'll come, or I shall be in the old doghouse.'

Cuthbert took the card and managed to hide his reluctance as he accepted 'such a kind invitation'. He was not a dinnerparty animal, and as Maxton-Forbes sauntered away, Cuthbert was already trying to formulate an escape plan that would allow him to make his apologies and stay at home with his Latin poetry.

He arrived back at the hospital mortuary late in the afternoon to find Morgenthal busy examining tissue sections at the microscope in the outer laboratory.

'Dr Cuthbert, I wasn't expecting you back this afternoon. How did the lecture go? Did you have them eating out of your hand again?'

'Dr Morgenthal, I don't seek to enthral my audiences, merely to inform them.'

'With respect, sir, I've heard you speak, and while it might not be your intention to enthral, you certainly succeed. When you spoke to our class at Guy's, I decided then and there that this was what I wanted to do. You inspired me.'

Cuthbert had forgotten that his first meeting with his assistant had been when he was a fourth-year medical student during his medical jurisprudence class. It was true: he always prepared thoroughly for his lectures and felt it his duty to impart not only the facts and figures, but also a sense of the excitement of his subject.

He had learned that from his own professor in Edinburgh, whose lectures he still thought about some fourteen years later. Cuthbert was not a sentimental man, but he was oddly affected by what Simon said. Perhaps this was his role from now on: to inspire the next generation rather than to contribute meaningfully to his own. He hoped that was not the case, as he still knew he had much to do. In fact, in his heart, he felt he had hardly begun.

'And as for coming back, young man, I wasn't aware that the work was finished for the day. Where are we with those bite marks? Do we have the casts to compare that I asked for?'

'They arrived while you were away, sir, and I've arranged them on the bench.'

Cuthbert had been examining the photographs of the bite marks on the three victims, and while they seemed to be almost identical, he wondered if further insight might be gained by obtaining three-dimensional representations of the teeth.

This, to his knowledge, had not been done before, and he was not even sure it would be possible. However, using his usual method of getting someone else as excited about his idea as he was himself, he had persuaded one of the mortuary technicians to make plaster casts of each of the marks.

Now, these lay before him. They were rough, probably because of the state of the tissues, but they seemed to confirm that the set of teeth that had made the marks was the same in each case.

As he studied each cast, there was something, however, that caught Cuthbert's attention. This was a detail he had missed when he had studied the bite marks themselves on the bodies and the photographs afterwards.

On one of the crescent-shaped bite marks in each case, there was an irregularity that he had previously attributed to the angle of the bite, but now that he could compare it with the plaster cast, he could see that there appeared to be an extra tooth mark on the right-hand side. There were the clear marks of four central incisors, but instead of the normal, single canine tooth to each side, on one side there were two.

Such supernumerary teeth were not unknown, but they were certainly unusual, and Cuthbert realised that the killer had effectively left his dental fingerprint behind on the body. For the moment, this piece of evidence would be of relatively little importance, but when they had a suspect, it would be invaluable.

He shared his findings with Morgenthal, who immediately got down their odontology textbook from the shelf. According to the book, such a finding was only seen in somewhere between one in twenty-five and one in a hundred individuals, and it occurred twice as often in men.

'Could you write up these findings, Simon? I think the detectives will need this as soon as possible. After that, get yourself home to that wife of yours. I see more of you these days than she does.'

'Certainly, Dr Cuthbert, right away, but just before you go, I wanted to share some news with you. I hope you don't think it's inappropriate, but I wanted to tell you that I'm going to be a father.'

Cuthbert took his assistant's hand and shook it with vigour. 'Congratulations, Simon. I couldn't be happier for you. You must be very pleased.'

'Oh, I had nothing to do with it.'

'Well, as medical men, I think we both know you had something to do with it, laddie. However, Mother Nature does place the burden of pregnancy on the female of the species. How is Sarah? Well, I hope.'

'Absolutely glowing. But then she always is.'

Cuthbert knew better than to ask how far along she was. After all, he had been at the wedding.

*

At the next case conference, Cuthbert passed around copies of the post mortem photographs of the bite marks and the plaster casts his technician had made at St Thomas's. He talked the group through the findings and even showed them a drawing he had made of what the dental abnormality might look like in the killer.

'As you can see, it is in the upper jaw on the right-hand side. Here, we have four normal front teeth and then on the right side a normal eye tooth or canine, and then the extra tooth, which most likely will look like this – a second eye tooth on the same side. It might not be obvious when the person smiles unless it is a very broad grin, but it would be easily detectable on examination.'

The young detective constable at the front felt his own teeth and nudged his colleague beside him to take a look.

Cuthbert could see the concern on his face. 'I should add, gentlemen, that this kind of abnormality does occur in a recognised number of the population, so on its own, it doesn't mark out our killer.'

The additional evidence from the dental analysis report was promptly added by Baker to the duty-room pinboard. Like Cuthbert, he could see that it was not going to be of immediate use. It was hardly going to be practical to study the teeth of every man in London, and even if they did, they would turn up hundreds with the abnormality. No, this was probably only going to be useful when they had a list of suspects to help eliminate people from their inquiries. He thought again and corrected himself – *if* we ever have a list of suspects.

Later, as Sergeant Baker was trawling his way through the Addicts' Index, he paused and frowned. They were looking for a man who had knowledge of, and access to, white drugs and who was frequenting Soho by night. Until that moment, he, like everyone else, had been thinking that the killer might well be one of the men from the smart set in the files. A known addict with more money than sense who, for whatever reason, had gone completely off the rails. But wasn't there another possibility?

The drug addicts of the upper crust who were pictured in the files were not the only ones who had access to white drugs or who had knowledge of the street girls in Soho. What about the coppers in Vine Street? There were a number of young men there, working vice, who all had an intimate knowledge of the workings of the drug scene and of prostitution. It would be easy for one of them to get hold of syringes and white drugs from anyone they nicked. It would also be easy for them to walk the streets of Soho and take any of the girls upstairs.

Baker knew that when they were short of money the girls often offered the coppers sex by way of a kickback. It wouldn't even begin to explain a motive for the killings or for how they were carried out, but it was surely a line of inquiry that needed to be pursued, even if it was just to exclude it.

He went to Mowbray to explain his thinking. The chief inspector heard him out, and when Baker had finished, his boss leaned back in his chair and put both hands behind his head.

'Let me get this straight, sergeant. You're saying we might be dealing with a bent copper from C Division. Maybe a detective constable, with ready access to drugs, say from the evidence store, who's taking things a little too far with the tarts when he accepts a fuck instead of a bribe.'

'I know it sounds like a daft idea, but I think it's a possibility.'

'Well, by all means, do pop straight over to Vine Street and caution all your colleagues before grilling them about their use of prostitutes and possible motives for multiple murder. And don't forget to question Chief Inspector Grant. He'll be especially amenable to all your questions.'

Baker bit his lip and left the office.

*

The following Wednesday, Cuthbert was still trying to decide whether to attend the dinner party or not. He was annoyed with himself. He should have sent his apologies before now because cancelling at the last minute would be nothing short of rude.

He was brooding over it in his office and decided to start polishing his boots. Normally, he spent the lunch breaks in his office attending to their shine. The high gloss on his footwear had become a distinguishing feature, and no one who had met him could ever recall even a smear on his toe caps.

While Morgenthal was lunching in the doctors' mess, Cuthbert would take the time to indulge his private obsession. At his desk, he would ritually untie his boots and take his wooden box from his bottom drawer. The mixture of black polish and occasional saliva was rubbed rhythmically into the leather, and as the mirror-like gloss appeared over the hour, he found it calming and necessary.

He managed to stop worrying about the dinner party, and even the details of his latest cases faded into the background. He told himself it was his meditation, when he knew in reality it was his addiction.

At the end of the work day, he left his department promptly. On his arrival at Gordon Square, Madame Smith informed him that his evening wear was pressed and ready.

Of course, she was really telling Cuthbert that it was high time he was getting ready for the dinner party. She had worked for the doctor for almost five years and during that time she had often lamented his lack of a social life. His life was his work, and she understood its importance, but she also knew that life was about more than books and medicine.

Theirs was a very unconventional arrangement and visitors were often surprised at her youth and attractiveness, expecting a housekeeper to be an elderly matron. She was younger than Cuthbert and he himself was only 35, so tongues wagged.

Madame Smith was Belgian by birth but English by marriage, or at least she had been before she was widowed shortly after the end of the war. A fiercely independent thinker with a very low tolerance for nonsense, she had found a niche in Cuthbert's household that she could not only fill but in which she could also excel.

He, for his part, had become reliant on her practical

assistance with his life and, increasingly, on her companionship. But theirs was a relationship that could never be described as romantic. They were close, but always at a very respectable distance. They knew the truth about themselves and cared little for how other people chose to see them.

'Thank you, madame. You know, I'm not sure I should go. I expect he only asked me to be polite and I barely know them.'

'Forgive me, Dr Cuthbert, perhaps it is because I am a silly foreigner, but is it not the point of going to a party, to meet people you do not know in order to get to know them? Now, please get ready or you will be late. And you know what you are like when you are late for an appointment.'

Cuthbert almost sulked as he was told off, and as he climbed the stairs to his room he muttered that no one should talk to him like that in his own home, but then he smiled and was quietly pleased that someone cared enough to scold him.

He came downstairs dressed in his full white tie, and when he was standing at the hall mirror, tidying his hair before leaving, Madame Smith took a long critical look at him. His jet-black tail coat with its sharp silk lapels starkly contrasted with his white waistcoat, winged collar and tie. His thick dark hair was oiled and slicked back with a perfect parting and mirrored the gloss of his boots.

She reached up on her tiptoes and smoothed his broad shoulders, before nodding her approval. He was just about to put on his overcoat and take his hat from the rack, when she tutted and indicated that he should stand still. She reached up again and this time placed a lavender rosebud in his lapel.

'There, now you are in a fit state to leave the house. Please do not return, Dr Cuthbert, without having enjoyed yourself.'

'Either with my shield or on it, madame. I hear you loud and clear.'

The taxi to Grosvenor Square only took fifteen minutes

and did not give Cuthbert enough time to fabricate any further excuses. He was met at the door by the maid, who took his hat and coat and led him through to the large drawing room.

Celia Maxton-Forbes saw him the moment he came through the door and rushed over to greet him. She was striking in a black satin silk dress that was completely backless and clung to the soft curves of her body. Her only jewels were diamond bracelets which she wore over long evening gloves and a matching necklace that drew attention to the line of her neck. Every other woman in the room was in bright, fashionable colours, but she was the one who stood out, and Cuthbert knew that was exactly her intention.

'Dr Cuthbert, how do you do? I can't tell you how pleased I am that you found the time to join us. I know how busy a man like you must be. There are a few others still to arrive, but in the meantime, let me get you a drink and introduce you to the gang.'

Celia took Cuthbert by the arm and led him over to a group standing around a grand piano. The carpet underfoot was thick, the décor modern and French, and the air in the room was already filled with laughter and cigarette smoke.

'Dr Cuthbert, do let me introduce you to Charlie's prodigal older brother.'

'How do you do, sir? Napier Maxton-Forbes, but please call me Napper, everyone does.'

'How do you do? It's a pleasure to meet you.'

Cuthbert had thought that Charlie Maxton-Forbes was attractive, but could see now that his older, taller brother was the real catch in the family. He was probably in his late twenties and was immaculately groomed in bespoke evening wear. He was tanned, wore a broad smile and his eyes were a sparkling green.

Cuthbert took his hand and enjoyed the brief moment of

warmth and firm pressure that Napper exerted before releasing him. The doctor knew he was going to have to be very careful with what he did with his eyes that evening.

Celia also introduced Cuthbert to three young women: Florence Parker, Elizabeth Hamilton-Jacques and Mary Edmonton. Although all three were slim, lovely young women with diamond smiles and flashing eyes, it was Miss Edmonton who was by far the most interesting. She engaged immediately with Cuthbert on an intellectual level that the others appeared to eschew.

'Please don't mind them, Dr Cuthbert. They'll giggle their way through the evening, but they're mostly harmless.'

'Mostly?'

'Well, you know what they say about the female of the species. And if you don't, I'm not going to be the one to tell you. But what are you doing here? Surely you have more important places to be.'

'Not at all. I can't think of a pleasanter way to spend an evening.'

'You're a good liar and I shall have to watch you, Dr Cuthbert, lest you become too charming. But, honestly, what are you doing here? This isn't your set, is it?'

Cuthbert explained how he had met the Maxton-Forbeses, at Simon and Sarah's wedding some months before, and how they had bonded over a shared ignorance of almost everyone else in the ballroom at the Dorchester.

'Celia does have an eye for talent, I'll say that for her. I do hope we're seated together at dinner. This crowd could do with a little new blood and strong muscle. And I see you have plenty of both.'

He rather thought she expected him to blush at the compliment, and the truth is he would have, had it been said by Napper. When the others arrived, Celia quickly gathered everyone and seated them for dinner, which was served by two staff and was as modern and French as everything else in the house. The wine flowed and encouraged the conversation to drift into increasingly more risqué realms.

'It's all the rage in Paris, you know,' said Miss Parker, seated opposite the doctor. 'I'm sure it would be delicious to try it. What do you think, Dr Cuthbert? Am I being too outrageous for you?'

'I'm sure I wouldn't know how to advise you, miss, other than to say that the use of such a substance does tend to lead to addiction that regrettably may prove fatal with time. And there is the distinct danger of overdosing at any stage.'

'Oh, you can't be serious. I've heard heroin is just the thing you need for a pick-me-up. You know, the morning after the night before, and all that. And, anyway, don't they sell it over the counter at the chemist? It can't be all that dangerous, surely.'

'It's true, it was readily available in the past, but in this country, I'm pleased to say, you have not been able to purchase heroin without a doctor's prescription for the last ten years.'

'Really?' said the Hamilton-Jacques girl. 'You do see a lot of it about. Tell me, have you tried it, doctor?'

'I have not, miss.'

Celia intervened, seeing that her guest was being ambushed, and changed the subject. 'This is really all too boring. Tell me, Napper, what should we be drinking this season? I'm simply dying to try something new. Do you have a new cocktail recipe for us from America?'

'Not from over there, darling, but I'm just back from Paris and amongst the other lovely things I brought back, I feel it is my duty to introduce the "Bee's Knees" to England. I tasted it at the Ritz Bar over there and to say it was divine is an understatement – gin, lemon juice and honey, but in secret proportions.'

Celia batted her eyelashes at the doctor by her side. 'What do you think of that, Dr Cuthbert? Are we on safer ground there? Almost sounds like a health drink!'

The laughter around the table saved him from answering, and Celia put her gloved hand over his on the table. She leaned in to whisper in his ear, and because Cuthbert knew he had heard her correctly, he wasn't at all sure how to answer. Eventually, he managed to stumble over a reply to her invitation.

'Regrettably, I think I must decline. It is really very kind of you, but I must be going soon.'

'You are a delight, Dr Cuthbert. I shock and appall you, but there isn't an ill-mannered bone in your body. Perhaps another time, another party. You would have such fun – I guarantee it.'

After dinner there were brandies and small talk and the group fragmented around the room. Cuthbert found himself beside Miss Parker, whom he had thus far avoided. As Miss Edmonton had warned him, she was indeed a giggler. She was giggling now, even as she spoke to him.

'It must be so interesting being a doctor. Do you get to do simply wonderful things – like save lives and all that?'

'Not quite, miss. You see, I work with the police a great deal, and there the focus is not so much on saving life but bringing criminals to justice.'

'A sleuth too. How marvellous! Lizzie, come and hear this. Our doctor has been hiding his light under the proverbial bushel. He's really a detective. I expect we're all going to be "run in", if that's the expression.'

'No, miss, I never said I was a detective.'

'Oh, nonsense, now you're just being modest. Lizzie, make him tell you.'

Cuthbert now found himself cornered with a girl hanging on each arm, but this time it was Napper who rescued him.

'Get off the man, you two. It's not a fair fight when you

hunt in packs. Here, Cuthbert, let me take you away from all this perfume and diamanté. I don't think you've met our friend Billy. That's the trouble with these dos – the tables are so bloody long you only get to talk to the blighters on either side of you. Here he is. The Honourable William Wellesley, but between you and me, Cuthbert, there's nothing honourable at all about Billy.'

'How do you do, Dr Cuthbert? Please don't listen to a word that reprobate says. Why don't you go off and mix a cocktail or something, Napper, and leave the grown-ups to talk. There's a good lad.'

'How do you do, Mr Wellesley?'

'Oh, Billy, please. I was interested in what you said earlier about all that stuff at the dinner table. I thought you were the voice of reason. There's an awful lot of nonsense going on in Mayfair just now. I mean these new drugs. Especially the young girls. They're so naive, and I was glad to hear your warning.'

'I hope I didn't sound too much like a spoilsport.'

'Not at all. You're a professional man with an opinion that should be listened to. Lord knows they don't listen to anyone else, this crowd. Look, Cuthbert, I'm off soon – I hope I'm not being too forward, but I'd very much like to get to know you a little better. You seem like a man who talks sense, and that's a rare thing around here. Here's my card. Perhaps we could have lunch at my club someday soon. If you would like, of course.'

Cuthbert took the card, which was embellished with an aristocratic coat of arms, and nodded in appreciation. 'I would be delighted, naturally. Please take mine and do call me whenever you would like to meet again.'

When Wellesley left him, Cuthbert only had a chance to take a sip of his brandy before he found another young woman at his side. She was as much perfume and diamanté as the others, but she just stood by him, sipping her cocktail silently.

He was unsure if she even knew he was there, but then she said, 'Please don't mind me, I'm just hiding.' Cuthbert was puzzled. He wondered how you could hide in a Mayfair drawing room during a party, but thought it would be impolite to enquire. Without turning to look at him, she said, 'You're being terribly decent about this. I expect you would like an explanation.'

She didn't wait for an answer and proceeded to tell Cuthbert that she was hiding from Napper. 'Like everyone else here, except you, he wants to tell silly jokes, and I've reached the end of my tether in that department. So that's why I've decided to wait it out in your shadow. No, don't move. Just stay as you are, and I think I might get away with it.'

Cuthbert did as he was told and sipped his brandy.

'I expect you'd like to know my name. I was going to introduce myself at the outset of my subterfuge, but things rather got away from me. It's Lucinda Bartleby, by the way, but call me Lucy for goodness' sake, and I know you're the dashing Dr Cuthbert, so no need to speak if you'd rather not. I'm already imposing upon you enough as it is.'

'On the contrary, Miss Bartleby. I feel compelled to tell you that I've never been used as a human shield before, and it's rather exciting.'

'Yes, isn't it? Life needs a little intrigue from time to time, just to pep it up. Uh oh, I think I might have been rumbled. I see Napper coming this way. Could I possibly ask you to kiss me passionately on the lips? I think it would confuse him sufficiently to make him lose his way. But I suppose that's an even greater imposition than asking you to hide me. Well, nothing else for it – better go and face the music, as they say. It's been a delight meeting you, all the same. We really should hide together next time, and just think, we could have a whole conversation without having to be funny. Now, wouldn't that be a novelty.'

The young woman slipped away from Cuthbert's shadow and back into the glare of the party, only to be pounced on by Napper Maxton-Forbes, who was laughing wildly at something one of the others had just said. Cuthbert found himself charmed by her, and he couldn't remember the last time that had happened.

*

When Cuthbert turned the key in his lock, he saw that Madame Smith's light was still on in her top-floor bedroom. It was very late, and he tried to make as little noise as possible. He placed his hat and coat on the side table in the hall and slipped into his study.

He was not ready for bed and wanted to take some time on his own to think about the evening. His housekeeper had been right; he didn't get out as much as he should, and he had indeed let his social life, if he'd ever had one, slide. He had not been looking forward to the party, but he found the evening strangely exhilarating. The new faces, the glamorous company, the connections to be made and the possibilities to ponder. All these thoughts were swimming in his head as he poured himself a whisky.

He had already drunk much more than was usual for him, but that only made it easier to have another before turning in. He sat in his chair beside the fireplace. The embers had died some hours ago and the room was cooling. He sipped the dram and savoured the burn as it slipped over his tongue and down his throat.

As he swallowed, he closed his eyes and thought of Napper Maxton-Forbes and his green eyes. There had been many men just like that over the years who had filled his imagination since his first and only love at medical school, and he knew that every man simply served to remind him of the one he had lost.

Every fantasy always ended with the same image burning on his lids – that of Joseph Troy, his tall, gangling roommate with the ginger hair who went to war and never came back.

While Cuthbert's early life had been filled with loss, it was losing Troy that cut deepest. And it was a wound that had never healed.

Some may have thought that the death of his parents might have been the defining tragedy in Cuthbert's life, but in truth he had never known his mother, who died giving life to him. And his father was the faintest of shadows because he had died when Cuthbert was only four years old. Now they were only names in his story, hardly memories, and all he had ever known was to be an orphan.

People, of course, would ask about his family, but Cuthbert never liked to discuss them. Not because of any discomfort, but rather because he had so little to say. He had no siblings, no cousins, no parents he could remember. If pressed, he could tell of the overwhelming love he had felt for his nanny, and of the greatest respect he had shown his maternal grandfather who raised the orphan child in his grand home in Edinburgh. But that was not what people wanted to hear. All such a tale would evoke was pity, and the last thing Cuthbert wanted, or felt he deserved, was that. So all he would ever do when asked the question would be to shake his head and change the subject. He had learned that it was easier that way, for everyone.

Chapter 9

London: 15 April 1930

The telephone rang at Cuthbert's home before he or his housekeeper were awake. He got up to answer it, knowing that the only ones to call him at such an hour would be Scotland Yard.

The detective constable on the line was sheepish about waking Cuthbert but explained that he had been given special instructions by Sergeant Baker to phone him at any time if there was a further murder. He had done so because a fourth body had been recovered in Soho in very similar circumstances to the previous three.

Cuthbert reassured the constable that no apology was necessary and took down the address. He rubbed his eyes and imagined what he would like to do to Baker.

*

Old Compton Street was one of the main roads running east–west through Soho, and even before six o'clock in the morning, horse-drawn carts and drays were trundling over the cobbled street and shop doorways were being sluiced by florid-faced women wielding mops and pails.

Cuthbert looked up at number 68. The blackened tenement had dirty windows with every set of curtains shut tight against the morning. He knew that up on the second floor one room was the scene of yet another murder. In just a few hundred square yards, he had already visited three similar scenes in three very similar buildings.

How was it possible, he thought, for one man to frequent so small an area and carry out these atrocious crimes without people noticing something out of the ordinary? But then he looked around, and the squalor of it all reminded him that at night this place was transformed into a much darker place than even the moon could penetrate. There was no 'ordinary' here.

Sergeant Baker met him with an apology about the hour. 'But I knew you'd want to know right away, sir. And it looks like it's him again.'

Cuthbert had managed to get over his initial irritation at being disturbed at five o'clock. Although he was still tired, he did not allow that to affect the thorough examination he made of the corpse and the scene. Sergeant Baker was of course correct, and everything at the scene pointed to it being the same killer using the same method.

'How was the body found so early, sergeant?'

'Just luck, sir. One of the other girls was bringing her punter up the stairs and got the wrong room. He got more than he bargained for, I shouldn't wonder. She found her like this and raised the alarm. The only name we've got for this one is Josie La Belle, but I think we can be fairly certain that's an alias. As usual, no one knows much, but I've still got a few of the girls to speak to, when we can rouse them, that is.'

'Well, we'll get busy at our end and see if we can get you any more to go on, sergeant, but so far everything looks as if it's going to be a carbon copy of the other three. You'll have a report as soon as we can get it done.'

Cuthbert packed his things and took a last look around. It was the same sad, dreary bedroom he had known from many of these cases in London. And it reminded him of another that had persisted in his memory for years. He shook away the thought, unpleasant as it was, and concentrated on getting out of the place.

He decided to go back home, as he had after all left without any breakfast. Madame Smith looked pleased to see him as he hung up his hat and coat up in the hallway. She prepared a pot of chocolate and warmed some croissants and laid them on the breakfast table with a folded linen napkin and the morning paper.

When he came in from washing his hands, she could see he looked weary and wondered if this case was proving to be too much. Despite her position as housekeeper, she resolutely refused to conform to the behaviour expected of a servant. She poured his chocolate and at the same time slapped the back of his hand as he reached for a knife to cut his croissant.

'*Monsieur!* Tear it! How many times do I have to tell you how to eat a croissant?'

As he was looking at her and deciding whether this was one admonishment too many, the house telephone rang, and Madame Smith hurried out to answer it. She took a note of the caller and told Cuthbert, who at first looked puzzled and then vaguely remembered the name before taking the receiver.

'Dr Cuthbert? Billy Wellesley here. I'm sure you've forgotten me, but we met at the Maxton-Forbes' do. Yes, that's right. Oh, you're too kind. Now, you said you'd have lunch with me at my club, and I'm calling you on it, old chap. How are you fixed for tomorrow? Excellent, it's the Chancellor's in Pall Mall. You know it? Righty ho. I'll expect you at one.'

Cuthbert did not eat lunch, had never heard of the club and could barely remember the man except for the intriguing coat of arms on his card. The house in which Cuthbert had been brought up counted good manners to be the earthly manifestation of godliness, and as an adult he found it impossible to be impolite. Unfortunately, that meant saying things he did not believe and often agreeing to things he did not want. His expression soured, and once more he was just a little disappointed in himself as he flicked through the directory to find the address of the club.

*

The next day, he arrived at the high-arched doorway and climbed the short flight of stairs through imposing red marble columns. The glass door was opened for him by an elderly liveried attendant.

'Sir?'

'I have a lunch appointment with the Honourable William Wellesley.'

'Indeed, sir. Please follow me.'

The silence of the entrance hall was broken only by the click of the two men's heels on the mosaic floor and the tick of the ornate clock above the fireplace. Cuthbert climbed the stairs behind the man and was shown into the members' lounge. This was a large ornate room, lit by five tall arched windows looking out on to Pall Mall. The walls were panelled oak and the high-backed leather chairs carefully placed around the room at discreet distances from one another.

Most of the faces were obscured by newspapers, but Cuthbert caught sight of Billy Wellesley at the far end. He had been watching and waiting for his guest and now rose to greet him. As he did so, he simply put a finger to his lips and took Cuthbert back out into the upstairs hall.

'Sorry about that, old chap. Can't break the rule of silence in there, or I'll be thrown into the street. How do you do?'

His handshake was warm and enthusiastic, and although Cuthbert found the whole rigmarole of the London Gentlemen's Club terribly English and faintly ridiculous, he would never say as much out loud.

'Not at all. One must obey the rules of the club if one wishes to enjoy the benefits of its membership.'

'Precisely – no matter how silly they might be. Let me take you into lunch, Dr Cuthbert. They do a rather fine lamb chop here on a Wednesday.'

The lunch was stodgy and over-long, the club having been designed for those with little to do during the day. Cuthbert, having accepted the invitation, tried to make the best of it and managed to leave his pocket watch untouched in his waistcoat throughout.

He declined all offers of alcohol, knowing that he would have to return to work at St Thomas's at some point, and sat at the end of the meal sipping only from a small coffee cup as Wellesley made his way through a large brandy.

'I just wanted to say again that I thought everything you said at the party was so helpful. There really is a lot of damage being done these days with all these new temptations. The booze is one thing, but these drugs are quite another. I've seen a few university chums quite frazzled by them, I can tell you. And I do worry about Charlie. You do know, don't you, that he's been dabbling?'

'Well, I had no firm knowledge of that, but . . .'

'You suspected, am I right? I mean, a medical man like yourself is hardly going to miss the signs. He has become quite the slave to them, I'm afraid, and I feel so sorry for them both. Celia does her best, but it's a losing battle sometimes.'

'Where does he get his drugs?'

'Oh, it's all above board. He has them prescribed by his doctor. As a diagnosed addict, it's all absolutely proper. He has a rather charming and most amenable doctor in New Bond Street: Dr Jackson Stark. Do you know him? He even telephones to tell him when another prescription is due. He overcharges him of course, but one does expect to pay for the convenience of it all, I suppose. Tell me, Dr Cuthbert, do you write prescriptions?'

'As a medical practitioner I have that power, but as you might imagine, most of my patients are beyond the need of any medication.'

'Of course, how silly of me. But you can write them – how interesting. I only ask because I'm so worried about Charlie, and it would be such a solace to know that there might be someone else, someone like yourself, that poor Celia could rely on if Charlie were to run out. I realise it's a frightful imposition, but you have met him, and you've seen for yourself that he is in genuine need.'

Cuthbert now knew what this lunch was about. For a plate of lamb chops, he was expected to sacrifice his professional standards, no matter how sweetly the idea was being wrapped up. He sighed audibly because he had reached the limit of his good grace, and no social niceties were about to lead him to compromise himself. He folded his napkin and stood up.

'I'm sorry, Mr Wellesley, it would be quite out of the question for one medical practitioner to encroach upon another's management of his patient. I am certain that Mr Maxton-Forbes is already receiving the highest standard of care. And I'm afraid I must now take my leave of you. Thank you for lunch, but duty calls. I do hope we meet again.'

Cuthbert did not wait for Wellesley to respond. He swept out, quickly retrieving his coat and hat from the doorman. On the street, he found the tarry fumes from the London buses and taxis refreshing after the stuffy air in the Chancellor's Club. He hailed a cab and returned to the hospital.

Shortly after he got back to his office, one of the mortuary technicians knocked on his door and led Sarah Morgenthal into the room. He was surprised to see her and rose to greet her, this time stretching his hand out to shake hers, keeping her at a distance in case she had any thoughts of repeating her actions at the wedding. But as he took her limp, almost perfunctory handshake, he could tell from her demeanour that she had no intention of kissing him this time.

'Mrs Morgenthal, what an unexpected pleasure. I'm afraid Simon isn't here.'

'I know. It's you I've come to see, Dr Cuthbert.'

As he asked her to take a seat, he could see she was breathing hard and looked to be steeling herself for a fight.

'And what can I do for you? Is it something important?'

'Do you honestly think I would come to this charnel house if it wasn't important? I want to know what you've been saying to Simon about me, and I want to know right now.'

Cuthbert remained still, and his voice was calm and measured. There was already enough excitement in the room.

'Mrs Morgenthal, I'm afraid I don't know what you're talking about. I have never discussed you or your personal life with your husband. That is not the nature of our professional relationship. What has prompted this?'

'Simon is never home, and when he is, he barely looks me in the eye these days. I know he's more interested in his work than his family and I think you're to blame. I think you've poisoned his mind against me. I know you don't like me, Dr Cuthbert, but I think it's unspeakably cruel of you to jeopardise our marriage.'

'I can assure you Mrs Morgenthal, nothing could be further from the truth. Simon is a young doctor, and he works very hard because he knows he has to if he wishes to excel in his chosen field. What he does is very difficult and highly specialised. He chooses to work long hours because he wants to. No one is compelling him to do this job, and certainly not me. We may not agree with the decisions of others, but surely we have to respect them.'

'Not when those decisions affect one's future.'

Sarah Morgenthal was flushed, and the tears were welling up in her eyes, but she was determined not to let go of her argument. 'Whenever I try to speak with him, he simply says it's because of his work. He's not home because of his work. He misses every Sabbath dinner because of his work. He's away all weekend because of his work. What am I to think? That you're a slave driver or that maybe you're encouraging him to spend more time with you than his wife?'

Cuthbert was uncomfortable about the direction these accusations were taking, and he knew he needed to stop her in her tracks.

'Mrs Morgenthal, I have never asked Simon to work all weekend, or in the evenings, and I have made especially sure that his Friday evenings were free for his family. If Simon is not home at these times, it is not because he is here and certainly not because I have asked him to be. Now, I think this conversation is over, and I would appreciate it if you could let me get back to my work. I suggest you have a fuller discussion about your difficulties with your husband in the privacy of your own home, without bringing them back here. Good day, Mrs Morgenthal.'

Cuthbert escorted her out of his office and asked one of his technicians to show her from the department. When the man returned, he made plain his annoyance that she had been admitted in the first place.

'I don't care whose wife she is. She is a member of the public and there is no admittance to this mortuary without my express permission and invitation. Is that perfectly clear?'

To everyone in earshot, it was. Cuthbert was a big man, and when he wanted to, had just as big a voice. He knew from painful experience that if he lost his temper, he could be fiercely intimidating to all around him so he rarely, if ever, raised his voice at work. He certainly had never slammed his office door before; when he did just that after he marched away from the humbled technician, all the staff knew he meant it.

It did not take him long to calm himself, and soon afterwards he was seeking out the mortuary technician who had been on the receiving end of his rage. Of course, he politely apologised for his outburst, but the technician was still quaking from being shouted at and now found the apology of the towering Scotsman almost as intimidating. Cuthbert could see he was not helping the situation, made his excuses and left the department for the short walk along the river to Scotland Yard, where he was expected.

He arrived for the case conference early, and as he crossed the duty room, he saw Sergeant Baker poring over a thick file at his desk. The officer was sitting with his head in both hands, and he was frowning.

'You look as if you need an interruption, sergeant.'

'Good afternoon, Dr Cuthbert. You never said a truer word, sir.'

Cuthbert came around behind Baker and looked at the series of photographs stuck to the pages in the file he was reading. They were all small head-and-shoulders shots, both full face and side profile for each person. Cuthbert was startled when he saw the photos at the bottom of the page.

'That's Napper Maxton-Forbes. What is this, sergeant?'

'According to this file, he's Norman Brown. Or at least that was the name he gave when he was nicked. This is the Addicts' Index from Vine Street. I've been working my way through it all day yesterday and all morning today. Pointless task if you ask me. None of the names are real, and all the addresses are made up.'

'But you do have photographs.'

Cuthbert looked more closely at the picture that had caught his eye. It was definitely the elder Maxton-Forbes brother. He certainly wasn't looking quite as polished as Cuthbert remembered him, but those eyes were unmistakable.

'Do you know this one then, Dr Cuthbert?'

'I suppose I do, sergeant. I came across him at a dinner party in Mayfair. Is he in the book because he's a known addict?'

'That he is, sir. It says here that he's had four offences in the last two years, including illegally bringing cocaine into the country from Paris and forging prescriptions for morphine. Each time he got off with a fine. You know what the magistrates are like with the posh boys and girls. One rule for them and one for the rest of us.'

Cuthbert began to wonder about Celia Maxton-Forbes's gang, as she called them, and he asked the sergeant if he might take a look through the file.

'There's a lot of it, sir, but you're more than welcome. What are you looking for?'

'I'm not sure, but we might at least be able to put a few more accurate names on the records.'

It didn't take Cuthbert long to find Napper's brother, Charlie, who was listed as John Foster in the file, as well as two of the young women who had been at the dinner party. The photographs of Florence Parker and Elizabeth Hamilton-Jacques were far from becoming. They looked haggard and their make-up was smeared, but they were instantly recognisable even though they were listed as Flora Green and Gladys Jackson.

They were obviously more experienced than the naive experimenters in white drugs that Cuthbert had thought them. The two women already had five convictions for prescription fraud. As Baker had indicated, none of these bright young things had suffered the indignity of a custodial sentence for their crimes, and all had escaped with, what must have been for them, the lightest of financial hand slaps. Fines of as little as one shilling were imposed, on the condition that they undertake a residential cure for their addiction.

Cuthbert thought of the Soho prostitutes living from hand to mouth who could expect to be fined forty shillings when they were found guilty of soliciting.

He looked further through the file – page after page of photographs of known addicts. All were young, and he was surprised by how many of them were women. But what most surprised him were the photographs on the final page of an Alfred Thompson, whom he knew better as the Honourable William Wellesley.

'Well, well, Billy, and what are you doing in there?'

Cuthbert now considered who was to be the real recipient of the prescription he had been asked to write over lunch. He was starting to see how Celia's 'gang' operated. It was a tight-knit Mayfair clique interdependent on the wiles of those who could inveigle themselves into the good offices of doctors who would ask few questions. The prescriptions, when issued, were doubtless altered and shared around the group.

He was still thinking about the photographs on his walk back to St Thomas's and about this world he had stumbled into when he arrived back at the hospital. His head was full of their faces, the lovely young women and the even more lovely young men.

Their vibrancy, he now knew, was fuelled by drugs and funded by their families' money, and he wondered just how long it would be before they would all look permanently like those mugshots taken in Vine Street late some night.

When he got back to his office, he saw his assistant, who had returned to the laboratory just before him from the seminar he had been attending.

'Dr Morgenthal, a word if you please. In my office.'

Simon Morgenthal was just changing into his white coat. He looked concerned; he was unused to this tone in his mentor's voice. He began running over in his mind everything he had done in the last few days and what could possibly have been found deficient.

Cuthbert sat with his elbows on the desk and his large hands clasped almost in prayer. 'I like to keep things separate in my life. My work and my home, as you will have observed, rarely cross over, and I have come to expect that from others too.'

Morgenthal had no idea what Cuthbert was getting at, but he nodded and agreed.

'I am not a married man, as you know. And as such, I am in no position to offer any kind of advice with respect to your domestic arrangements, but when any problems you are having turn up in my office, I do feel the need to say something.'

'Dr Cuthbert, I don't know what you're referring to. Have I offended you in some way? Please forgive me if—'

'Your wife was here.'

'In your office?'

'She arrived when you were over at the university. And she came to see me. She has a great many grievances about your lack of attentiveness and lays the blame squarely at my door. I am supposedly keeping you from her day and night and even, it seems, at weekends.'

His assistant hung his head.

'Perhaps you would like to explain to me how I have become the fiend in all this?'

'It was never right between us, even from the start. You could see that – everyone could. I even had doubts. When we were first engaged it was wonderful, but I suppose I changed.

She wanted one thing, I another, and I thought I could make it all work, but I can't. Whenever we're alone together, we fight. I just can't be the kind of person she wants me to be. All her silly friends irritate me more than I can say. Everything about the life she wants for us is so shallow. So I stopped going home, and made excuses. I said it was because I had to work. I even said that you had asked me to work. At night, I try to go home after she's in bed, so we don't have to fight, and I've been spending time at my parents' house at the weekends and with some university friends. I haven't been seeing anyone else if that's what you think. It's nothing like that.'

'I would sincerely hope not, Simon, but as I'm trying to make clear to you, it really is none of my business. I'm disappointed that you deceived her into thinking I was the cause of this. I said to her that you both need to speak to one another and sort out your difficulties, and I will say the same to you. In God's name, man, she's carrying your child.'

Simon blanched. He had never heard Cuthbert speak like this before. He mumbled another apology and looked at him, appealing for some form of forgiveness, but Cuthbert wanted actions rather than words from his assistant.

'Get your coat and go home to her. Sit down and work this out. This is not just about you and her now; there is a third person to consider. I expect you to be back here tomorrow morning, and I do not wish to hear any more about it. We have important work to do in this department, and I cannot allow you to be involved in that if you are distracted by your personal life. I hope I've made the position clear, Dr Morgenthal. Please close my door on your way out.'

Before Morgenthal could leave the office, the phone rang. Cuthbert composed himself and answered calmly and professionally.

'Cuthbert, this is Mowbray. I have a question about the drugs.'

'Of course, chief inspector. How can I help?'

'I know you've confirmed that there were traces of white drugs on the bedside table of the first victim, but not at any of the other scenes.'

'That's correct.'

'And I know you've found needle marks on each but – here's what's worrying me – can we be certain that drugs were actually injected into these women?'

'We can test the routine blood samples we collected from the victims. With our current methods, I'm afraid it's not possible to quantify how much might have been administered, but if we get a positive test at all, it means that they were injected. In fact, we should have done this already for you. You shouldn't have had to ask.'

'Well, you've had your hands full. Just when you can, doctor.'

Cuthbert would have assigned the assays to Morgenthal, but he was keen to see the back of him for the day, so when he had gone, he undertook them himself.

He repeated the drug testing protocols his assistant had already followed. The only difference was that this time he took small samples of each of the victims' blood from the refrigerator, added a precipitating reagent to each in order to bring all the blood proteins out of solution, and then spun them in the small mechanical centrifuge on the bench. This forced the now solid proteins to the bottom of the tube, leaving an almost clear liquid with which to work.

The colour spot tests confirmed that each of the women had traces of morphine and cocaine in their blood. Although the analysis of the white powder had also suggested the presence of heroin, he knew he would not find that in the victims' blood samples as it was broken down rapidly in the body to a form of morphine.

He concluded that they had indeed received an injection of a cocktail of the white drugs. He wrote up the report including the precise details of the methods he had used and the results obtained, and then he phoned Mowbray back with the answer he needed.

Almost as soon as he hung up, Cuthbert's office phone rang again. He thought it might be Mowbray with another query, but he was surprised to hear Sergeant Baker's voice instead.

'Dr Cuthbert? Sorry to bother you, sir, but I needed to check something with you . . . Remember the Addicts' Index, sir? Well, I seem to recall that you recognised one of them and knew his real identity. Napper someone?'

'Yes, sergeant, Napper Maxton-Forbes. I only met him the once, but his face was quite memorable.'

'Would you mind re-identifying that photo for me, sir, if I brought the file to you at St Thomas's? The thing is, one of the witness statements from the Josie La Belle murder mentioned someone called Napper. I thought it was maybe too much of a coincidence, especially considering the drug angle in all this. And I thought it might be useful to have the gentleman in, but of course we need his real name to find him.'

'Of course, sergeant, and I'll come to you. There were a few others in the file that you should know about too – they all belong to Napper's set.'

*

Before setting off for the Yard, the following morning, Cuthbert looked in to see if his assistant was at his bench. Morgenthal had arrived early and was already busying himself with preparing the dissection tray for the next post mortem.

Cuthbert had asked him to take the lead again in the examination of the fourth victim. In his mind, he had already moved on from the unpleasantness of Sarah's visit to the department, and he was keen to get his young assistant back to work.

When the corpse of the woman known as Josie La Belle was delivered to the hospital mortuary, after Cuthbert had sent Morgenthal home the day before, he had made a preliminary examination. He had checked for all the hallmarks of the murders – signs of asphyxiation by smothering, bite marks and the single hypodermic needle wound. But even in such a cursory examination, there was something different about this body that puzzled him. However, he said nothing and left Morgenthal to it to see if he came to the same conclusions.

'Dr Morgenthal, I shall be at Scotland Yard this morning. On my return I would appreciate your post mortem report.'

'It will be ready for you, sir.'

The young man was brisk and professional and was keen to show that nothing was distracting him, even though nothing at all had changed in his domestic affairs.

On Cuthbert's return, Morgenthal was waiting with the pathology report already typed up. He had completed the external and internal examinations of the corpse and had ensured that the body had been carefully and respectfully reconstituted. Cuthbert, however, was preoccupied as he had been during the whole walk back from the Yard. After his discussion with Baker, a number of questions were still buzzing in his head, and he barely noticed his assistant as he came in.

'Dr Cuthbert. The report is ready for you, sir.'

'Oh yes, of course. Right, let's have it.'

Cuthbert started to read over the findings, and Morgenthal sat in silence watching him for any sign of approval or otherwise.

'The bite mark, this time high on the left breast – did you think it looked like the others?'

'I did, sir. I've had it photographed, so we can compare

them directly, but to the naked eye it certainly looked to be the same, right down to the supernumerary canine.'

'Yes, I would agree. And the needle mark, is it a single hypodermic stab wound as before?'

'Undoubtedly, sir.'

'It all seems entirely consistent with the three other victims, right down to the method of killing. But there is just one thing.'

Morgenthal knew that Cuthbert would find something in his report to question, if only to remind him that his work and his attitude to it were still under the closest of scrutiny.

'In your examination of the vagina, Dr Morgenthal, what's missing?'

'I'm sorry, sir, I was very thorough.'

'No, I don't mean what did you miss, I mean what was missing? To be plain, what about the cervix? Was it like the others, consistent with at least one previous pregnancy?

'Yes, sir, it was. All four women have definitely had children.'

'And when you examined the cervix did you have the same problem visualising it as before?

'No, I didn't. You're right, sir, there was no semen. None at all.'

'Exactly. This time he didn't have sex with her, and probably because it was earlier in the evening, he must have been her first client of the night. Which raises an interesting question: was any of the previous semen we recovered from the other bodies his at all? Did he have sex with any of the prostitutes, and, if not, why not? I'm beginning to wonder if this case has anything to do with sex at all.'

Cuthbert took the latest pathology report personally to Scotland Yard as he was due to attend another of Mowbray's case conferences. As always, he was early, and he took a seat at the far end of the duty room in front of the pinboard bearing the details of all the cases. Cuthbert found himself alone for once before the board, and it gave him the opportunity to study it in detail.

It made grim viewing, and no clear picture was emerging from the maze of coloured strings and labels that were used by Baker to connect the victims with any of the other individuals on the board.

What possible motive, he wondered, could there be for anyone to kill these women? As he stared at the post mortem photographs, there was a tap on his shoulder, and he glanced up to see a somewhat nervous-looking Sergeant Baker.

'Dr Cuthbert, I wonder if I could run something by you, sir.'

'Of course. Shall we wait till the chief inspector gets here?'

'If it's all right with you, sir, I'd like to show it to you first.'

'No point in getting the Pie all fired up over nothing. Is that it?'

'How well you know us, sir. The thing is, I've been going over some old files. It was the bite mark, see. There was a case a while back and it rang a bell. Anyway, I've dug out the file and this is the post mortem photo here. This is the bite mark on the woman's thigh. I think it looks a lot like the ones we're dealing with.'

Cuthbert took the photo and scrutinised it, and then went over to the pinboard and matched it with the photos of the bite marks on Dutch Edie, Jeanette X, French Renée and Josie La Belle.

'You're absolutely right, sergeant: it's the same. Tell me what else we know about this victim.'

'That's just it, sir. The similarities don't end with the bite. She was also a prostitute, thirty-five to forty years old, worked in Soho and was found in the room she rented for trade.'

'And the cause of death?'

'That's where it differs, sir. This woman had a serious head wound and was strangled with a length of electrical cable.'

'Needle mark?'

'None according to the pathology report. But might it have been missed? That's what I really wanted to ask you.'

'Who was the pathologist?'

'Dr Strangford at Guy's, sir.'

'Then the answer is no; he wouldn't miss that. He's one of the best. But the other similarities are too much to be a coincidence. Maybe this was the first victim, and he hadn't perfected his technique yet. I think you need to bring all this to Mowbray's attention.'

'I was worried you might say that.'

'Sergeant?'

'You see, sir, it was one of the chief inspector's own cases.'

Chapter 10

London: 6 May 1923

The St Pancras Workhouse was a very different institution from the Foundling Hospital. The five-storey red-brick edifice squatted near the rail tracks north of the terminus.

On the February morning in 1912 when the 3-year-old Robbie Compton was delivered there by his foster mother, she took the small amount of money that was owed to her for his upkeep and did not look back as he burst into tears and raised his arms to be picked up. He was taken to the children's ward where he was put on the floor beside several other toddlers.

The room was bright with large windows that also made it cold, but there was a nursemaid who tried to soothe his tears and feed him along with another small boy. The two looked at each other and held out their hands, unsure of what they were seeing.

Both were new arrivals and had been weaned in isolation away from any other children. As their little fingers found each other, they giggled and lost interest in the spoonfuls of porridge offered by the nursemaid. She allowed them to discover each other and smiled as they touched each other's hair and faces.

Not long after Robbie arrived, the guardians of St Pancras

decided to move the younger children out of the overcrowded workhouse to an industrial school in Leavesden, near Watford.

They were duly dispatched to the quarantine cottage there, where they would stay for three weeks before entering the school proper, such was the concern that infectious fevers might be brought from the city. Soon, Robbie and the others settled into their new home, and the boys who had met on the floor of the children's ward grew up together.

When they started their lessons, it was Robbie who took the lead, for he was a bright boy, eager to learn and interested in everything. The boys learned their scripture and about the expanse of the British Empire on the world map hanging on the classroom wall. They memorised their times tables and recited them each morning. There was singing and drawing, and they were encouraged to play football and cricket in the grounds.

When the two friends turned 7, they joined the older boys and had to spend an hour a day between breakfast and the start of lessons at nine o'clock working either in the carpentry shop, the blacksmith's forge or the farm. Robbie always made for the farm and tried to feed the squealing piglets just so he could hold them and feel their warmth.

When they were 14, Robbie and his classmates were instructed on their future by the headmaster. Mr Gresham was a stern young man with a deep gruff voice, but the boys all knew he was fair.

Gresham had been on the Western Front in the war, and although he never spoke of it, the boys imagined he had been a fearsome warrior. His left arm, which hung withered by his side, was a testament to his exploits in battle, and they would often re-enact his imagined days and nights on the Somme in their dormitories.

Gresham was a realist and cared a great deal more for his

fatherless charges than his demeanour suggested. In his address to them, at the end of that term, he was honest and made it clear what their options were.

'Boys, you are on the brink of manhood and very soon you will leave the Industrial School. Some of you are prepared for this, but many of you are not. You will all need to make your own way in life, and make no mistake that will be hard for all of you.

'You have led different lives from those of other boys. You have had no mothers to soothe you, and no fathers to guide you. But here we have tried to be the parents you have lost, in the full knowledge that we can never fully take their place. You have received a rudimentary education, but it has been more than that given to many other boys outside these walls. You have learned to work hard, and perhaps that will stand you in greatest stead.

'None of you are privileged or rich. All of you are alone, and whether you sink or swim will be entirely dependent on your own efforts. In the next few years, you will grow into men and be able to take your place in the world, but those first few years will be your hardest. No longer children, but not yet adults, you will have to live and work in a world where many will seek to take advantage of you. Be watchful, boys, work hard, give your trust sparingly and always remember your bible.'

As the boys walked back to the refectory from the headmaster's address, there was much discussion about his meaning. They knew that over the next few weeks they would be leaving the school, and they were all filled with a mixture of excitement and apprehension. Gresham had reminded them that until now they had been protected from the outside world, and now that world was about to be unleashed on them.

Robbie's best friend, Michael, pulled him back from the others. Both boys were tall for their age and physically mature.

They knew their strength could not yet match the blacksmith in the forge, but they could already wield the largest of the hammers without difficulty.

'What will you do, Robbie?'

'I dunno. There are the mines. They're always looking for young ones down there. Or the barges. They say that's a good life. Maybe even the merchant ships. I fancy seeing some of that Empire on the map. What about you?'

'I don't know either, but whatever you decide to do, I'd like to go with you. Mr Gresham said we're alone, but we're not alone, Robbie. We can stick together. What d'you say?'

'Let's do just that. We could get down the docks and sign on to the first ship that's going far away. We might see China or the South Seas – remember *Coral Island*? – or even South America. Do you remember the pictures of the Amazon in the *Daily Graphic*? Imagine seeing that for real! Think of the adventures we can have! We can be family – like proper brothers.'

The two boys laughed together and rushed to find seats at the refectory benches to eat their supper.

As chance would have it, they were both released together and given ordinary but second-hand clothes to wear in place of their school uniforms. They stood together in the dormitory sizing each other up. Each wore a rough canvas jacket and twill trousers, and their shirts were darned but clean and white. To top it all off each wore a flat tweed cap.

'You look like one of the gardeners, Robbie.'

'And you look like his little sister.'

The boys started to wrestle and the caps went flying, but the laughter soon subsided and they were on their way. They walked and then ran south to the river and followed it along to the docks in the East End.

As Robbie and Michael were walking wide-eyed along the dockside in Stepney trying to find out which was the largest and fastest of all the merchant ships, Lizzie Compton was washing the blood from her hands as Walter lay dead in his room. The night before, she had had five of the sailors from the SS *Normanstar*, including the one who had been careless with his knife.

Now, the two boys were looking up at the large red funnel of the same steamship and its huge blue star in a white circle. They called up to be allowed on board and learned that she was a refrigerated cargo liner bound for San Francisco through the Panama Canal. All 4,300 net tons of her would be setting sail with the next morning's tide and, yes, they could use two more cabin boys.

'How old are you lads?'

'Sixteen, sir,' said Robbie before Michael could offer him the truth.

'Sea legs?'

'Not our first time out, sir. And you can count on us working hard.' Michael knew the game now and nodded in hearty agreement.

'Hard work is the very least you'll have to do in the middle of a force ten in the Atlantic. Get yourself up here so I can get a proper look at the pair of you.'

The mate sized them up and pinched their arms to satisfy himself that they could pull their weight. He nodded and said, 'Get yourself a berth and don't expect much. We leave tomorrow at dawn with or without you, so if you're out on the poke make sure you're back.'

'Yes, sir, we won't let you down,' said Robbie. After the mate had left them, Michael asked his friend what he meant. 'What's out on the poke?'

'Bleeding hell, am I going to have to explain everything to you. The girls on the docks, that's what he was meaning. What do you reckon? Should we have a go?'

Robbie counted the coins in his pocket while his friend looked nervous and blushed at the thought.

'You mean go with one of them? And do what?'

'What you've been doing all by yourself under the blankets. Only instead of using your hand, you get to put it up her. Don't you know all this?'

'Of course I know. I just don't think I want to, that's all. Not with one of them.'

'Well, it's one of them or nobody, and anyway, I'll keep you right. Besides, we're going to be at sea for a while. Come on, let's get the berths sorted, and then we can see what else we can find.'

Michael reluctantly followed his friend below and then, as dusk fell, out along the dockside. The first of the prostitutes looked old to the boys, and they moved further along the river. When one of the younger girls caught Robbie's eye, and he went over, but she frowned when she saw him in the light.

'Does your mother know you're out on your own, sonny?'

He opened his palm and the silver shilling glinted in the gaslight.

'And what about your pal? Is he looking for a short time too?'

Robbie nodded on Michael's behalf and the girl shouted along the quayside, 'Annie, got a pair here. D'you want one of 'em?'

The two prostitutes took the boys round the side of the warehouse. Robbie reached out to touch his, and she swatted him away.

'Business first, young 'un.' She took his shilling and put it in a small purse she had sewn in her dress, and then pulled up her skirt and leaned against the barrels.

Michael watched wide-eyed as Robbie undid his trousers and let them fall to his knees while the woman took hold of him and guided him in. His own prostitute had her hand out, and she was telling him she didn't have all night, so he gave her his shilling, and she took up the same pose only yards from Robbie, who was now working hard like the ram in the farm at school.

Michael fumbled with his buttons and tried not to look at her. In her impatience, she reached out and pulled him towards her, his body jerked, and he came in her hands.

She wiped her palm on his trousers and said, 'Well, that was a quickie, but no refunds. Away you go!'

Michael could see Robbie slapping against the girl and then grunting as he arched his back and thrust forward for the last time. She pushed the boy away, wiped between her legs and straightened her skirt. She was already walking back out into the gaslight on the quayside with her companion while he was still breathing heavily. Michael watched as Robbie straightened and pulled up his trousers. He was wearing the broadest of grins.

'How was yours? Mine was great. Never thought it would be as good as that.'

Michael muttered something about wanting to go back and get cleaned up. Under the gaslight, Robbie looked at the stains on Michael's trousers and then at his hangdog expression, and he understood. The friends walked back to the ship in silence and mounted the gangplank, and as the sun rose the following morning, they were already steaming past Greenwich on their way to the New World.

*

As the boys stood on the deck of the SS *Normanstar*, Marie was waking up in the single room she had rented on Romilly Street. On her walk from Stepney to Soho the day before, the chrysalis that was Lizzie Compton had cracked open and

Marie de la Rue had emerged to take her place. She found the accent easy and decided that Marie walked differently, held her handbag differently and even smiled differently from the little girl she had once been.

She knew of Soho and what happened there, but her days of taking men up alleyways and being scraped against brick walls were over.

This second-floor room would be her workplace for a while, at least until she could afford something better. The other girls on the street were suspicious of her that first night, but they soon learned that she was no real threat for she charged too much. They asked for five bob a time, and she wanted double.

'What does she give 'em for half a knicker, that's what I want to know. I mean, what's she got under that skirt, two pussies?'

'Well, whatever she does, she gets some of 'em to pay it. She does half the work as us and makes the same money, so maybe we should be taking lessons from her.'

But none of them dared ask her outright what services she offered, and her air of mystery grew. They did learn that she carried a razor in her garter and had a knife in her room. And the rumour was that she wasn't afraid to use them.

A grudging respect grew between her and the other girls, which gradually over the weeks turned into friendship. She never once let her accent slip when she was in their presence, and everyone regarded her as an authentic French girl. Sometimes, if one of their clients asked if there were any foreign girls, the other prostitutes would even recommend Marie.

Eager and curious, the men would pay their money, and Marie would give them the illusion of the exotic and use all the tricks she had learned from the foreign sailors in the docks. Every one of her clients left satisfied and word soon spread about the beautiful French whore on Romilly Street.

With the money she earned, she bought better clothes and

expensive French perfume. Everything she did was to improve the illusion, and the stronger the illusion, the more she knew she could charge, because she understood the one thing about men that the other girls on the street had failed to recognise.

She knew from that very first night that her profession was nothing to do with sex and everything to do with power. These men were not buying her body to use for ten minutes; they were buying the fantasy of her body. Sex was little more than the friction of skin against skin, but what she sold was far more exciting than that.

When one of the pimps approached her and told her she was working for him from now on, she smiled and asked him to come away from the light so they could talk. As she turned, she pulled the razor from her garter and slashed at his upper arm. She cut through the fabric of his jacket and deeply into his skin. He grabbed at his arm in pain and felt the blood seep through his fingers. He moved to strike her, but she raised the razor and fearlessly told him if he touched her, he would lose his nose, then his dick and then his life. He cursed her but retreated into the shadows and did not bother her again. Nor did anyone else: not because they knew she carried a razor, but because they knew she was fearless.

She soon learned there were other opportunites available to her, and as her sole aim was to earn enough money to move on, she took advantage of every one of them. She worked with petty criminals in the area and received stolen goods, passing them on in the bars for a cut. She took commission from the illegal gambling clubs to steer her clients there.

She had started to attract some more well-heeled clients and could purr in their ears as she felt for their wallets. As well as stealing cash from them, she could persuade any of them to take her to the clubs where she received five shillings for every man she brought to the blackjack table.

The bars were another racket, and the owners soon came to rely on her abilities to provide them with a regular stream of men with more money than discretion. They overcharged them for watered-down gin and the customers would never notice as long as she was sitting on their laps.

She even worked with the taxis. When the drivers were asked in a nervous whisper if they knew anywhere their fares could go to have a special time, they would bring them to her door and she would split the fee with them. It meant she no longer needed to walk the streets because her trade would now come knocking at her door. And it also had the advantage of leaving her less vulnerable to the occasional sweeps the police made of the area, when they rounded up the street girls and bundled them into their black vans.

As Marie gathered a regular clientele, she moved from one room into two and then three, but she remained in Soho. She had the rooms cleaned and bought fresh linen. And she found a gramophone in the local sale room on which she only played French music.

Every move was designed to increase her value and to nurture the deception. But under even the cleanest, crispest pillowslip, she always kept the knife she had used on Walter, and it still had traces of his blood on it. She knew that she could slit a man's throat, and she was ready, if it were ever needed, to slit another.

During the day, Marie slept well on clean sheets, and in the afternoons, she spent her time watching the women shopping in Fortnum & Mason, strolling through Hyde Park and taking tea in Selfridge's. She studied the way they sat and held their cups, how they smiled, how they laughed and how they crossed their legs. She followed them into the powder rooms and noted their cosmetics and how they applied their lipstick. She eavesdropped on their small talk.

Every day she learned a little more about how to look and act and sound like one of them, for already she was laying the groundwork for her next metamorphosis. She didn't have enough money yet, but soon she would, and then it would be time to move again.

Occasionally, when she was away from Soho and doing her research, she would drop her French persona and practise her new one. She would watch the faces of shop assistants and waitresses, looking for any trace of recognition or suspicion.

When she was sure of her new accent, and the gestures she knew needed to accompany it, she would even join in the chatter in the powder rooms and occasionally even initiate a conversation in the park or in front of a painting in a gallery. She knew she was almost ready. Once she was out of Soho and earning real money, she would be able to start looking for Robert.

She had already asked those street girls who had been brought up in orphanages around the city if they remembered a boy called Compton, but she was unsurprised that none had. It was a big city and many years had passed. As the matron at the Foundling Hospital had warned her, her brother could be anywhere in the world by now, assuming he was even still alive.

She put that thought aside for the time being and knew she had to concentrate on the present. As darkness fell, she would sit by her window and watch the girls one by one take up their spots. At night, she knew the city transformed into something monstrous. It moved like a hungry beast rasping smoky breath in the feeble moonlight, heaving and watching those who ventured out.

Only with the dawn were the slimy streets turned back into grey cobbles and the rank, fleshy buildings turned back to stone. And only the morning rain would wash away the night soil. The animal would sleep in the light, hiding from all in plain sight, until the sun went down again.

*

After another month, Marie knew she was ready. On her return from one of her field trips around the National Gallery, walking along Old Compton Street, she paused to look at the jewellery in a pawnbroker's window. Amongst the rings and bracelets were necklaces and pendants. She looked closely to see if there were any gold chains that might be suitable, and she saw one at the back.

The elderly gentleman behind the counter looked up and smiled at the young woman. She used her French accent and asked to see the tray from the window. She explained that she had inherited an old necklace, just a little family trinket of no real value except of a sentimental nature. She wanted to wear the pendant, but the chain had been broken ever since she had been given it.

'Let me see, mademoiselle.'

She produced the small 'C' pendant and placed it beside the fine chain she thought might match.

Marek Jankowski took the pendant and held it close, so he could see it clearly. Could it be? 'Mademoiselle, where did you get this?'

'Oh, monsieur, it is nothing. It was my mother's when she was young.'

'And she was French?'

'But of course. Now I think I will take the chain. No need to wrap it – I will just put it in my purse.'

He took her eight shillings and gave her the chain.

'*Au revoir, monsieur. Merci bien.*'

Marie left the shop and paused in the covered doorway before stepping back out onto the pavement of Old Compton Street.

Mr Jankowski moved to his window to look at the young woman standing outside. She had taken the chain from her purse and was already putting it around her neck. She adjusted the pendant until the letter 'C' rested against her skin. She caressed it and then put on her gloves and left. The elderly pawnbroker thought for a moment, then shook his head and scolded himself for being such a silly old fool.

Chapter 11

London: 22 April 1930

The police file on Mary Jones, also known as Belgian Marie, was disappointingly thin. There were no other photographs of either the corpse or the crime scene beyond the one of the bite mark that Baker had shown to Cuthbert, and the written descriptions were sketchy at best.

Cuthbert looked for the pathology report which had been written by his counterpart at Guy's Hospital. At least it was thorough and properly reported.

The victim was a Caucasian woman, probably in her late thirties, who was poorly nourished and showed evidence of multiple old injuries. She had a fractured right temporal bone and had been strangled with a length of electrical cable which was still twisted tightly around her neck when she was found.

Her external and internal examinations confirmed death by asphyxiation. However, there were a number of other injuries that were consistent with defensive wounds. Two of her fingernails were broken and there was skin under three others. There was also fresh bruising on her chest which would have been consistent with downward force, perhaps another person pinning her to the bed.

Internally, there were various findings consistent with excessive alcohol consumption and signs of secondary syphilis. Importantly, there was no mention of any hypodermic needle marks, although as Baker had pointed out, there was a bite mark. It was described in the notes, and unlike those that Cuthbert had recently been dealing with, it appeared to have been inflicted post mortem because of the absence of associated bruising around the wound.

Baker had delivered the file at Cuthbert's request and was now standing behind the pathologist as he read it in his office at the hospital.

'Thank you for letting me see this, sergeant. It certainly looks like this might be the work of our perpetrator. There are too many similarities to my mind for it to be a coincidence. The profession and age of the victim, but most importantly the bite mark. There are of course some problems. Unfortunately, there is only a very perfunctory description of the scene and no photographs, but I wouldn't be surprised if this woman put up a fight for her life. She looks to have been forced onto the bed and she would have left some marks on her killer.'

'Before I take it to the chief inspector, is there anything else I should know?'

Sergeant Baker was clearly dreading the confrontation with his superior about one of his old cases, especially one that looked to have been poorly investigated and reported.

'I think you already know what I'm going to say, sergeant. This is quite a botched job, and if you were to put in a report like this on a murder, Mowbray would go for your throat. It's really most unlike him. Is there any explanation?'

'The body was found on the fifteenth of December. That was the day they hanged Freddie Dawson's murderer, if you remember, sir. I know the chief inspector was very tied up with that case, and I think this one came in when his full attention was elsewhere. It was Sergeant Hills who led on it, and he retired a few weeks later due to ill health. In fact, we heard he died last month. So, a combination of things, really, sir. Sometimes things just slip through the cracks. And with a prostitute there's rarely anyone shouting for answers.'

'That might explain it, but it doesn't excuse it. He's not going to take this well, is he? Doesn't like admitting a mistake and certainly not to his junior officers. Look, sergeant, I know this is a bit unorthodox, but why don't we say I dug out the file, and it could all come from me? He'll still be furious, but he can't stay angry at me for long. He needs me and my department.'

The relief on Baker's face was clear. 'I can't tell you how grateful I am, sir. It would make a huge difference to me and the lads if you would be prepared to do that.'

'Sergeant, we're a team and we need to work together if we're to get things done. Sometimes, it's a little easier for one person to do something than another. Besides, I might just enjoy this one.'

Cuthbert had Baker return the file to the archives and then put in a new request for it himself, along with five other old cases where Soho prostitutes had been murdered. When it arrived back on his desk with the others, there was a clear paper trail to show that he had initiated a review. He waited a day and then phoned Mowbray.

*

'Chief inspector, good morning to you. I hope you are well.'

'People who enquire after my health, doctor, are usually after something, so what can I do for you?'

'I'm looking for a little of your time. I've been reviewing some old murder cases and there's one that caught my eye. It was actually one from December last year — a Mary Jones. I wasn't involved in it – my colleagues at Guy's handled this one – but there are some interesting similarities with our Soho killings. Do you think it might be worth going over?'

Mowbray was silent at the end of the phone while he searched his memory. He could not recall the killing of a Mary Jones at all. What on earth could he have missed that had prompted Cuthbert's interest? He agreed as casually as he could that, of course, he'd be happy to consult with the pathologist.

That afternoon, Cuthbert had to go through the usual rigmarole at the reception desk in the Yard to gain admittance to the building, but once inside, he leapt up the stairs to the second floor and Mowbray's office. Since Cuthbert's phone call, the chief inspector had been going over his own notes but was dismayed to find no record of the Jones case. He knew he couldn't ask old Jack Hills as he had attended the officer's funeral three weeks before. Whatever it was, he was going to have to play it by ear in order not to appear a complete incompetent.

'Take a seat, doctor. Remind me, which case is this you're interested in?'

'Mary Jones, although Belgian Marie was her street name. She was a prostitute strangled with a cable and was found in her room in Soho on the fifteenth of December. You'll certainly remember that day. It was the conclusion to our last major case.'

The penny dropped. Mowbray had not attended the crime scene and had not even seen fit to get the duty-room pinboard up for that one. He'd left it to Sergeant Hills, who concluded it was a punter who had gone too far and they had nothing that might help them find him.

It was one of the many such cases where the police knew they had no chance of a conviction so it was reported and shelved. Mowbray knew he must have read his sergeant's report to sign it off, but he couldn't remember any of the details.

'Ah, I do recall it. But tell me, what was it about this case that piqued your interest?'

'Well, the bite mark, of course. It's described in the pathology report and fortunately there is a post mortem photograph of it. It's not the best quality, but it does show the same pattern of teeth we've seen in the other four cases. What do you think?'

Mowbray had no memory at all of there being a reported bite mark on the body and was beginning to wonder if he'd even read the report. He was finding the whole conversation deeply troubling. 'And the other details? Did you see similarities there too?'

'She was strangled rather than smothered and she probably put up much more of a fight than the others, probably because there doesn't look to be any drugs involved. What I mean is that she wasn't unconscious when she was killed. And that bite mark, although similar to the others, was inflicted after death – he seems to have bitten her corpse.'

'No needle marks? Could that have been missed?'

Cuthbert answered the same question for a second time, assuring the chief inspector, just as he had Sergeant Baker, that with a pathologist of Dr Strangford's experience performing the post mortem examination, this was highly unlikely.

Mowbray went back to the photograph, still puzzling over why he could not remember something as important as a bite mark. He asked Cuthbert to show him the whole file, and he turned to the page with the senior officer's approval. It was certainly signed 'J. Mowbray', but it wasn't his signature.

What had Hills been playing at? he thought. His sergeant had never submitted the report for sign-off, and it looked as if he had done it himself and then buried the shoddy piece of investigation in the archives.

As Mowbray flicked through the pages, he was appalled at the standard of the documentation. He would never have allowed this to get through without serious revision. Noticing the chief inspector's deepening frown, Cuthbert began to wonder how he was going to explain it. He knew this was not Mowbray's style, but how would he defend it? The answer was not at all.

'This report is a disgrace. It has my name on it, and even though this isn't my signature and I've never set eyes on it until now, it remains my responsibility. I am not about to blame anyone else, and I apologise that you've had to waste your time reading it, Cuthbert.'

'I don't need your apologies, chief inspector, but perhaps Mary Jones does.'

'Tarts die every night in this city, Cuthbert, and every other city I don't doubt. It's a perilous game they play trying to get money from dangerous, vicious men. And some of those men are only going with the likes of these women because they want it rough and get their thrill from thumping them or throttling them. But, yes, you're right, of course you are. We should have done a better job on this one. How certain are you that this is an earlier killing by the same man?'

'Nothing is ever certain, but that bite mark looks to be too close a match to be a coincidence. So, yes, I think it's the same killer and that means we've got five murders now.'

This was the last thing that Mowbray needed. The chief constable and the deputy commissioner were already breathing down his neck and now he had to report that not only was there another one to add to the death toll, but that it had been sitting on their shelf at the Yard for nearly five months.

He knew the only way to deal with this was to conceal these facts in a wrapper of more interesting ones. And that meant progress and, if at all possible, some suspects.

'I need to review everything and decide on the next steps. Can you stay on and join us at the board, Dr Cuthbert? I'm going to call everyone in, and we'll be staying here till we've got a plan. If you're here as well, it might go a lot quicker.'

'Of course – just let me make a phone call. I'll need to let my housekeeper know not to expect me home for dinner.'

'And will she be terribly disappointed?' Mowbray raised an eyebrow.

'Don't be tedious, chief inspector. You know we've been through all that. She's my housekeeper and nothing more. She's not my lover, my mistress, my concubine or any other less agreeable word you might want to use. She runs my home for me because I am incapable of doing that for myself. I am a single man who spends too much time working and too much time reading books to remember to buy lamb chops, and one that has led too privileged an existence to be able to know what to do with them if I did.'

'All right, all right! I was only asking to be polite.'

'No, you weren't. You were asking because you have a prurient interest in my personal life which has exercised your imagination since we met. I expect I do not fit your idea of how a man should live, and I am afraid I can do nothing about that. Now, shall we see what we can do about catching our killer?'

Mowbray knew he had touched a very raw nerve and agreed to get on with organising the men for an unscheduled case conference, but he also made a mental note of everything Cuthbert had just said.

At the impromptu meeting in front of the case board, it was Mowbray, to his credit, who described the murder investigation from December. He highlighted the similarities with the more recent cases and openly admitted the investigation had been seriously lacking. True to his word, he blamed no one but himself for the failing.

'Regrettably, we don't even have a photograph of the

woman to pin on our board, but, sergeant, I would be obliged if you could make sure her name is added.'

They reviewed all the evidence and walked over the same ground again in case anything had been missed. However, the same conclusions were reached: the focus would remain on the smart set who were known addicts.

In particular, they would look at the young men and try to ascertain what links, if any, they had with the Soho prostitutes. And, of course, some of the girls might have a story to tell about their boyfriends, so they needed to put some pressure on them too.

When Sergeant Baker told Chief Inspector Mowbray about the latest witness statement from the Josie La Belle murder that mentioned a young toff named Napper, he agreed that they should have Maxton-Forbes in for a chat. The chief inspector also said that he would conduct the interview himself.

'These people need the fear of God putting into them, and I'm in the mood to be a frightful God today. Get him in pronto and let me know when he's here, Baker.'

*

It wasn't difficult to locate the suspect once Baker knew his real name and address. He was at home when the sergeant and a uniformed constable called, and he agreed to come to the Yard 'for a chat' without even asking what it was all about. It was only once he was seated on a hard seat in an airless interview room that he started to ask questions.

'You didn't really say what this was all about, sergeant. I'm sure I can't help you but, of course, I'll do my best. What is it you need to know?'

'Detective Chief Inspector Mowbray will be conducting the interview, sir. It's best if I let him explain.'

For a further fifteen minutes Maxton-Forbes was left to sit

alone in the room and he occupied himself with chain-smoking three cigarettes. When Mowbray arrived, he introduced himself and went straight to his questions.

'Mr Napier Maxton-Forbes, do you also go by the name of Napper?'

'Yes, everyone calls me that, why?'

'And have you also called yourself Norman Brown?'

'I'm sorry, I don't know what you're getting at. Who's Norman Brown?'

'You are apparently, sir. At least, that's the name you gave my colleagues when you were arrested on suspicion of prescription fraud on the ninth of May 1928 and again in August of last year. Does that jog your memory?'

'Ah, I see. There's clearly been a bit of a mix-up. I might have been a little drunk when that happened and—'

'And you forgot your own name, sir.'

Mowbray sat waiting for a better explanation. Maxton-Forbes tried smiling, but the chief inspector was the very last person who might find him charming.

'No, I don't mean that. I mean I was terribly embarrassed by it all and I didn't want to drag the family name through the dirt. And, I mean, imagine if the papers had got hold of it.'

'Yes, imagine. What were you doing in Soho on the evening of Thursday the twenty-fourth of April?'

'I don't know. I wasn't in Soho then or anytime. You must believe me.'

'Must I? I should believe someone who by their own admission lied to the police on more than one occasion? Think again, sir. Where were you on the evening of Thursday the twenty-fourth of April?'

'I don't recall. Probably at some party or perhaps a club, but I know I wasn't in Soho.'

'We have a witness who places you at the scene of a murder

in Old Compton Street that evening at around nine o'clock. So, sir, you need to do better than give me a line about some party or some club. I'll let you reflect on that.'

Mowbray stood up and looked at Maxton-Forbes, who was no longer trying to smile, the gravity of the situation starting to register in his eyes. The chief inspector left the room and instructed the constable on the door to make sure his interviewee didn't go anywhere.

'We need to let him stew a while. That should soften up the meat a little. I'm going for my tea.'

On his way back up to his office, Mowbray met Cuthbert on the stairs coming down. As the Scotsman greeted the chief inspector, he quickly repositioned himself two steps lower so he could look the man in the eye. Cuthbert knew this wasn't the moment to use his height as an advantage.

'I've just been speaking with Sergeant Baker, chief inspector. I understood you were busy in the interview room, or I would have waited to speak to you.'

'Yes, we've got one of your chums down there. Napper Maxton-Forbes. Why do these posh boys have such fucking stupid names?'

'I can't shed any light on that, I'm afraid, and, please, he's no chum of mine. I met him once at a party, as I explained to your sergeant, and I happened to catch sight of him in that rogues' gallery you have of known addicts. I hope you're getting what you need from him.'

'Oh, he thinks he's just going to smile and flash those big eyes and we're all going to offer to shine his shoes for him. Well, he's come to the wrong nick for that. I'll keep you posted though.'

Cuthbert was surprised to be so included in the investigation and thanked the chief inspector before apologising for keeping him.

Mowbray continued up to his office and took longer than usual over his tea. He knew from experience that suspects responded much better if they were left alone to think about it all than if they were hectored and abused. Fear of not knowing what was next was a much more powerful torture than anything Mowbray could inflict with his fist.

When he did go back down, a good hour had passed. He entered in silence and sat opposite Maxton-Forbes. As he expected, Maxton-Forbes began to talk.

'I'm mixed up in booze and drugs and I can't get myself clean. I've tried, I've done what the judges have told me to do and I've been to God knows how many places to get cured, but nothing works. All that matters when the hunger is on you is to get the next injection or snuff. I cash the prescriptions I can get at the chemist in Piccadilly – you know, the one that opens all hours. You'll see a lot of the addicts there any given night. Sometimes I go to Soho afterwards. There are some drinking clubs there, you know, bottle parties. They're supposed to be private parties, but you pay to get in and that covers the booze. It's just a scam to get past the licensing laws, I suppose. But I've never done anything like hurt anyone. I've certainly never killed anyone.'

'Would you know that for sure, sir? When you're high from the heroin or the morphine or the cocaine, or even all three, would you know what you've done at all? I have a woman dead and mutilated by one of your gang, and I think it could very well have been you. She was a prostitute, and I wouldn't find it hard to believe that a man like you might like to go slumming it on occasion.'

'No, you're wrong. I've never been with any of that sort down there. You see them on the street, of course, but I'd never go with one of them. They're disgusting.'

'So disgusting perhaps that you'd like to get rid of a few of them, eh, sir? Clean the streets up a bit? Was that it? Was that what made you do it?'

'I didn't do anything. I'm a drug addict, yes, but I'm not a murderer. You must believe me.'

'Yes, sir, so you said already.'

Maxton-Forbes was sweating and agitated. He could see the chief inspector didn't believe anything he said, and he could conjure up no alibi for the time and date of the murder.

'Have you ever injected white drugs into another person?'

'No. Is that how this woman was killed?'

'Do you know if any of your associates are in the habit of injecting others?'

Maxton-Forbes was reeling and didn't know what was happening or why he was being asked these questions.

'No, that's not the way it's done. People inject themselves, but we don't do it for each other. Why is this important?'

'Let me decide what's important, shall we, sir? Now, I need the names of your close associates, and by that I mean the other addicts you hang about with. Write them all down: names – real names – and addresses.'

'But you can't expect me to shop all my chums.'

'I think I can, sir, and that's just what I'm expecting you to do because if you don't, I will assume that you have something to hide or perhaps that you're protecting someone else who does. Either way, you'll be spending a lot longer in my company. So why not make it easy and give me the fucking names!'

The young man was rattled as Mowbray screamed inches from his face, spitting as he shouted. And then he took up the pen and immediately began to write.

*

Charlie Maxton-Forbes proved harder to track down than his brother because he was apparently in the country, according to his wife. However, two days later he also found himself sitting across the table from Mowbray in the same interview room.

He started off much as his brother had, using the charm and the smile that had helped him out of so much bother in the past. And just as quickly as his brother, he discovered its complete futility in this room with this man.

'Have you ever used a prostitute, sir?'

'I say, that's a very personal question.'

'Murder, I find, is a very personal business, sir, but I'll take it from your refusal to give me a direct answer that you mean yes. Now, have you ever used the same prostitute with your brother?'

'Steady on, what do you think we are?'

'That's what I'm trying to determine, sir. Now, please answer the question.'

'No, emphatically no. I don't know what Napper gets up to, and I've certainly never been with him and a tart together. I want to go home now.'

'I'm sure you do, sir, but I still have a few questions, so if you don't mind . . . Now, where were you on the evening of Thursday the twenty-fourth of April?'

'I don't have a clue. Why?'

'That was the evening when a working girl in Soho was brutally murdered. That was the evening that your brother was seen in Soho. That was the evening when your gang was at a jazz club on Dean Street. So where were you, sir?'

'I don't remember, I honestly don't. If we were all at the Gargoyle, I suppose I must have been there too, but I had nothing to do with this murder you're speaking of. I just go for the fun.'

'Yes, your lot do like their fun, don't they? It's just that sometimes people get hurt when people like you are having fun. In case you're in any doubt, let me make things clear. You are a suspect in this murder inquiry and I'm going to need some better answers if you want to walk back out that door a free man. I'll leave you to think about that for a moment, shall I?'

Mowbray decided to use the same tactic he had employed with the brother, and he left Charlie Maxton-Forbes to sit on his own in the interview room for over an hour. When he returned, he found the young man in tears and ready to tell him anything.

Unfortunately, nothing he said was new or of much interest. He confirmed that his brother Napper was a regular user of the street girls, and, yes, he had, on occasion, used them too, but he still vehemently denied sharing one with his brother. He was often in Soho and had almost certainly been there the night of the murder, but he was so high on cocaine that he couldn't remember. He said that Lizzie Hamilton-Jacques was with them, as well as his wife. Although Celia never used white drugs herself, she kept a check on him and his habit.

'She's an angel, and I don't know what I'd do without her. She certainly deserves a better man than me.'

Mowbray couldn't help thinking he was right. He also thought that this weakling was a very poor fit for his killer and decided that his brain was so rotten from the drugs that any statement he gave was likely to be inaccurate and therefore useless.

'You can go now, sir, but please do not think my interest in you is over. We will certainly be speaking again.'

The last of the Mayfair set was seen by Sergeant Baker as the chief inspector looked on through the observation window in the interview room. Elizabeth Hamilton-Jacques was like the others: in her twenties, refined, expensively outfitted and adorned, and thinking that coming to Scotland Yard was such fun – before it turned out not to be. She broke much sooner than the two Maxton-Forbes brothers and was eager to reveal the set's dirty little secrets in order to get away.

'Napper often leaves us when we're in the Soho clubs. He goes off for maybe half an hour at a time and never explains where he's been when he comes back. He does it when he's high. He uses a lot of morphine, but it's mostly cocaine when we're out. I don't know for certain, but I think he goes with the street girls. I think he gets a thrill from it.'

'Are you not Mr Maxton-Forbes's lady friend, miss? How does his behaviour make you feel?'

'I'm most certainly not his "lady friend", as you put it. Napper doesn't have such civilised or normal relationships. He likes drugs, he likes the clubs and he likes sex. And if he can get them all in one evening, so much the better. And he is also rather perverted. You should know that he likes not just one at a time. He even asked me to go with him, you know, with one of the prostitutes. He asked me more than once and probably asked others too. I can't speak for them, but I never went. I can't even imagine anything as ugly.'

'Do the members of your set inject each other, miss?'

'No, I've never seen that. People inject themselves, usually in private but not always. Some of them are attention seekers, you know, and like to flaunt it. I was even at a dinner party once when this woman injected heroin at the table, right there in front of everyone. I do think there's a limit.'

Behind the glass the chief inspector laughed and shook his head. 'These fucking people.'

Afterwards, Baker compared notes with Mowbray, and they both agreed that she was likely telling the truth for the most part, but they doubted whether she was entirely honest about her goings-on with Napper.

'She's been up those stairs in Soho. Christ knows what they do when they get there, but she's shared a tart with Napper the lad or I'm a monkey's uncle.'

'Is your money still on him for these murders, boss?'

'He's got to be in the picture. The thing is, I just don't like these people and I'm trying hard not to let that affect my judgement. It's always a fatal mistake to let emotions get in the way of good detective work. Looked at objectively though, I'd say he was our best bet so far. And if he's guilty, some of the others are going down with him because they'll be involved in this as well.'

Chapter 12

London: 5 May 1930

At the morning case conference, the recently completed interviews with the Maxton-Forbes brothers and the Hamilton-Jacques girl were the focus of attention. Baker summarised the findings as he put up their photographs on the pinboard.

'First we have one Napier Maxton-Forbes, also known to his chums as Napper. He is a convicted addict who, surprise, surprise, does not appear to pursue any occupation. He denies all knowledge of Soho and the girls there and claims that the addicts never inject each other.

'This one is his younger brother Charles, or Charlie, who is following in the family tradition by also being a drug addict. Like his brother, he sees himself as a charmer, but he wasn't feeling that charming by the time D.C.I. Mowbray had finished with him. He came across as a weakling, playing second fiddle to his big brother. He denied everything that was put to him. I think if we'd asked him in a gruff enough tone to confirm his name, he'd have denied that too. Compared to his brother, he seems a very unlikely suspect for all this.

'One of the other members of this set who Dr Cuthbert was able to identify from the Addicts' Index was this young woman, Elizabeth Hamilton-Jacques. She tells a rather different tale from old Napper. Apparently, he had a liking for the working girls, especially when he was high. She says he was often in Soho clubs and that he had even invited her to join him with one of the prostitutes. Apparently, he was looking for a little threesome. She claims she never did such a thing even though he asked her on several occasions.'

One of the constables couldn't help himself and let slip, 'Dirty bugger!' Mowbray glared, which was more than enough to silence him, and Baker continued.

'Napper also kindly gave us a list of his closest friends and allies, and so far we have spoken with five of them. Three young women, one man and one rather effeminate gentleman called George Royce-Blunt who gave his name, when questioned at his home, as "Rosie Bothways". I'll leave that one to your imagination, gents.

'Pretty run-of-the-mill stuff – more money than sense, the lot of them, all into morphine mainly, but the girls admitted they had been to heroin snuff parties in the West End. The man, Michael Torridon, was probably the most interesting. He confirmed that they all regularly frequented the jazz dives in Soho. He also said he had known Napper Maxton-Forbes since school and was very keen to share stories about his past.

'He certainly confirmed what the Hamilton-Jacques girl said about Napper's interest in threesomes, but apparently he wasn't overly choosy about who the third one was. He'd asked Torridon on a number of occasions to join in as well. The gentleman of course denied he'd ever gone along with him, but having spoken with him, I have my doubts. There was certainly something odd about him although I can't quite put my finger on it.'

Mowbray looked around the group and realised he was a man missing.

'Where's Cuthbert today?'

'Teaching, sir. He sends his apologies,' said one of the constables, only to receive his second scowl of the morning.

'This is all very entertaining, sergeant, but all it's doing is confirming that this bunch of raging addicts are exactly the perverted piss artists we thought they were. It's not getting us any closer to who did this. Any one of these toffs could have got drugged up and three-effed these tarts. He found them, fucked them and forgot them. Only he might also have forgotten the state he left them in. But we're none the wiser as to who it is yet. Baker, is there nobody on that list whose head isn't addled by drugs?'

Baker scanned the names Napper had written down and cross-checked it with the list Cuthbert had found in the Addicts' Index.

'There's Celia Maxton-Forbes. She's Charlie's other half. She doesn't have a record with C Division, but she's certainly at the centre of the set. Maybe she'll tell us what we need.'

Mowbray examined the pinboard, which was a mess of photographs and loose connections. By this point in an investigation, he expected to have a working theory, a list of plausible suspects and at least an idea of what was going on. In this case, he had none of these.

He looked around the group again and cursed silently. He missed the calm calculating brain of his Scottish pathologist but knew he had to keep the investigation going forward.

'Right, let's have the wife in. But, Baker, get me a little background on her first. I want to go in knowing what I'm dealing with.'

*

When Celia Maxton-Forbes walked into the interview room, she studied it before taking a seat. She sat without leaning back on the chair, crossed her ankles and turned her legs to one side.

Mowbray entered the room and could not help but be taken by her poise. She did not turn to look at the chief inspector, and when he sat across the table from her, she barely raised her eyes. When she did, she said nothing.

Perhaps it was on account of her physical beauty that Mowbray started gently on his questions, or perhaps it was because he could not imagine a woman like this being involved in such a case.

'Thank you for agreeing to this interview, Mrs Maxton-Forbes.'

'Not at all. I'm only too happy to help in any way I can. It often saves time, I find, to sort out these little misunderstandings face-to-face.'

'Indeed, madam. I wonder if you could begin by telling me how you know Napper Maxton-Forbes.'

'Oh, that's easy. He's my brother-in-law. That is to say he was forced into my life as a side effect of my marriage to his brother, Charlie.'

'You sound as if you have little regard for him.'

'Oh, he's a scoundrel of the first degree, but he's family, so what can one do? The brothers inherited a lot of money and they've never really been forced to grow up like real men. It's just their toys that have changed. You obviously know about Napper and his drugs. How could you not? I'm guessing that's why I'm here after all. Am I right?'

'We do have an interest in Mr Maxton-Forbes, and that interest does in part relate to his use of white drugs.'

'But there's more, isn't there? If that's all there was, I doubt you would be wasting your time speaking to me. What's he done this time? It can't be money. Lord knows he's got plenty of that, so it must be sex. That's his other little vice. Yes, I can see from your face, I'm getting warm. Now, let me guess. Has he got another baronet's daughter into trouble? No, that wouldn't interest Scotland Yard. What about forcing himself on a young innocent? No, I'm not sure he has the energy to work that hard. Oh, I know, has he been caught with some ladies of the night? Yes, that's it, isn't it? I had heard that he rather enjoyed paying for it. What was she, a five-shilling whore in some sordid little room in Soho?'

'And how would you know how much a Soho prostitute charges for her services, Mrs Maxton-Forbes?'

'I expect Charlie told me.'

'Is he also in the habit of frequenting prostitutes?'

'Of course not, but men just know these sorts of things, don't they?'

She looked at Mowbray knowingly with her eyebrows raised, and he found her gaze so disconcerting he had to look away to his notes. She always enjoyed the power she could exert over men with her eyes, and even sitting on the wrong side of the table in a Scotland Yard interview room, she was in control.

Mowbray regained his train of thought. He would come back later to Napper and his appetite for street girls. For now, he needed to know more about this woman.

'Tell me, Mrs Maxton-Forbes, what's your story?'

'I wish I had something as grand as a story to tell. I was born in England, but we moved soon afterwards to the United States. My mother was American, you see, and she and Papa rather fell out of love. He went one way, and my mother and I went another.

'We lived in New York, and that's where I started school, but of course because my father was still paying for my education and by now hated everything about America, he insisted I be brought up in England. I wasn't party to the discussions, as you can imagine, but some sort of compromise was reached between them and I ended up at boarding school in Switzerland.

'All very cosmopolitan but all rather dull, I'm afraid. The girls, me included, I suppose, were lost souls, with families who didn't quite know what to do with them. After that, Papa arranged for my coming out, and as a result of that particular cattle market, I was hitched to Charlie. Great family, oodles of cash but hardly a brain cell between them. And there you have it. You're up to date. Sorry – no international intrigue, no vice ring, no drugs and, even now, very little sex. Perhaps I married the wrong brother.'

'Tell me more about Napper and your relationship with him.'

'Oh, there is no relationship. I'm not at all his cup of tea.'

'Meaning?'

'Nothing, other than that my brother-in-law has particular tastes, shall we say, when it comes to women, and I'm not one of them.'

Mowbray found it hard to believe that any man would not find this woman desirable and suspected that she was lying. Hers was not a world in which he had ever moved, let alone lived. She was rich and privileged and like all her class was used to those around her doing her bidding. And that didn't just mean her domestic servants. She was used to getting her own way in her dealings with professionals and that included the police.

Her story was plausible but would be difficult to corroborate. And in any case, he wondered if the details mattered. But what interested him more at the moment were her dealings with the drug gang. Was she one of them? Her mugshots were conspicuous by their absence from C Division's files, but that might just mean she was smarter than the others and had avoided the inconvenience of arrest.

'Have you used drugs, madam?'

'Oh dear, you can't seriously think I'm like those silly little girls and boys whom I happen to live amongst? I'm so disappointed in you.'

'Then you won't object to showing me your arms, madam.'

'I do object because it's an outrageous imposition, but, here, take a look, if you must.'

She removed her matching silk coat and gloves and placed her slender white arms on the table. There were no blemishes of any kind, let alone needle marks, and Mowbray nodded his acknowledgement and invited her to put her coat back on.

'I apologise, madam, but it was necessary.'

'Only necessary if you choose not to take my word for it. Now, is there anything else because I am starting to find all this just a little tiresome.'

Mowbray was pleased that she was becoming irked as that meant her guard might fall. He was increasingly of the opinion that there was more to this woman than she was letting on. So he decided to press on without explanation. 'Tell me about Elizabeth Hamilton-Jacques, madam.'

'What can you possibly want with Lizzie? She's just one of Napper's girls. At least one that he doesn't pay for, that is. Or to be more accurate, one he doesn't pay for with money. Another wretched addict, I'm afraid. The Hamilton-Jacques are a respectable family. The father is a barrister, I believe, but it's the mother who has the money. I don't know much more than that.'

'So she is Mr Napper Maxton-Forbes's girlfriend?'

'Oh, I think that's putting it a little delicately. She sleeps with him, if that's what you mean.'

'I thought you said he paid for sex?'

'Oh, he does – all men do, one way or another. Lizzie doesn't always have the prescriptions she needs, and Napper always seems to have some to spare. It's just a business arrangement, really. I do think she's innocent though, unless of course being stupid is a crime.'

'Have you ever been to Soho, madam?'

'Of course I have. I've even been with Napper. That's where some of the best clubs in London are. We would usually start with the Gargoyle on Dean Street, but if the night was really heating up, we'd head over to the Blue Lantern in Ham Yard or even Uncles on Albemarle Street.

'Sometimes he would stay with me and the gang, and sometimes he would drift off. You know, to satisfy one or other of his little appetites. There was always booze, but it was mainly the music I went along for. They have some wonderful Negro bands from America and it's all so joyously alive.'

'Do you know on what dates you would have frequented these clubs with your friends, and especially with Mr Napper Maxton-Forbes?'

'Well, I'm not really that sort of person. You'll be asking to see my diary next. They would go when the mood took them, and I would follow along. That's really all I can say.'

'Tell me more about your husband.'

'Charlie is the second son and that really tells you all you need to know. He didn't get the looks or what little brains there were to share out, and he rather dotes on his older brother, who has led him decidedly astray.

'I'm sorry to say that my husband is also an addict, and it's probably my fault. I've known about Napper all along, and I should have kept them apart. A woman should be able to control her husband, but trying to manage Charlie has always been rather more difficult than I expected. He spends far too much time with Napper, so I try to go out with them whenever they hit the clubs, even if it's just to keep an eye on Charlie.'

'Does he go off as well, madam?'

'Yes, I'm ashamed to say he does. On more than one occasion I've come home alone in a taxi from Soho, my ears ringing and my furs reeking. Charlie and Napper might appear hours later, but my bedroom door will be locked by then.'

'You said earlier that your husband did not use prostitutes. Are you changing that story now?'

'Did I? I expect I didn't want to admit such a thing to a man. It makes one feel terribly inadequate as a woman, you know, realising your husband would prefer to have sex with one of those harlots. I expect it's the thrill of the forbidden that excites them. What they can take at home probably seems too easy, too ordinary after a while. But we've not even been married two years. That's what I didn't expect.'

Mowbray was watching her closely as she spoke. He could see the mixture of annoyance and failure in her eyes. Yet, again he was struggling to believe her. Her husband frustrated her — that much was plain — but did her disappointment in him run even deeper?

'Do you help him with his addiction?'

'If you mean, do I care for him when he is suffering from withdrawal, or do I encourage him to seek professional help, then yes very much so. But I rather think that wasn't your question. You were asking if I procure drugs for him. You know very well that the drugs he needs can only be obtained with a prescription. And not being a member of the medical profession, I am hardly in a position to help in that respect.'

'Indeed, madam, but you would be in a position to sweet talk a willing medical man into providing you with a prescription for your husband, or even for the others.'

'I'm not sure what you're implying. Perhaps you think I go around batting my eyelashes and men just do what I want.

If only that were true, life would be so much simpler. No, I admit I've carried them in my handbag for him when we go out, but I've never "sweet-talked" anyone, to my knowledge. I'm sure I wouldn't know how.'

Mowbray, however, was just as sure that she would be able to give lessons. As the interview looked as if it might go on for some time, he offered her tea, which she politely declined.

'Now, can we go back to your own background. You said you were born in England – what year would that have been?'

'It was 1908, and it was the eleventh of December in case you're thinking of sending me a card.'

'Yes, that's what we thought, but I've had my men do a little checking with Somerset House and we can't find any Celia Amersham – that was your maiden name, according to your statement, I understand – or indeed any Amersham at all born on that date. Can you explain that, madam?'

'I think I may have misled you when I said I was born in England. The truth is I was born while my mother was in America, and she brought me over here as a babe in arms.'

'Is that so? There is also another inconsistency that I need to iron out. You said you were schooled in Switzerland, but no passport was ever issued to a Celia Amersham in the last twenty years. How exactly did you get to and from your school if you were domiciled in England? And before you tell me you travelled on an American passport, we've checked with our colleagues at the Embassy in London, and they've never heard of you either. All this leads me to ask: who exactly are you, madam?'

'We all need a little mystery about our lives, don't you agree? I've just added mine myself.'

'So are you telling me you have lied about your past, madam?'

'I don't think it's a crime to have a past – do you?'

'That depends entirely on how you spent your time back then, madam. Perhaps you'd like to revise your story.'

'If you insist, but it's a much gloomier tale. I was born in England, that much is true, but very much on the wrong side of the sheets, I'm afraid. I never knew my father and my mother was a domestic servant.

'I was left to my own devices while she worked to keep us fed, and I had to learn fast like any young girl on the streets. The only way I could stay out of trouble was by being cleverer than them. And that I found easy to do.

'It wasn't long before I realised that I was really quite gifted at getting men to do what I wanted, without ever having to give them anything in return. I stole money from men who didn't even know how much they were carrying, and I stole it so that my mother wouldn't have to wash other people's underthings.

'We moved around a lot, and I met even richer men, and they were just as easy to dazzle and rob. Once you have the right clothes and you fake the right accent, the moves are easy to copy. Just watch them, these ladies of leisure in Mayfair, and you'll see their repertoire is pretty limited. It didn't take long before I could pass for one of them, and that's when I met Charlie.'

'Did your new social set not question your origins, madam? Did they never suspect you were just a fake?'

She frowned slightly at his use of the word but did not allow it to break her composure. And that was exactly how she had managed to pull it off – by detaching everything she was feeling inside from her outward appearance. She took her gloves from the table and very slowly put them back on, interlocking her fingers to make sure they were a snug fit.

'They don't want to know. They have no appetite for the impoverished. They simply don't see those at the bottom of society. In fact, they look right through those invisible men, women and children living on the streets of London nowadays. So, no, I could never have told them that's where I came from.'

'Does your husband know?'

'Oh, Charlie is such a sweet darling but ever so slightly dim. I told him one story and he believed it. The same one I told you about my American upbringing and Swiss schooling and then I threw in a car accident that got rid of Mummy and Daddy. He never really asks any questions. I suspect that's because he can never think of any to ask. I'm decorative, you see, and I look and sound the part. That's all that matters to these people.'

'You sound as if you despise them, madam.'

'Oh, I do, chief inspector, but needs must. Might I have a cigarette?'

Mowbray looked at the woman sitting opposite him as she took a cigarette in her blue gloved hand and put it to her lipsticked mouth. She waited, without asking, for him to offer her a light, and when he did, she drew on the cigarette and held the relaxing smoke in her lungs before softly exhaling.

Mowbray now knew she was a fake, as he had put it, but he also knew that there was nothing inauthentic about her beauty. Her complexion was perfect, and her dark violet eyes invited his gaze. She oozed elegance. There was no whiff of the back streets about this woman, nor any trace of her past in either accent or bearing. She had reimagined herself and through careful study and imitation had metamorphosed into the half-American debutante she claimed to be and the society wife which she undoubtedly was.

'As I said, it is hardly a crime to conceal one's origins. I'm sure it even happens with detectives.'

She smiled at Mowbray, who was stopped in his thoughts. Could she possibly know about his own past? How, when he was a child, his father had murdered his mother and her sister and had gone to the gallows for the crimes.

Mowbray had spent half his life running away from his past and concealing it from view whenever he thought it might get in the way of his progress. No one at the Yard knew of his family history, and he made sure no one asked.

How could she possibly know? Was she simply reading him, looking for the smallest of clues in his expression and his voice as she edged towards an imagined truth? In fact, she could know nothing about him at all, but she did know that everyone had a secret, and sooner or later they will tell it to you even if they try their best not to. Mowbray put his feelings aside and composed himself.

'Indeed, madam. Everyone has a past, but not everyone lies about it to the police. I think that concludes our interview.'

'I would normally say, "I do hope we can do this again sometime," but you'll forgive me if I don't. Charming as all this has been, I'm not sure I'd want to repeat it.'

'I hope we won't need to speak with you again, madam, but we know how to get in touch if we do.'

She lowered her head and caught him with her half-shut eyes. He did not give her the satisfaction of seeing him swallow hard but instead busied himself with his papers. She pulled her blue fur collar up around her exquisite face and left like a cat who had just failed to stifle the life from a small bird.

Mowbray was still preoccupied when his sergeant met him outside the interview room, and Baker had to ask him twice how it had gone before he got an answer.

'She's one of the best liars I've ever seen — partly because not everything she says is a lie. I know she's lying to my face, but it's impossible to tell which are the lies and which are the truths. She's certainly not what she seems — she admitted as much — but I'm sure there's something else too. And she's a stunner, which always complicates matters. What's Cuthbert's take on her?'

'I'm not sure he has one, sir. He had more to say about the Napper chap.'

'Yes, not so much of a ladies' man is our doctor. But I'll wager he'll have an opinion. When is he next over here?'

'This afternoon, sir. He's coming to speak with the new intake of constables about crime scene management.'

'Poor sods, they'll love that. Catch him when he's here and ask him to come up, will you?'

*

Later that day, Cuthbert paused in Mowbray's doorway and waited in silence to allow his presence to be felt. Without looking up from his paperwork, the chief inspector said, 'Good afternoon, doctor, it could only be someone as big and ugly as you casting a shadow like that on my desk.' He looked up at the towering figure in black and grinned as he invited Cuthbert in to take a seat.

'Thank you for coming up. I was hoping to get your opinion of one of our Mayfair set. I interviewed Celia Maxton-Forbes this morning, and let me just say, it was interesting. What did you make of her?'

'I've only met her a couple of times, but each time she was the brightest thing in the room. She's not just beautiful, she's luminous. Men swarm around her, but none of them know quite how to deal with her.'

'I didn't have any difficulty knowing how I'd like to deal with her, I don't mind telling you.'

Cuthbert didn't join in on the joke and tried hard not to look disapproving. 'Did you learn anything useful from her, chief inspector?'

'Indeed, I did. I learned that she's a liar, and an accomplished one, and that she's been lying to everyone for years. She's not a toff at all, but a con artist and petty thief. Illegitimate, from the

East End and crawled her way up the greasy pole using nothing but her wits and her looks.'

'Do you think she's mixed up with the drugs?'

'No, she's much too clever for that. And I checked her arms – nothing. She did say some interesting things about the Maxton-Forbes lads. Apparently, both have been regularly dipping their wicks in Soho, even though they both denied it when we first spoke with them. That puts them both firmly on my list of suspects. Both white drug users and both frequenting the girls. It might even have been the two of them, and if it was, there'll be a double hanging to look forward to.'

Cuthbert was not so sure. Having met both the brothers, he still found it hard to believe they would resort to prostitutes to satisfy even their most base desires. And what could possibly be their motive for killing the women? He thought this case was about something far more complex than sexual desire. However, he had no evidence yet to counter the chief inspector's conclusions, so he knew he would have to be patient.

*

The next morning, Cuthbert arrived early at the department and was surprised as he opened his office door to see a lamp still lit on the other side of the laboratory. It was one of the large equipment cupboards, and he made a note to have words with the janitor, whose job it was to make sure everything was switched off at the end of the day.

As he was turning the key in his office door, there was a rustle from the same direction. He picked up a large metal retort stand and raised it in readiness to bring down any intruder. He crept across the lab and threw open the door to find Morgenthal lying on the floor in a mess of blankets.

'What on earth is the meaning of this, Simon? Have you been sleeping here all night?'

Morgenthal looked up from the floor in shock. His mentor appeared even taller and darker than usual from this angle. He mumbled an apology but was barely able to say anything before Cuthbert hoisted him up and pushed him out into the laboratory.

'I will not be having a discussion with a man in his bed. Explain yourself, doctor.'

Morgenthal was unable to meet Cuthbert's fierce gaze. He knew telling the truth was the only possible option with this man, and he began falteringly. 'I . . . I did sleep here last night, Dr Cuthbert, and I apologise for that. I couldn't be at home and my parents have forbidden me to visit them. They say I should be at home with my wife.'

'And so you should. You are a married man, with commitments and obligations to that young woman, and what's more you have a child on the way.'

'But you see, sir, she's thrown me out of the house. She says she never wants to see me again and that she wants a divorce.'

'You fool, what have you done?'

Morgenthal straightened the clothes he had slept in and smoothed down his hair in an attempt to make himself more presentable. He was unshaven, and Cuthbert thought he looked much older than his years. He had been worried about his assistant for some weeks now, and in a way, he was glad things had finally come to a head.

'I've done nothing, sir. And that's the problem. Sarah wants me to give all this up and I've said I won't. She wants me to take up general practice and I've said I won't. She wants me to take more of an interest in her friends and I've said I won't. I've done nothing that she wants me to do and because of that she's said it's over.'

Cuthbert watched the young man crumple before him and fall into a chair. He looked dreadful. In the last weeks, he had lost the sparkle that was such a part of his smile, and even though his joviality had often irritated Cuthbert in the past, he now missed it.

'Simon, everything seems so final, so irrevocable, when you're young, but she doesn't mean it. She's frightened of what you've become and what that means for the life she had planned out for you both. And remember she's pregnant with her first child. Try to imagine what that must feel like, not really knowing what's to come, with your head full of horror stories about childbirth.

'The girl is terrified, and she needs you to help her through it all. I know she's angry just now, but very soon she will regret the harsh words she has said, and you need to be ready to go home.'

'But she's said she doesn't want to see me again. Where do we go from there, sir?'

'Give her a day, maybe two, to think about what's been said and then go home to her and apologise. I know you think you've done nothing wrong, but you have, at least in her eyes. You've confused her, overlooked her, deceived her even.

'You're still maturing as a man and as a doctor. She thought you would be the smiling Simon she met and fell in love with for ever, and she's just realising that you're not. But whether she knows it or not, she's changing too, and the biggest change of all will be when she becomes a mother. You may have to forgive each other and fall in love all over again.

'But in the meantime, I don't expect my assistant to have a five o'clock shadow at eight o'clock in the morning, so take your bags and go to my house. I'll call Madame Smith and tell her to expect you. Wash, shave and change and be back here by ten. This evening you can stay with me, but tomorrow night you will be sleeping in your own home.'

Morgenthal took Cuthbert's hand and shook it, but he would have liked to embrace the older man to express everything he felt for him — respect, thanks and something close to love.

That evening Madame Smith served dinner to the two gentlemen and listened as they talked. She found it rather endearing how much the younger man hung on every word her employer said and couldn't help thinking her Dr Cuthbert would be such a good father. And then the thought was tinged with sadness as she realised that would never be.

Chapter 13

London: 8 July 1925

Sipping the Earl Grey tea with lemon from the fine bone china cup, Esme reflected on how far she had come. She sat by the open window of her Mayfair flat and enjoyed the late morning sun on her face. Her poached eggs had been served by Louisa, her maid, and she glanced at *The Times* which lay neatly folded beside her crisp linen napkin.

She paid twelve guineas a week for the flat and its furnishings and a further twenty-five shillings a week for the maid. Then there were her laundry expenses, her clothes, cosmetics, perfumes and the gin and whisky for the crystal decanters on the sideboard that always had to be full.

She knew precisely what she spent, down to the last penny, and understood exactly what and how much she needed to do to earn it. But the way she still calculated it all was to equate it with the work she would have needed to do in the Stepney Docks as a shilling whore.

Now, she charged two guineas, sometimes three, and was also happy to receive gifts of jewellery from her admirers who vied with each other for her attention. Life, Esme thought, was almost sweet.

Six months earlier, Marie de la Rue had packed her things in Romilly Street and taken a taxi with her three suitcases the short drive from Soho to Mayfair. She had already signed the lease for the furnished flat as Esme Elizabeth Henderson, and as the taxi rolled out of Soho, she shed the accent she had used to wish the other girls *au revoir*.

By the time they were driving through Piccadilly Circus, she had replaced it with her clipped, upper middle-class English vowels, and as they drove along Brook Street, she even changed out of her French silk gloves into soft cream kid leather ones. If the cab driver noticed, he didn't say, but she brought him into her confidence and made sure he knew her new address and telephone number and exactly how she expected him to use it.

The flat was bright and airy and close to the square. She knew other girls worked the area, but she also knew she would never meet them outside. Gaslights in this part of town lit the streets, not those who stood underneath them. Now, she had a telephone and cards printed with her name and address, which she would share discreetly to build her new client list.

The men she had serviced in Soho could not afford her now, and she needed to meet gentlemen who could. That would require expensive new clothes and even more expensive outings. However, she had carefully planned the move and was sure her savings were equal to the task. This was, after all, an investment in her future. But first, she lay in her new bath and luxuriated in water that had come hot from the tap and then, wrapped in a silk robe, she wandered around her new accommodation.

There was a spacious lounge, a well-appointed kitchen and two bedrooms – one for her alone and one for them. She was particularly pleased that she would no longer have to sleep in the same bed in which she worked.

She lay on the divan and smelt the new sheets she had brought with her and promised herself that she would never again sleep on linen soiled by men. The workroom would need some reorganisation, but she was confident she could make it just as much an illusion as before. This time, however, she was planning to sell something rather more lasting. This time Esme was looking to weave her spells for someone special. This time she wanted someone for whom money meant nothing because for her it still meant everything.

*

It took her the rest of the summer, but once she was established, Esme's thoughts turned more and more to finding her brother. She barely knew where to begin, but she knew his name and his age and the one piece of information that might be the key – the name of his orphanage in London.

She paid a visit to the St Pancras Workhouse, and as she was escorted along the corridors to the governor's office, she caught sight of the thin, blank-faced men and women moving in regiments to their workrooms. Her rage almost choked her, but she had learned to hide any emotion that might be inconvenient.

'Miss Henderson, it really is very generous of you to consider making a donation to our institution. As I am sure you have seen, we do rely very much on the kindness of our benefactors.'

'And the children? Where are they, Mr Samson?'

'I'm pleased to say that most of the young paupers of our parish receive their education at our Industrial School in Leavesden. Do you know it?'

'I'm afraid not, but I think I would very much like to visit. Could you arrange that for me? You see, my family are especially interested in improving the lot of the children.'

'I quite understand. Let me see what I can do.'

On another afternoon, Esme took a taxi and found herself in another, equally bland office. The man behind the desk was probably only in his early forties, but he looked and acted older. She studied the withered left arm hanging uselessly by his side and calculated that it must have been a war wound.

'How is it I can help you, Miss Henderson?'

'Oh, you'll think me a rather silly girl, but my mama and I have this notion that we'd like to give something to the school. You see, Mr Gresham, we once had a connection. It was a few years ago now, but one of your boys used to work for us. He did some gardening, and we did grow rather fond of him. I'm sure you won't remember him – his name was Robert Compton.'

As she said her brother's name, she truly expected nothing in return but was heartened to see a flash of recognition in the headmaster's eyes.

'Yes, I remember young Robbie. He and his friend Michael were as thick as thieves. They went off together, what, it must be three years ago now. Good-looking lads. "Gardening", you say? I recall their talking about going off to see the world.'

'So you called him Robbie here? How interesting. We always called him Robert. And his friend, this Michael, what about him?'

'Oh, same story, I'm afraid. He was a foundling like Robbie, and they spent their years here before going out into the big bad world when they were both fourteen. I never worried quite so much about either of them. They were big and strong for their age, and I knew they would be able to make their way. Some of the others are innocents when we discharge them. They're the ones who keep me awake at night.'

Esme could see the headmaster had genuine concerns for his boys and in her head silently thanked him for everything she knew he must have done for her brother. She left Gresham's office promising to be in touch, but just before she went, she asked, 'What was Michael's name?'

'Torridon, I think. Yes, Michael Torridon.'

Esme now had more facts but was as far as ever from finding her brother. She did not know where he had gone, but she was comforted to think that he had not been alone on his journey.

*

Her Mayfair clientele grew along with her reputation, and in time she could be more and more selective about the men she entertained. She concentrated on the rich, knowing they would never miss the five-pound notes slipped from their wallets. And as a by-product she learned that money was no indicator of sexual taste or ability.

She knew a great deal more about these men's bodies than they did themselves, and she found she could manipulate their desires in ways they had never imagined. Soon they were clamouring for her attention.

Eventually, one evening, what she had long been hoping for happened. One of her wealthiest clients, an older man in his late fifties who visited her Mayfair flat every Thursday, was lying panting and spent on the bed in her workroom. When he regained his breath, he said he no longer wanted to share her.

'But, Henry, you know how it is. I'd simply love for it to be just us. Think how marvellous that would be. But I have to work to pay my rent, my maid, and all the hundred and one other domestic expenses one has to deal with.'

'Stuff and nonsense, Esme. That's just vulgar money talk. I'll deal with all that, but I want you to see me exclusively. What do you say, my darling?'

'Well, if that's the way you feel about it, Henry, it would be wonderful. But, I mean, are you sure? You do know that the rent here is really quite expensive.'

'No more talk of money, my sweet. Gives me indigestion. And don't talk about rent. I'll buy you a flat, a better one. And an allowance, whatever it is you need.'

And with that, Esme entered the next phase of her ascent. She moved to a larger, more luxurious apartment on the square and now, as well as her maid, she had a cook. She carefully made sure all the paperwork for the new flat was in her name, and the promised allowance turned out to be around three times what she had previously been earning. All that was required of her was that she was freely available every Thursday to do what she had always done for Henry – make him feel young and virile again.

She now had much more free time and again turned her attentions to the search for her brother. She could now afford to engage the services of a private investigator, and she provided him with the names of both her brother and his friend. After two weeks, he came back with the report of his first results.

'Miss Henderson, I'm pleased to say I've made some headway. I've been following up your lead about the boys possibly going to sea. I've been checking through the crew lists of merchant ships leaving London since 1922. It's taken a while, but I've found a Robbie Compton and Michael Torridon on board the SS *Normanstar*.

'It's a Blue Star merchant ship that does the regular voyage from the Port of London to San Francisco. They're first listed in May 1923, but their ages are given in the crew lists then as sixteen, and according to the dates you gave me, they would only have been fourteen at that time. My guess is the lads lied about their age. A lot of the young cabin boys do that.

'They're listed in different ships over the next year, all Blue Star merchant ships going to various places. Last summer, I lose track of Robbie Compton, but Michael Torridon is still listed and most recently he was on the SS *City of Oregon*. She's at sea just now but due to dock in London on the fourteenth of October, next Wednesday in fact.'

Esme listened with interest. If she could meet Michael, she would at least learn more about her brother and maybe even his current whereabouts. She paid the investigator in cash and asked him to keep looking for Robbie, but in the meantime to make the necessary arrangements for her.

'Perhaps you could meet the ship when it docks and identify young Mr Torridon for me. I would be so very grateful if you could, and then bring him to meet me. I don't know, maybe you could offer him some pretext about a long-lost relative and a small legacy. That should serve to attract him, don't you think?'

'It certainly will, and I would be happy to do so. If you wish, I will also stay with you when you speak with him. You can never be too careful with men you know nothing of, miss.'

Esme, who still kept a bloodstained knife under her pillow, was touched by his concern.

'Thank you, but I don't think there will be any need for that. Just find him and bring him here. I'm sure I'll manage to do the rest.'

*

The following Wednesday, Esme took her breakfast late and spent longer than usual on her hair and make-up. When the doorbell rang, her maid answered it and led the two men into the lounge.

The young man looked about him, unsure of what was going on, but as soon as Esme appeared in the doorway, he was shocked. Although he had never met her before, he had looked into her eyes many times, for they were Robbie's. On Esme's nod, the investigator made his excuses and left them alone together.

She looked the tall, tanned youth over and appraised his strength and character. He had remained standing, not wishing to dirty the furnishings in so grand a room, and Esme could see he was nervous. She was well used to soothing young men, and she smiled her warmest of smiles and explained.

'I do hope you can help me, Mr Torridon. May I call you Michael? You see, I believe you may know my brother, Robbie.'

The young man stiffened and looked away, and Esme could tell something was very wrong. She did not reveal the panic that seized her inside but put out her hand to take his.

'Please tell me what you know. And do sit down.'

He sat on the very edge of the seat and put his head in his large rough hands and covered his eyes. His story was fragmented and at times difficult for her to understand, but she learned that she would never meet her brother.

'It was in the Atlantic, miss. The waves were high and white, and the swell was something to see. Robbie was lashing some of the deck cargo to secure it, and one of the steel cables snapped. It was under such tension that it sprung back and hit him square on the chest. He didn't stand a chance. He was thrown back against the gunwale and his back cracked. When we got to him, he was already dead. I'm so sorry, miss.'

She could see the memories were fresh and still raw for the young man, whose eyes were filling with tears as he spoke. She, however, felt only a numbness she had not expected. She had spent so many years now thinking about her brother and then searching for him that she knew this was always going to be a possibility. But here in this room overlooking Grosvenor Square, the reality of it all was lost on her.

She had never seen Robert and never known him, so did that mean he had never truly existed for her? However, she knew, looking at his friend sitting opposite her and now crying openly, that he had most certainly lived.

Quietly and gently, she probed. 'Would you tell me about him, Michael? What was he like? You see, I never got to know him.'

'He looked like you, miss. Exactly the same eyes. He was big. Bigger than me and strong as an ox. We were only fourteen when he got us on that first ship, but we could both pass for sixteen easily. He was always the one to push me forward. I wouldn't have done half the things I have or seen half the places if it hadn't been for Robbie. We were raised in an orphanage, you see. We were like brothers he said and, well, I loved him like a brother, miss. We did everything together – saw the world just like he said we would.'

The young man was crying harder than ever. Esme was touched by his sorrow and decided she could not let him go.

'Tell me, Michael. What is life like for you now?'

'Miss?'

'I know I have no right to pry, but I imagine life at sea can be hard.'

'Yes, miss. It was an adventure when I was with Robbie, but when I lost him, all the enjoyment went out of it. Now, it's just drudge. Hard manual labour for a pittance and every now and then some shore leave to ease the monotony. But half the time, I don't even know what port I'm in. They're the same everywhere in the world. Watered-down whisky and drunken fights. I want to come home and start again.'

'My associate, who met you, did he tell you about your relative and the legacy?'

'He said something, but there must be a mistake, miss, for I don't have any family. I never have had.'

'Well, I admit he might have got some of the details wrong, but if you like, I could be your family. You said you loved Robbie like a brother. Well, I'm his sister, so that makes you my brother too, Michael. Can we help each other? I need to feel closer to my brother, and you're as close as I'm ever going to get. And you – you need that new start. As you can see, I have money, more money in fact than I need, and I want to help you. What do you say? Will you stay? Will you be my brother?'

Michael Torridon looked at Robbie's eyes sparkling in the beautiful young woman's face, and he knew he could not refuse.

*

Esme quickly found Michael rooms nearby and spent every day except Thursday with him, showing him how to be a gentleman. She bought his clothes and took him around London on her arm teaching him how to observe the rich young men and study how they walked and talked and smoked.

He was a quick learner, but as the weeks went by, he started to wonder about their situation, although he never once queried how Esme financed their lives.

'Esme, you have done so much for me. I can't take any more from you. It isn't right that a man should live off a woman. Let me pull my weight. Tell me how I can help you.'

'You help me every day, Michael, just by being with me. I don't feel alone any more. That's more precious to me than anything.'

'But–'

'But nothing. Now, there are a few things I need to tell you, my darling. You've been so kind not to ask, and I suspect you've guessed much of my story already, but if we are brother and sister, I want to tell you the truth. Do you think you're ready for that?'

'I don't want you to do or say anything that would upset you. If you want to tell me something, that's fine, but I don't think I have any right to your confidence.'

She smiled at his grace, this big strong-muscled seaman in his elegant new suit, and she told him everything that had happened to her since she left the Foundling Hospital. He listened in silence as she recounted the unvarnished tale of her fall and then her rise, of the hurt and the degradation and then the reclamation of her life and her dignity.

'I'm sure dignity is not the word many would use to describe my circumstances, but I am the mistress of my own fate now and that for me is everything. Have I shocked you? Or is it that I have disgusted you?'

'No, Esme, never that. If I hadn't had Robbie to look after me, I can't say where I would have ended up when I walked out of the orphanage. And if I had been a girl, your path might very well have been mine. Only, I know I wouldn't have had your guts. You deserve the life you've made for yourself. I just don't think I can be another man who takes from you.'

She took his hand and said that everything she had told him was so that there would be no secrets between them.

'That's the way this family should be and that's what we are – family, just like Robbie said. I know you have your pride, and of course this arrangement has only ever been a temporary one, just to get you established. Now that we've got those fingernails of yours under control, it's time for you to start earning your own living. I've been doing a little work in the background on that and there's someone I think you should meet. Let's just say he owes me a little favour.'

'But, Esme, I can't ask you to do any more for me.'

'You don't have to. I've already done it, and next time you can take me out to tea. And I expect Claridge's, so you'd better work hard.'

*

The following month, Michael Torridon began working as a result of a connection with one of Esme's former clients. He had been a regular and had fallen for her very badly, but like the others he had been sidelined when Henry claimed exclusive rights to her company. He now saw this as a way to get back on her client list after she had announced that she could no longer see him.

He had many important friends, one of whom owned a bank, and after one phone call Michael found himself suddenly on a board that seemed to require nothing else from him except attending the occasional lunch and always looking the part. The latter was easy, as his natural good looks had been groomed by Esme into those of an Englishman with breeding. She had taught him the rules of this silly society game, and, like her, he found he could pass unremarked in their circles.

He offered to repay Esme every penny she had spent on him, but all she asked for was his continued friendship and for him to tell her occasional stories of their brother.

*

When Henry failed to turn up one Thursday, Esme wondered what had happened to him. He was a man, so he might simply have grown tired of her and shifted his attentions elsewhere, but as she looked at herself in the wardrobe mirror, she very much doubted that.

She knew her looks would not last for ever, but she was only 18, and she knew she had several years left yet. No, something must have happened, she thought.

He had a wife and a large country house as well as his own flat in the city, so any number of things could have held him up. But he had never been late before, not once.

The phone call, when it came, was from his valet, who knew more about his employer's movements than most. He called simply to say that with regret he had to inform Miss Henderson of Mr Latchford's passing two days before. Esme made all the right sounds on the phone and thanked the manservant for his thoughtfulness in calling.

When she hung up, she sighed with relief that she had been spared the awkwardness of Henry dying in her flat, or, worse, in her bed. She was glad she had made sure the apartment was hers outright, for she knew that one day Henry would stop coming.

Similarly, the furs and the jewels were hers, but she could expect no further allowance, so she turned her thoughts to a change. It was time again for Esme to assume a new persona. There would have to be new clothes and a new past, and it would all be to attract a new kind of client altogether. This time she was looking for a husband.

She told Michael of her plans, and he was excited by the games she played with life for it reminded him so much of the way Robbie used to speak. They sat together over afternoon tea in the foyer of Claridge's and turned their attention to finding a new name for her.

'I think I might keep Henderson as a surname. After all, I don't plan to have that for very long for I'll soon be a Mrs Something or Other, but I think it's time to put Esme away. Do you think I look like a Lavinia or a Margery?'

'I've never met anyone less like one of those. No, you need something simple, modern, but at the same time a little timeless.'

'Edna?'

'Don't be silly. I have it.' He said her new name with different voices and different accents to let her hear how it would sound on the lips of others.

'Yes, that will do very well. Now, all I have to do is sort out Mr Right.'

'Now, there I can help you. It's the least I can do after everything you've done for me.'

'It's very kind of you, Michael, but I'm not marrying you. That would practically be incest. Besides, you're as poor as a church mouse.'

'Not me! There are a couple of likely candidates on the board at the bank. They're the right age, good-looking and most importantly they've got oodles of family money. I think they're on the board just to keep them off the streets. Not the sharpest tools in the box, but then you can't have everything.'

'Why not, Michael?'

'Because that would be greedy and that's not the new you. You're a young lady of good breeding and wealth but with no family. A poor little rich girl in need of love and protection.'

'I can be that. When do I meet them?'

*

Michael trailed the story of his cousin from the country, Miss Henderson, at the next of the board's luncheons. He wasn't overly effusive, but instead just hinted at her beauty and her poise.

'In fact, she really knows no one in town, so I'm thinking of throwing her a little party. Can I count on you to come and offer her a little distraction?'

As he expected, it wasn't difficult to whet their appetites for someone new, and he was confident that once they met her, they would need no further encouragement.

That weekend, Michael hosted a cocktail party in his flat and introduced the new Miss Henderson to the young gentlemen and their various friends. Unsurprisingly, she fitted right in. She enchanted all the girls and had the men eating out of her hand before the night was out.

The next day three of them called to ask her out. She walked out with them all and within the month she had selected the candidate she wished to marry. He was from a good family, and she had made sure with the help of her private investigator that they were thoroughly solvent.

His manners were charming and he asked so little of her, although he obviously found her attractive. He knew not to press a girl like her too hard, and when she politely refused to sleep with him until they were married, he knew she was a lady of virtue and he respected that.

Despite his thwarted desire, on her wedding night, her new husband did not make love to her. Instead, he slept slumped in a chair, his face on the table beside a syringe, which still contained some of the heroin he had injected, and a dusting of white powder that he had been snorting.

She had known that he drank and took drugs, but she had not let it distract her from her purpose. She looked at her wedding ring and then across at the young man she had married for convenience only hours before, and she thought about the journey she had taken from that doorway in Old Compton Street.

She thought, as she often did at night when sleep eluded her, about the mother who had left her twins there. She thought of just how desperate that girl must have been to abandon her own flesh and blood on that winter's night, and she felt so dreadfully sorry for her.

She knew that just as she had searched for her brother, she now needed to find her mother, if she was still alive. But where could she possibly begin? She thought of Michael and of all the support he had given her and wondered if he might help her once more.

Chapter 14

London: 16 May 1930

Sergeant Baker hung up the receiver and rushed to Mowbray's office. 'Chief inspector, it's just been phoned in by uniform. Looks like we've got another one in Soho. But this one he didn't finish. She's still alive.'

Mowbray stopped what he was doing and immediately looked up from his desk. His eyes were bright and eager for more information. 'Can she talk, Baker?'

'I'm going over to the hospital now to check. They took her to St Thomas's.'

'That's handy. Get Cuthbert involved and see if he can check her over when you're there. It'll be a nice change for him to have a warm one.'

Within the hour, Baker was knocking on Cuthbert's office door in the pathology department, so he could explain the situation to him. The pathologist became as animated as the chief inspector had been by the news, and he made a quick phone call to the house physician in the receiving ward and arranged to take the sergeant up.

As they walked along the windowed corridor from the mortuary block that housed Cuthbert's department to the medical wards, Cuthbert asked more questions.

'Do we know what state she's in, sergeant? I mean, how far did he get before he was disturbed? I assume that's why she's still alive, that he got interrupted?'

'That's the story we're getting from the woman that found her.' Baker consulted his notebook. 'According to her statement, the victim was in the upstairs room with a punter. One of the others happened to pass the door and said she heard some moaning, but, and I quote, "not the usual sort". Said she knew something was up and knocked hard on the door and asked Belle if she needed help.

'When she got no answer, she tried the door. It was locked from the inside, which apparently none of the girls ever allowed. She raised the alarm, and then the door flew open and a gent in dark clothes pushed past her and the others and ran down the stairs and out onto the street.

'When she looked into the room, she saw the victim lying on the bed, and she said the woman was moaning in a strange way. They tried to rouse her, but her eyes were rolling up into her head and she was breathing strangely.'

'Sounds as if he injected her with his usual cocktail of drugs. Listen, sergeant, let me go in first,' said Cuthbert. 'Given who she is and what happened, she might say more to a doctor than a policeman at this stage. Would that be acceptable to you?'

'Of course, doctor. This is your patch after all.'

The woman had been placed in a side room when she was admitted, and when Cuthbert entered, he saw that she was similar in age to the other victims. She was extremely pale, probably because she was anaemic as so many of these women were.

She was lying with her eyes closed, but Cuthbert could sense she was not sleeping. He glanced at the buff cover of her hospital notes where she was listed as Isobel Buckman.

'Good afternoon, Miss Buckman. My name is Dr Cuthbert. How are you feeling?'

'Oh, doctor, I'm sorry I didn't see you there. I've been cleverer, and that's the truth, but I'm still here, ain't I?'

'Indeed you are, miss. I know you've been examined by the young doctor, but I wonder if I could take a look too. Would that be all right?'

'Go ahead. I'm used to men taking a look.'

Cuthbert flinched at being casually grouped with the rest of his sex, but he knew this woman had more cause than most to think that all men were the same. Without touching her, he stood close on her right side and looked at her eyes and the skin of her neck. He looked at her bare arms which were lying on top of the bed sheet with the sleeves of her hospital gown rolled up. He spotted the red hypodermic needle mark in the fold of her right elbow that he had expected to see.

'May I open your gown, miss? I need to check for any other marks left by the person who attacked you.'

Cuthbert looked at the case notes and read the house physician's examination notes. When Isobel Buckman was admitted semi-circular bruises over her left breast had been noted.

He untied her gown at the neck and gently lowered it to expose her breast. He knew immediately that this was a bite mark. It was not as deep as the others and the individual teeth marks were difficult to distinguish, but he was fairly sure that when they compared it with the post mortem photographs from the other five victims it would be a match.

He studied the woman who had again closed her eyes and was grimacing. 'Are you in much discomfort, Miss Buckman?'

'You know, that's the thing. I didn't feel anything for a while but now I'm starting to ache all over.'

'I'll speak to your doctor, and we'll get you something for

that. The important thing is for you to rest and get some of your strength back. Now, there is a policeman here to see you. His name is Sergeant Baker, and he's a good man whom I know well. Would you be able to speak to him for me about what happened?'

The woman looked up at the tall doctor and sensed this was one she could trust. His voice was as gentle as his touch, and in her line of work that was a rare thing. She was not overfond of the police, having been hauled into the Vine Street Station by her hair on more than one occasion. However, she knew that what had happened was not a normal roughing-up by a punter and the other girls might be in danger.

'Yes, if you think it might help. Can you help me make myself decent first?'

Cuthbert carefully fastened her gown at the neck, smoothed the top sheet and rolled her sleeves down to cover her bare arms. He went out into the corridor and brought the sergeant in and instructed him to sit at the bedside.

'I'll leave you to speak to Sergeant Baker, Miss Buckman, and I'll arrange for some pain relief for you. Remember, if you feel tired, just tell the sergeant and he'll come back another time.'

The sergeant had never seen Cuthbert's bedside manner before because he'd never seen him with a living patient, and he was fascinated by just how courteous and respectful he was. He knew that Cuthbert would expect him to extend the same level of courtesy, and he tried not to disappoint him.

'Miss Buckman, could I ask what name you use in your work?'

'You'll have me in your records as Belle Fleur. That means beautiful flower, sergeant, and that's a bloody laugh, ain't it? Look at me – not so belle any more.'

'How long have you been a working girl, miss?'

'Twenty-odd years, dear. Seen it all, done it all, had it all done to me.'

'Can you remember much about what happened last night?'

'Some of it. I started as usual about seven o'clock, just when it was getting dark, you know. Had a couple of quick ones right at the start – blokes finishing work, looking for a bit of relief before heading home to their wives. After that, I was just standing in the street for a while and trade was slow all round. It wasn't until about ten o'clock or thereabouts that the other one approached me.'

'Can you describe him, miss?'

'Oh, it wasn't a man, sergeant. It was a lady.'

Baker stopped writing in his notebook. Had he heard her correctly? 'You mean there were two of them and it was the woman who approached you?'

'No, it was just a lady on her own. Your face – it's a picture! Did you not think we got that kind of trade?'

Baker did not answer, but the fact was he had never even contemplated that a woman would go to a prostitute. He knew there were lesbians, just as he knew there were homosexual men, but this was beyond his experience.

He had nicked women dressed as men and men dressed as women during raids on Soho bottle clubs, but he had never thought too hard about what they might be doing with each other or more probably with the girls and indeed boys on the streets.

'Do you often get women seeking your services, Miss Buckman?'

'Oh, it's not that often we get a lady, but when there's one on the street and we know what's she's looking for, there can be a right old scramble. They sure smell a lot better than the men, I can tell you, but they can also be harder work. Some of them just want to watch you touching yourself up, but others want a lot more. But the good thing is there's never any rough stuff. Or at least that's what they're usually like.'

'And this one, what did she want from you?'

Baker's imagination was not up to the task of sorting this one out. He was having a hard time processing this new twist in the case and all the time was wondering what these women could possibly do together. Nevertheless, he had learned early on at the Yard that it was his job to listen to things he didn't particularly want to know about.

'To be honest, I didn't even know it was a lady at first. Came up to me at the corner of Old Compton Street and Frith Street, my usual pitch, and I thought she was a gent. Very dapper, I must say, and it was only when I saw her face in the gaslight that I knew it was a woman. Didn't bother me, just thought my luck was in. Said she wanted to talk – a lot of 'em say that, sir, but they've got a funny way of talking when you get 'em upstairs, if you get my meaning. But when I got her up to the room, she gave me a ten-shilling note right off and sat in the chair while I got on the bed.'

'And what did she want for her ten bob?'

'Well, it wasn't what you think. She really did want to talk. Just prattled on and on. I couldn't understand half of what she was saying. But she did ask me if I was really French on account of my name, see. I told her it was just what I called myself. Then she showed me a necklace and asked if I recognised it. It were a pretty little thing, but I'd never seen it before. Then she asked if I'd ever tried this, and she produced a whatchamacallit, a doctor's needle.'

'Was it a syringe, miss?'

'That's it. Asked if I wanted to feel good, and, well, who doesn't want that? I wasn't sure what she was up to, but she came over and stroked my arm ever so gentle like – beautiful hands – and then I felt a little prick. I don't know what she did, but I suddenly came over all warm and woozy. Never felt anything like it. I must have gone to sleep 'cause the next thing I know there's all this effing and blinding and Betty's shaking me.'

There was a knock on the door, and Dr Cuthbert came in with a nurse, who appeared agitated in his presence.

'I'm so sorry to interrupt you and Miss Buckman, sergeant, but I think it would be best if we could ease Miss Buckman's discomfort. Sister Evans here will give you a small injection, miss. Will that be all right?'

'The last little injection I got ended me up in here, so I don't suppose it can be worse than that. But my chest's starting to hurt something awful.'

'Sister.'

Dr Cuthbert nodded to the nurse, and she quickly administered the injection, which rapidly eased the woman's pain. He turned to the sergeant and suggested they all leave the patient to sleep. Outside in the hallway, Baker learned why the nurse was so apprehensive.

'Now, sister, that wasn't so difficult, was it? I simply do not care what your personal opinions are of this woman; she is a patient in your ward, she is in pain, and she needs regular pain relief. I will be returning later today and if I find you have again deliberately withheld the medication that the house physician has written up, I will see to it that you are removed from your position in this hospital forthwith. Have I made myself quite clear?'

The nurse glared at Cuthbert but nodded curtly and went back to her duties.

Cuthbert turned his attention to Baker and without any further explanation asked about his interview. 'Was she able to tell you anything about the man who did this?'

'Yes, sir. She was able to tell me it wasn't a man at all.'

*

They both returned to the Yard and shared their joint findings with Mowbray, who took them out to the duty room to go through it all again.

'And was she absolutely certain it was a woman? She did say, after all, that she was dressed as a man. Couldn't he just have been an effeminate type? I mean, what sort of woman could do all this?'

As he spoke, he indicated the array of post mortem photographs pinned to the board showing the bite marks and the results of asphyxiation.

'That might be the point, chief inspector.' Cuthbert was studying the pictures too. 'I think none of us here can imagine a woman doing this, and that's exactly why she did it. She knew we would be thinking like this and would never consider a female suspect. With all women off the list of suspects, she would feel quite secure in the knowledge that she would never be brought to justice.'

Mowbray was frowning more than usual and running his hands through his hair, trying to make sense of it. 'But, Cuthbert, if it was a woman who did this, why? What does she get out of it all? Is it a sexual thing? I'm serious; please help me out here, gentlemen. I've seen a lot in this game, but this takes the cream cracker.'

Cuthbert had ideas, but all of them he regarded as rather too far-fetched to be of use, so he suggested the simplest explanation he could think of. 'It looks to me like this woman wanted these particular women dead. Their deaths were not accidents in some sexual game gone wrong; they were all deliberately asphyxiated. That much we know. In all but the first case, white drugs were administered by injection, which would have rendered the victims drowsy and incapacitated.

Again, in all but the first case, the bites were inflicted before death but probably after the injection.

'Now, one question that has puzzled me from the start is, why do that? Why not kill the woman first and then do the rest? But I think our killer is clever and knows that wounds inflicted after death look different from those made while the person is still alive. I think the reason for the elaborate staging of these murders was to make us think she was a man who had forced himself violently on these women and then killed them. But I don't think this killer had any sexual motive at all.

'I also don't think she wanted to hurt the women and that's why the drugs were used. Remember, these drugs are expensive, and no addict is going to waste them. Based on what we learned from Miss Buckman, she was clearly given a big enough dose to knock her out completely, and she has no memory of the injuries being inflicted. I suspect that was the case with all the women who had needle marks. The killer drugged them first so she could stage the scene convincingly.'

Baker had been listening intently to the doctor and was going over the latest statement in his mind.

'Miss Buckman did say that the woman had paid her ten shillings upfront and seemingly had only wanted to talk to her in the privacy of her room. That would support your theory, Dr Cuthbert, that there was no sexual motive.'

Mowbray quickly responded, 'And what did she talk about?'

'We didn't get very far with that, sir. Miss Buckman said she didn't understand what she was saying. And it was only then that she suggested making her feel good with the injection.'

Cuthbert knew they would never know what went on in the other rooms unless the killer told them, but he suspected it would have been the same performance repeated over and over again. He went back to the board and looked more closely at the first victim, Belgian Marie.

'Why was the first one different, do you think?'

'How would we know, Cuthbert? We don't think like they do.'

'But don't you think we need to try, chief inspector? Imagine yourself for a moment in the killer's shoes and it might help us to work out what's behind all this.

'First of all, you are a woman who can afford expensive clothes and has access to white drugs, and, what's more, you know how to use them. Then, for some reason, you want to speak to prostitutes in Soho. The only time of the day you can ever see them is at night when they're working, so you resolve to pose as a client to meet with them. While you can't pretend to be a man, you can pretend to be a woman looking for sexual satisfaction from another woman. Such a thing in Soho is not common, as our latest victim has confirmed, but it certainly isn't unheard of.

'You approach the prostitute on the street and arrange to go back to her room. You pay her and then you speak with her. For some reason, whatever is said cannot be said out in the street. You deliberately sought the privacy of her room to have the conversation, and whatever was said also meant that the prostitute couldn't be left alive to repeat it. For one thing, we would immediately know the culprit was a woman and perhaps she had even revealed her identity to them. So where does this leave us?'

Baker, who was following the argument closely, said, 'We're looking for one of the smart set who's into drugs and knows about the Soho sex scene. We're also looking for someone who is clever, and I would say fearless. Those streets are dark and dangerous places when there's no moon, especially for a woman on her own.'

'I agree, sergeant: fearless or perhaps even desperate. Desperate enough to risk Soho at night to get something from these women. And as for clever, certainly, which I would say considerably narrows the field when we consider some of the young women of that social set whom I've met and you've had to interview.'

The chief inspector, although listening patiently to all this speculation, found it hard to swallow. 'No, there has to be a man involved too. What about Napper and that part-time girlfriend of his? This looks like it could be right up their street, especially with his penchant for threesomes. If it's prostitutes, it's sex and there's no two ways about it. These women are low-class tarts – no one's going to pay ten bob for a cosy chat with any of them. I just don't think they've got that much conversation in them.'

'Not conversation, perhaps, chief inspector, but maybe information.'

'But what do they know?'

'They know about their clients. They know about the crime in the area. They even know about bent policemen. There's a great deal they know – information that someone might be willing to pay for. Let's not dismiss them as nobodies, chief inspector. I know you think of them as just so much human waste, but they're people and they have eyes and ears.'

While Mowbray was digesting that observation, he began to wonder just where this case might be leading. If someone was trying to extract sensitive information from these prostitutes, he had to admit it could be explosive. He knew there were all sorts who frequented the girls in Soho because it was an anonymous world in the dark. But what if it wasn't quite so anonymous? What if these girls could name names?

'Do you think that's what this is all about? Using the girls on the street to collect information?'

'I don't know yet, but these women knew something their killer wanted. She didn't just want a chat with them. These were not social calls.'

'What, if anything, do these women have in common?'

'Take a look at your board, chief inspector. The prostitutes are all older. It's been difficult to be certain about their ages, but they all appear to be in their mid-thirties, and some are perhaps older. They're all getting near the end of their looks and with that their livelihoods.

'All are fairly low types, most poorly nourished. We can tell that they have all had at least one pregnancy. They've all been using street names so we don't know who they were or where they were from originally, but their names certainly give the impression that they might be foreign. Beyond that, we're in the dark.'

Mowbray concluded the discussion and told Baker to take a closer look at the women's names on the list of addicts that had been supplied by Napper Maxton-Forbes.

'We've wasted too much time in this case already hunting down a fox when we should have been looking for a vixen. Get them in and grill them on what they know. And while you're at it, what about that club in Chelsea where the women go?'

'You mean the Archways, sir?'

'That's the one. Where all the lesbians go. If this is a woman, she's got to be an odd one and that place is full of them. Get down there as well and turn over a few stones to see what crawls out.'

When Mowbray had gone back to his office and closed his door, the long-suffering sergeant just shook his head. Baker knew there were over twenty women on Napper's list. So far, they'd only spoken with Elizabeth Hamilton-Jacques and now he also had to find time to go over to Chelsea as well.

Cuthbert saw the man slump wearily in his chair. 'Yes, I know, Baker, it's easy to scream for work to be done when you're not the one who has to do it. Do you want me to take a look at that list with you, and perhaps we can focus on the priorities? Remember, we agreed whoever it is has to have some functioning grey matter and that's got to shorten the field.'

Baker smiled and nodded his appreciation and pulled up another chair for the doctor at his desk.

'I only know some of these girls, but I would suggest that these two might be at the bottom of your list. But this one, Lucinda Bartleby, might be worth speaking to. And what club was he talking about?'

'The Archways, sir. You'd never have heard of it. It's a private members club, and all the members are women, and a lot of them like to dress like men, if you understand my meaning. There's been times we've had information that it's just a fancy knocking shop for that sort, but it's more like a safe place where they can do what they want. As long as they're not hurting anybody, I don't see why we should be interested. At least that's my way of thinking. I don't imagine we'll get much joy there with this one though. It's not their style.'

'So there's a club where women go to be with other women, in an intimate way?'

'Yes, doctor. I don't know what they do with each other in the dark, but that's what it is.'

*

When Baker first met Miss Bartleby, she was being ushered into the interview room. Like all of the others of her class that he had met, she looked as if she was enjoying the thrill of seeing the inside of Scotland Yard for the first time.

She was in her early twenties and elegantly and expensively dressed. Her short-sleeved jacket was navy blue with prominent white buttons arranged diagonally across her bodice. Her matching hat was small and close-fitting and her short white gloves were soft leather.

'Miss Lucinda Bartleby?'

'Oh, do call me Lucy, simply everyone does. Goodness, what a depressing room this is.'

'I'm sorry it's not quite up to your standards, miss, but we do our best. Thank you for coming in for this interview.'

'Did I have a choice?'

'You did, miss, and I'm pleased you made the right one. Now, can you tell me about your relationship with Napper Maxton-Forbes?'

'I barely know him.'

'Well, he certainly knows you, miss. Indeed, he gave us your name. So perhaps you do know him.'

'I have met him, of course. One can't avoid bumping into people at parties and the like. You know how it is.'

'You use white drugs, miss.'

'I realise that's not a question. You know I do – I'm in your files, after all.'

'And you frequent the clubs in Soho.'

'Again, not a question because you already know I do. We all do – the set I mean. That's where all the best music is, and, of course, a few other delights.'

'Sexual delights, miss?'

'That's very forward of you. I'm sure I don't know what you could possibly mean.'

'I think you do, miss. We know Mr Maxton-Forbes enjoyed the company of the prostitutes in Soho, and we also know he would involve others in your set in his liaisons. So my question would be, did you ever join him?'

'That's a loathsome suggestion. You don't know what you're saying. Napper never went with those tarts. Why would he? Look at the beautiful girls in his own set. He didn't need that sort.'

'And what about you, miss? Did you ever seek out any of the prostitutes?'

'What? What are you saying? Prostitutes are for men.'

In Baker's opinion, the young woman looked genuinely appalled by his line of questioning. Gone was the air of quiet superiority with which she had entered the room; now she wore an expression of despair.

'Miss, I'm sorry, but I have a few more questions. We are conducting a multiple murder inquiry, and we have reason to believe that our killer is someone of your class and someone who has an intimate knowledge of white drugs. Do you remember anyone in your set speaking inappropriately about Soho and the goings-on there? Someone who seemed to know more than they should about the prostitutes there. Perhaps even someone boasting about their involvement with them?'

'I don't know. I don't think so. When we went to the Soho clubs, we would see them on the street, of course, and occasionally a comment would be made. I can't be certain, but I think Lizzie might have gone with him.'

'Lizzie?'

'Lizzie Hamilton-Jacques. She's one of the gang, and I think she went with Napper when he asked her to. I mean, with the tarts. He would talk about *ménages-à-trois*, and I think he might have got her to take part.'

Now, the young woman was flushed and clearly very uncomfortable, but Baker pressed on.

'Do you think Lizzie might ever have gone back on her own?'

'No, absolutely not. She hated it. She as much as told me so. It was simply vile. Everything about it. Napper is an animal – they all are.'

'They?'

'Men, wretched men.'

The sergeant took down all the details in his notebook and tried not to take her outburst personally. He had been called worse in that interview room.

'And was there anyone else?'

'Michael was always with us, and he would often go off too. Sometimes with Napper and sometimes on his own. But I don't know what he got up to. I did see him once or twice talking to the girls, but I never saw him actually go with one of them. That's really all I know. Please believe me – I had nothing to do with this and I can't imagine any of my friends being involved. It's all too gruesome. We only go to Soho to have a little fun.'

'Of course you do, miss.'

Baker was becoming irritated by her attitude and he tried to suppress it, remembering his boss's words of advice about mixing emotion with detection work. He probed further and asked her about her addiction, her procurement of drugs and the nature of her relationships with every other name on Napper's list. She confirmed much of what Baker already knew but claimed not to recognise some of them.

By the time the sergeant had finished the interview, her face was blotchy and she was close to tears. When he told her she could go, she left in a hurry and with nothing like the self-possession with which she had arrived.

Chapter 15

London: 21 May 1930

Morgenthal heard the women's laughter in the room before he opened the door. He had come home early from the hospital hoping to spend some time talking with his wife alone. Immediately after he had moved back in, things had been very cool between them. They slept apart and exchanged only the most perfunctory of words.

In the last week, however, he had detected a slight thawing. It was only little things. She offered to pour his tea at breakfast, he opened a door for her, she asked about the weather, he asked about her mother. These smallest of concessions in what had seemed to be a war of attrition between them were welcome on both sides, and he thought to build on them.

He did not recognise the voice but knew it must be one of Sarah's friends. She had lately been receiving more attention because of her pregnancy. She was the first of her set to be expecting a child and there was understandable curiosity and even concern.

Her friends, however, had been one of the major stumbling blocks of their marriage. They had been his friends too, but in the last year he had come to see them as little more than spoilt children, who used their money and their position to justify their behaviour. His work as a doctor and especially his exposure to the darker recesses of human nature in his time at the forensic laboratory had opened his eyes to just how superficial these people were.

He steeled himself and forced a smile as he opened the drawing-room door. He had expected the voice to belong to one of Sarah's old school friends, who were popping in on a regular basis now, but the beautiful young woman who was perched on the edge of the chair was unknown to him.

'Ah, I do hope I'm not interrupting, darling. I didn't realise you had a visitor.'

'Simon, don't be so bashful. You remember Mrs Maxton-Forbes. She and her husband were at our wedding.'

'Oh, I doubt you'll remember me. It was such a glittering day and there was so much going on. How do you do, Dr Morgenthal? Your lovely wife has been telling me all about you and of course the happy event to come.'

Morgenthal was captivated by her violet eyes as she spoke. He found it hard to believe he had not noticed her at his wedding reception, but as she said, there had been a great deal going on that day. She held out her gloved hand. He took it and bowed his head slightly as he held it. She was in the palest of pinks, almost white, and the rich fur of her collar framed her face.

'Simon, we were just about to have some tea. Why don't you join us?'

'Of course, my darling.'

The maid brought the tray and Sarah poured for all three of them. Morgenthal couldn't help feasting on the sight of this striking woman. He could smell her perfume as he sat close to her and could almost taste the mouth-watering fragrance. She sat upright, barely using the chair for support at all, and she moved with deliberation. Sarah, sitting opposite, was already showing her pregnancy and looked to many eyes even more beautiful than ever, but it was Celia who drew his gaze.

'Tell me, Dr Morgenthal, what can we expect of the summer? I am so concerned with the state of things at the moment.'

'The state of things?'

'The economy, of course. I was just saying to Mrs Morgenthal before you arrived how bleak the outlook is for the manufacturing industry. Without that, what are we as a country? A few green fields and a crowd singing "Rule Britannia". No, this "slump", as they call it, looks to me to be developing into something much more serious, don't you agree?'

Morgenthal had not expected this. He was more used to being asked for his opinion on the latest developments in hem length or how dry a martini cocktail should be. He was also surprised to learn that his wife had been engaged in such a conversation.

'I think you're right. This is going to get a lot worse before it gets better. The signals from the United States are truly awful. There is talk that London might escape the worst of it, but what of the Midlands and the North? That's where the engine of our economy is, and if it falters, so do we.'

'Indeed, we do. Mrs Morgenthal, if you feel up to it, you must come along with me to the Commons gallery. Prime Minister's Question Time can be most enlightening. Ramsay MacDonald is such a compelling speaker.'

'But it's a Labour government. Surely you can't support them?'

'Well, I am rather of the opinion that irrespective of the colour of their rosettes, they are all the same under the skin. It's what they actually do that concerns me, not what they might promise to do. And Mr MacDonald has already made history by appointing the first woman to his cabinet. Did you know we had a female Minister of Labour? I think we can agree that's a step in the right direction. If there were more women in power, we might be in a very different place right now.'

Morgenthal nodded in agreement, but it was his wife who demurred.

'I'm not so sure that women have a place in politics. I think we should leave that to the men, don't you, Simon?'

Morgenthal had both women's eyes on him. He knew that whatever he said would annoy one of them, and he dearly wanted to please them both.

'I can see both points of view. Women are enfranchised, which to my mind is a great step towards making this a modern country, and as such women should be properly represented by their own sex. The elevation of women to positions of political leadership, however, has undoubtedly led to discord, yet it must surely be inevitable. Perhaps one day we'll even have a woman prime minister.'

'Nonsense,' said his wife sharply, while Mrs Maxton-Forbes smiled at him with those eyes. He thought it best to shift the subject onto safer ground, such was the delicate balance of Sarah's mood.

'Tell me, Mrs Maxton-Forbes, will you be going to the Flower Show at Chelsea this weekend? Sarah and I unfortunately might miss it, but I hear it's going to be bigger than ever.'

'Oh yes, we never pass up the opportunity to admire their geraniums.'

Celia knew she was being steered away from politics for the sake of a marriage and was happy to comply. She had an inexhaustible store of small talk accumulated for just such occasions. The tea was refreshed, and the chat turned to gossip.

'You don't mean to say he actually married her!'

'Not only that, Mrs Morgenthal, but they say that afterwards she still carried on seeing the other one.'

'Scandalous!'

'Yes, but delicious too. I mean how thrilling to have one husband for weekdays and another for weekends.'

The women laughed again and then remembered Simon was with them. Sarah bit her tongue in embarrassment. Simon was just happy to see his wife laughing and could forgive them anything.

'Now, I've kept you from your husband long enough, Mrs Morgenthal. I came for ten minutes and seem to have stayed over an hour. How rude of me. So I must be going.'

'Do let me show you out, Mrs Maxton-Forbes.'

Morgenthal accompanied their guest to the hallway, where she paused before the large mirror and adjusted the tilt of her hat. She noticed her lipstick was slightly smudged and took a handkerchief from her bag to dab her mouth. She reapplied a fresh coat to her lower lip and pursed her mouth to even it out. Then she smiled broadly to check there was none on her teeth and that's when Morgenthal, who was standing behind her and to the right side, saw it.

As she peered into the mirror, he saw the extra eye tooth, exactly as Cuthbert had shown what it might look like in his drawing. He knew, of course, that it meant nothing on its own, but he shivered nonetheless and showed the young woman out with slightly less warmth than before. When he went back to his wife, he immediately asked how they knew the woman.

'She's Ruth's cousin, I think. Or maybe cousin once removed, whatever that means. I'm not sure we ever met before the wedding, but it was Mama that put them on the list, or maybe it was Papa. Anyway, she is an interesting woman, don't you think? Full of very modern ideas though.'

'Yes, she certainly is, although in a good way. But I didn't know you were interested in politics, Sarah.'

'There's a lot we still don't know about each other, my love.

I've been thinking and I've come to the conclusion that we were too young when we got married. No, don't look alarmed. I don't regret it, but I think it explains things. I think we have to forgive each other a little for not always being the children we were as we grow into the man and the woman we're to become.'

'I am the one at fault, Sarah. You shouldn't reproach yourself. I'm going to try harder to find some compromise.'

'I don't want you to compromise. I don't want you to be unhappy. And I realise that all the things I thought were so important don't count for that much, not when you have this.' As she spoke, she caressed the growing child she was carrying. 'I want a home and a family, Simon, and I want love to surround our child. I want us to find each other again, and I want to be held by you at night.'

He said nothing but came over to her chair, knelt and put his head in her lap. She stroked his hair and they stayed like that, enjoying the warmth of each other until he was jolted by the smallest of nudges.

'Did you feel that, darling? He kicked me. I felt him.'

'Yes, there really are three of us now.'

*

When Morgenthal went to the hospital the next morning he was smiling. He had spent the first night for many weeks in his own bed sleeping with his wife, and he was beginning to see the glimmers of hope for his marriage and their lives together.

When he saw Cuthbert studying pathology reports from the recent series of murders in his office, he was brought back down to earth and remembered what he had seen the afternoon before. Before he even took his coat off, he knocked on the office door, went in and explained.

'Are you sure, Simon?'

'Absolutely positive, sir. She had a supernumerary upper right canine. I know there must be many people with that particular abnormality, but I thought you should know. If you think it's important, you can decide whether to pass it on to the chief inspector.'

'The chief inspector has already interviewed Celia Maxton-Forbes and I think he was rather taken with her, but you've met her and you're a man, so you probably don't find that too surprising.'

'She's utterly ravishing, sir. I've never seen eyes like them. And intelligent too. She's very interested in politics and has the highest regard for our Scottish prime minister.'

Cuthbert raised an eyebrow, unsure if his assistant was being pejorative with his reference to the prime minister's origins. However, he let it go as he had other concerns.

'I'll let them know at the Yard right away. It will be Mowbray's decision whether they have her in again.'

When Baker passed on the new information to his chief inspector, the senior officer was perplexed. Surely, it had to be a chance finding and of little relevance. He knew Celia Maxton-Forbes was not all that she seemed, but that hardly made her a cold-blooded killer.

He was having a hard enough time coming to terms with the idea of the perpetrator being a woman at all, never mind a woman like her. Sergeant Baker, however, had been less swayed by the woman's beauty and urged the chief inspector to reconsider.

'I think we should see her again, sir. I know you think she's very low on the list of suspects, and I know she's not even an addict, but surely this new development changes things. Even if it's only to eliminate her from our inquiries, it would be a good use of our time. Otherwise, I fear she might become something of a distraction.'

'And who exactly is she going to distract, sergeant? Do

you think my head is that easily turned? Get her in and get Cuthbert over too. I want him to watch and, if necessary, have a look at her teeth for us.'

*

Celia Maxton-Forbes was wearing red when she arrived at Scotland Yard for the second time. She moved as elegantly as ever to take her seat in the interview room. Mowbray had forgotten just how lovely she was and checked himself for thinking of her as a woman rather than as a suspect.

'Before we begin, I must tell you, madam, that you are being interviewed under caution. This means that you do not have to say anything unless you wish to do so, but what you say may be given in evidence.'

'So if I don't wish to say anything, I can go now?'

'Not quite, madam. You are still required to listen to my questions, and I do hope you will do me the courtesy of answering them.'

'Courtesy? That's a little rich coming from you. There's nothing remotely courteous about any of this.'

She looked about the room and thought that it was just as dreary and tired-looking as when she was last there. The walls were stained, the chair still hard and the table between her and the chief inspector as much a barrier as before. Nevertheless, she didn't show any of her apprehension, and wore her most relaxed smile tinged with only the faintest expression of distaste.

Mowbray offered her a cigarette before she asked and lit it for her. He pushed a clean ashtray across the table. She nodded and with her red gloved hand pushed it slightly back towards him.

'I have asked to see you again, Mrs Maxton-Forbes, because there have been a number of developments in our inquiry. Most importantly, we now know that we are looking for a woman as the killer.'

'And you think it might be me? Do you really think I look like a murderess?'

'In my experience, madam, murderers come in all shapes and sizes. Now, can we go over your previous statement?'

Mowbray read sections of the transcript from her previous interview and asked her to clarify the times she had visited the nightclubs of Soho with her set and pressed her on whether she ever went back alone.

'I hardly think that area is a place for a woman to be on her own, unless of course you're suggesting I'm a whore.'

'No, madam, I am not suggesting any such thing, but I would like you to answer the question: have you been in Soho alone?'

'Of course not. As I told you, I've been many times with the gang and mostly to keep an eye on my husband, but the thought of going unaccompanied is quite absurd.'

All the time, Cuthbert was watching the interview from the adjacent observation room. There was the same poise and the same measured tone of voice he remembered from their previous meetings.

She spoke with only the mildest outrage at being asked such questions, but as he studied her from behind, he could observe her back becoming taut with each of the chief inspector's probes.

'And the last time we met, you gave me two rather different accounts of your background, madam. So I feel justified in not necessarily believing what you tell me. I would remind you that you are under caution and what you say here may come back to haunt you.'

'Oh, I'm already haunted.'

'Meaning, madam?'

'Simply that we all have our demons. We've all done things that we're not proud of, perhaps things we wish we could change. Maybe even a whole life we wish we could relive.'

'And what do you regret, madam?'

'I'm not sure I'd know where to begin with that, but my marriage has certainly been a mistake. I thought he would be a great deal more of a catch than he turned out to be. But if you're going to regard a bride's disappointment as a crime, I think your cells might be filled to overflowing.'

'You said before that you had married the wrong brother.'

'No, I don't think Napper would have been much of an improvement.'

'Because he uses prostitutes?'

'All men use prostitutes because all women are prostitutes.'

'You can't possibly mean that, madam. You're a respectable married woman.'

'Really? How do you think I get these clothes, this jewellery? They say women like me live a life of leisure, but let me tell you, I work for everything I have, and that's always been the way of it.'

For the first time, she wasn't smiling, and her eyes had hardened. Mowbray knew he had angered her. Now perhaps he might be getting somewhere. But just as quickly as she had lost her composure, she recovered the softness of her expression and the slightest pout of her perfect lips.

'Of course, I don't quite mean that. I just get so annoyed when I think of how Charlie is throwing his life away. He won't last, you know; none of them do. And then where will I be? A slightly soiled socialite with only one careful owner, while he's lying dead in a corner from an overdose.'

She dabbed the innermost corner of her eye, but Mowbray was doubtful there were any tears to dry. The more he saw of her, the more he thought that everything about this woman was a performance. She was resistant to his questioning and could turn on a sixpence if he was getting too close. And he could hardly employ his more heavy-handed tactics with a woman.

He needed a new approach and knew just the person who might suggest it. He made his excuses and left Mrs Maxton-Forbes alone in the interview room, partly to let her worry about what was to happen next, and partly to allow him to confer with Cuthbert outside. From the observation room, Cuthbert saw Mowbray get up to leave and he made for the door too, meeting him in the corridor.

'Well?'

'I don't think she's as cool and calm as she's pretending to be, chief inspector.'

'That's just it — it's all an act. But what's she hiding? She certainly knows more about all this than she's letting on. She's maybe even in it up to her pretty little armpits. The Maxton-Forbes boys are still my prime suspects even if there is a woman involved. Maybe she's the accomplice — I don't know yet, but I've got to get her to talk. Any ideas?'

Cuthbert paced up and down the corridor outside the interview rooms trying to tease it all apart. He agreed with Mowbray that there was more to all this than she was saying, but how on earth to get her talking?

'Could you simply wear her down, chief inspector? Everyone has their limits, and if you tire her out, she might trip herself up. If she is involved in the murders, she might inadvertently reveal some detail that's not been in the public domain.'

'Sometimes that works, but usually with the more stupid ones, and she strikes me as very far from stupid. But it's worth a try, I suppose. Keep watching her for me, Cuthbert.'

The two men returned to their respective rooms and Mowbray resumed the interview. When he sat down again opposite Celia Maxton-Forbes, she barely raised her eyes from the compact mirror which she was using to check her lipstick. Other suspects fidgeted and sweated in this room but not her. She sat as still as a painting, her own work of art. She was barely breathing, and Mowbray had to look closely to convince himself she was real.

'Mrs Maxton-Forbes, I'm so sorry about that interruption.'

'Not at all. I'm sure you have a great many more important matters to attend to than me. You really mustn't let me keep you from them.'

'Madam, today you are my number one priority. Now, if we could just go over a few of the details again.'

For the next three hours, Mowbray made her retell her entire life story more than once. He asked her about every detail of her engagement and marriage to Charlie Maxton-Forbes. He asked again about how she had managed to squeeze her way between the cracks into his social circle and how she was able to fool everyone about her background. As he expected, she never faltered once, and her story was word-perfect every time. Finally, he broached the subject of her husband's drug habit.

'As I mentioned earlier, this case involves white drugs – the kind of drugs your husband and your brother-in-law use. You have admitted that you frequently carried these for your husband, but did you ever prepare his injection for him? Indeed, did you ever inject him with his dose?'

'No, that was never one of my little tasks. I wouldn't have the first idea how to do such a thing. All that mixing of powders and drawing it up into a syringe.'

'But surely you have seen your husband do it.'

'Yes, I have, but I don't pay attention to him when he's like that.'

'And you say you've never injected him, but again you will have seen how he did it. Is that not so?'

'Yes, I have seen that, but again, I pay little heed to the details. It's really all too sordid.'

'So, if you wanted to, you could mix a dose of white drugs for injection using a hypodermic needle.'

'I suppose I could, but why would I? Remember, I'm not a user of those vile poisons like them.'

'Oh, not for yourself, madam. I meant for someone else.'

Mowbray could see a trace of annoyance creep out from the edge of her smile and he pushed harder.

'If, say, you wanted to knock out a Soho tart before assaulting her, you could do that.'

'This is preposterous! What exactly are you suggesting? That I took one of those drabs up their stairs, drugged her, bit her, before, what, smothering her, slitting her throat? Please can we come back to the real world.'

'Biting, madam?'

'What?'

'You said "drugged her, bit her". Why would you think the murderer bit the victims?'

'Well, that's the kind of thing these savages do, isn't it? Obviously, I had no idea that's what really happened.'

'And you said "smothering her". Again, a detail we've never released to the press. So how would you know that's how they were killed?'

'I believe I said smothering or slitting her throat. They must be the two most common ways of killing a woman, surely. But what do I know? I am merely speculating.'

Celia Maxton-Forbes's back was rigid, and Cuthbert could see from behind that she was twisting her feet on the floor beneath the table as she spoke. Suddenly, she relaxed, and Cuthbert saw her lean towards the chief inspector.

Mowbray could smell her perfume as she whispered through the most seductive of smiles that she had been such a silly girl. She had promised Napper not to tell his little secrets, but she just wasn't strong enough to resist a man like Mowbray. He knew what was happening, but he kept quiet and allowed her to fill the silence.

'You see, he must have told me. I can't really remember when, but it must have been him. He does like the sound of his own voice. Surely you learned that about him when he was in here. When he gets high, he likes to talk about what he does to them. It's all ghastly, of course, but that's where I must have heard it. Imagine biting them! He said he wanted to leave his mark on them – what an animal.'

'Really, madam? There is only one small problem with all that. You see, Napper Maxton-Forbes couldn't have bitten the victims because he doesn't have the teeth for it.'

She stared at the chief inspector, who was now smiling, and removed her red leather gloves. She needed to have something to do with her hands.

'I can see I have puzzled you, madam. Please allow me to explain. The murderer unwittingly left a signature on those women. Distinctive teeth, you see, and Napper, well, he doesn't have them . . . But you do.'

She ran a finger along her teeth until it came to the small bump on the right side and smiled before shaking her head. 'Ah. To think, all that hard work and it comes down to a tooth.'

'I don't think you work that hard, madam. Certainly not as hard as those poor women who were killed. We've got five in the mortuary and one half-dead in the hospital.'

'Oh, I assure you I know exactly how hard they work in Soho. I know, you see, because for years I was one of them.' As she spoke, she touched the pendant at her neck. On the fine gold chain hung a delicate letter 'C'. It was mounted with a small, bright diamond, and she rolled it between her fingers, as if seeking comfort in it.

'Do I shock you? I don't mean to, but I think it's time for some truth. Such a rare commodity these days, and almost startling when you hear it. Though the truth has such a habit of being bitter on the palate. Lies, on the other hand, are so much sweeter, don't you think? But you're the wrong person to ask, I suppose. In this room, you trade in the truth, or at least you think you do. Well, it's finished now, and I'm tired, so what would you like to know? I promise to tell you no more lies if you give me another cigarette.'

Mowbray glanced to where he knew Cuthbert was watching and indicated the door. Before he excused himself, he gave her another cigarette and lit it.

In the hallway, Cuthbert was waiting for him. He knew Mowbray had called him out to seek his opinion, but he wasn't sure about what. Was he on the brink of getting Mrs Maxton-Forbes to confess to the murders? It looked as if she was about to tell him everything for the price of a cigarette. But if she had done it, what could her motive possibly be? Cuthbert didn't have time to ponder the questions, such was Mowbray's urgency.

'I still don't believe her, Cuthbert. She's been lying in there since she came in, and last time was just the same. If she confesses, that could be a lie too. She might be protecting someone. And as for working on the streets – have you ever seen one that looked like her?'

'Chief inspector, I agree she's a good liar, but she'll hang for any confession. I'm not sure there's anyone worth protecting that much. I think she could well be our killer. She's clever, she has ready access to white drugs, and she has the dental anomaly. I have no idea why she would kill those women, but it looks as if she's going to tell you. I suggest you simply let her talk and we might get the whole picture. If she does have a past as a prostitute, that might well have something to do with it.'

'Oh, I'll let her talk all right, but I'm not buying it, Cuthbert. I'm not buying it at all.'

Mowbray took his seat in the interview room and apologised again for keeping her waiting. He glanced at the ashtray now on her side of the table. She had finished the cigarette and he offered her another. This time, she politely declined. He decided to waste no time.

'Why did you kill them, madam?'

'"Why" is a rather complicated word when you think about it. It wasn't just one thing – one cause leading to one effect. It goes back to the beginning, really – my beginning, that is. I *was* born in England, I didn't lie about that part, but I never knew my parents at all. I was brought up in an orphanage after being left in the doorway of a shop on Old Compton Street. Apparently, it happens all the time. The Soho street girls give birth, and they have to get rid of the babies so they can go back to work. Can you begin to imagine how painful that must be for these mothers? To give up their babies so they can go back to those awful rooms. But, whoever she was, she must have felt something for me because she left me this.'

She showed the chief inspector the pendant she had been toying with. 'I've had it all my life and it's my only connection with her. It's nothing really, just a piece of cheap jewellery, base metal in fact. I had it gilded and later had the diamond added, but it's her initial, so later I made it mine.

'At the orphanage they didn't tell me much – I don't suppose they knew a lot – but they did like to taunt you with anything they thought could hurt. She was a tart, they said, and a foreign one at that. French, as if that made what she did even dirtier. So I grew up there, the French tart's little bastard, and they must have known all along but never told me.

'By the time I was fourteen, it was time to go. I couldn't wait to get out of there. How stupid I was – but not for long. The first man I met made sure of that. He seemed to be kind, offered me shelter and then raped me that first night, again and again. The second night his friends raped me, and he took money from them. The next day I was working the streets of Stepney for him, earning a shilling a time. There were at least a dozen a night. I was only fourteen, and they all used their fists when I cried.'

Mowbray listened as she calmly told her story, and he was forced to agree with Cuthbert: this was the truth, and, indeed, it was as bitter as she had said. Cuthbert for his part was listening just as intently on the other side of the glass and was equally sure that this was her testament.

'It was months before I could escape him . . .' She sighed, pausing for a moment to remember the circumstances. 'There's no need to bore you with the grisly details . . . I was only a girl and I had nowhere to go and nothing I knew how to do except what I'd been forced to do for him. So I carried on. I learned, I studied the rich, their silly habits, and I managed to make my way to the West End and then to Mayfair. The clients changed along the way, but what they wanted didn't. Eventually, I met Charlie at a party and, well, you know the rest.'

'Not quite all the rest, madam. What exactly took you back to Soho and into those prostitutes' rooms?'

'Oh, forgive me, I thought I had explained. I was looking for my mother, of course.'

Mowbray was surprised but did not show it. He nodded and urged her to tell him more.

'I was fourteen before I knew anything of my mother. I had always assumed she was dead. Can you imagine what that was like? Suddenly, to have your whole life turned upside-down and to realise she might be alive? Of course, when I was forced into prostitution, it didn't take me long to work out that she was likely to have been only a child herself when she had me, and, if that was true, there was a chance she might still be on the streets. That thought filled me with horror. To have to spend a lifetime like that. I had to find her, I had to save her, but I knew that would only happen if I first saved myself.

'As soon as I could, I starting looking, but I had so little to go on. She worked in Soho – she must have done to leave me where she did. I thought there might be a chance that she was still there because so few get away. But I didn't know her name, only her initial and the fact that she was French, and, of course, that she had to be old enough to have a grown daughter.

'I got Michael to help me. Michael Torridon, whom I believe you have interviewed. Michael is like a brother to me and was such a help. It was so much easier for him to ask around and find any likely candidates. They needed to be in the right age range, of course, ideally with some sort of French connection, and they needed to be mothers.

'He did it so well. I don't know what he said to them – it's so very difficult to get anything approaching the truth from those girls – but he brought me some names and then I took the next steps. I don't suppose I'm telling you anything you don't know, am I?'

'And did Mr Torridon know of your intentions, madam?'

'Absolutely not. He knew I was looking for my mother and agreed to help me. That's where it ended. I was just using him like all the others.'

'You said you took the next steps. What were they?'

'I realised I would need to go and meet them in person and that I would need to buy the information. After all, money is the only thing working girls understand. I couldn't pose as a man, could I? So I decided to go as a Sapphic. I knew from experience that the girls would be keen on my trade when they realised I was a woman.

'I found the ones Michael had spotted for me, and once we were in their rooms, I overpaid them. I thought I should at least make them feel good. I asked them questions and even spoke a little French. I explained who I was and what I was looking for. I showed them the necklace. But none of them gave me what I needed.

'I'm not sure what I was expecting – that one of them would suddenly recognise her long-lost daughter? But I thought if I asked enough of them, I might find her. Even if she wanted nothing to do with me, I might still be able to help her get off the streets and away from that hell. All I really wanted was to meet her, even once, to show her that I had survived, to tell her that I understood why she had to leave me in that doorway. I suppose I wanted her to know that I forgave her.

'The first one Michael found looked a likely candidate in the gaslight, but it soon turned out she was no more French than you, chief inspector. But after I'd told her my story and revealed altogether too much about myself, she turned the tables on me. I can't blame her – she saw an opportunity to make some extra money and I would probably have done the same. She knew I would pay a pretty price to keep my little secrets. A bit of blackmail to supplement her earnings. I should have been prepared for that, but I wasn't. All I knew was that I had to stop her talking. I panicked, and the only thing to hand was the table lamp in the room. I hit her with it very hard on the side of the head and then tied the flex around her neck. It was messy and very difficult, and I'm sure she suffered. I don't expect you've ever strangled anyone, have you?'

She looked at him in earnest and waited for his reply.

'No, madam, I can't say I have. I was in the war and all my killing was done at a distance with my rifle.'

She nodded sympathetically, almost as one murderer to another.

'Once she was dead, I started to think clearly again. I realised I needed to cover my tracks. It was really only then that I hit upon the idea of trying to make it look like a man. I know what men are capable of doing to women, so I thought I would add the bite just to finish things off and leave you in no doubt that you were dealing with an animal – I'm sorry, I mean a man.'

Mowbray never enjoyed an interview when it got to this stage, when the killer would calmly catalogue their crimes. It was the nauseating detail they would offer that he found so disgusting.

This woman had killed in cold blood, yet he had no doubt she was sane. That said, she had become hardened to the point of stone by her life experiences and had nothing but contempt for men. Cuthbert had been listening too and could not quell the feeling of pity for this woman that was welling up in him. He knew she was a killer and had shown no regard for her victims, but he could not escape the thought that she had been damaged beyond repair by the countless men who had brutalised her.

'After that, I resolved to do it differently. That's when I decided to take along Charlie's drugs. I couldn't stomach any more struggling, and I honestly didn't want them to suffer. God knows those poor souls have all had enough of that. And I had read something that your Dr Cuthbert was able to confirm for me later.'

Cuthbert, who had been looking away, was suddenly alerted by the mention of his name.

'We met, you know, at Simon and Sarah Morgenthal's wedding. They're a charming couple and expecting their first child. We were chatting, as you do at these affairs, and I was being interested in what he was saying. Men do so like that, don't they? He was telling me about how you can tell the difference between a wound inflicted before a person has died and one inflicted afterwards.

'I had already come across that in a murder mystery I was reading, but to tell you the truth I wasn't at all sure if it was true. However, it turns out to be a fact, so after the first one, if they turned out to be wrong, I invited them to take a little trip with me. While they were asleep, I made sure it looked like they had been bitten while they were alive. And then all I had to do was put a pillow over their faces. A little helping hand.'

The chief inspector looked up from his notes. She was almost describing putting someone to sleep and he was not going to leave it there.

'But why were you so brutal?'

'Brutal? I wasn't brutal at all. After I botched the first one, I made sure those poor women never suffered – unlike anything their trade made them endure. There was no pain. Yes, I did have to misdirect you. I had to make you think it was a man. And only men would do what I did. I should know. Do you not think I've been bitten, violated in the worst and most agonising ways? Do you not think they've tried to suffocate me? I know exactly what men, and only men, are capable of. No, those women felt nothing. That was the least I could do for them.'

'Surely the least you could have done was to spare them their lives.'

'Lives? I saved them from those so-called lives. You haven't the first idea of how such women live. I got away from Soho; they didn't. Every night on those streets, in those filthy beds, with those vicious animals. Year after year. I put them out of that misery. It was mercy.'

Mowbray saw her expression shift. Now she was telling the truth as she saw it. And she was angry. Even her well-practised accent was beginning to slip.

'Be that as it may, it was, of course, also a convenience. For you that is. By your own admission, you couldn't allow them to live. You killed these women so they couldn't blackmail you and spoil the life you had created for yourself. These were not mercy killings. You were saving your own skin. You murdered these women to silence them! Didn't you?'

She sat, her head now bowed, not meeting his eyes as he shouted at her. Cuthbert leaned into the glass to study her reaction even more closely. She was completely still, but then he saw her shoulders begin to tremble and then to heave. Was she crying? Mowbray was also watching her across the table, judging the right moment to demand an answer, but she spoke before he did.

'Yes. You're right. Of course you're right. I was only thinking of myself. But, you see, that's what I've had to do every day since I was a child.'

The young woman before him was no longer smiling, no longer the assured society beauty. She was leaning back in the chair now, almost slumped, and tears were welling up again in her eyes.

She dipped into her bag, found a small lace-trimmed handkerchief bearing an embroidered initial exactly like the one she wore around her neck and dabbed her eyes.

'And in spite of everything, it was all for nothing. I never found her, and anyway she had probably died on the streets years ago. I do wonder though if we had ever met without knowing — she on one street corner and me on another, plying our trade together in Soho's feeble moonlight. I'll never know now, will I, because for me it's finally over. Ultimately, a man will get to take my life. It was always going to be that way — it was only a matter of when.'

'Celia Maxton-Forbes, I am arresting you for the murder of Mary Jones, the murders of the women known as Dutch Edie, Jeanette X, French Renée and Josie La Belle, and the attempted murder of Isobel Buckman. You do not have to say anything unless you wish to do so, but what you say may be given in evidence. Constable, take her down to the cells.'

Chapter 16

London: 23 September 1930

The trial was swift, and when the verdict came through it was no surprise that Celia Maxton-Forbes would hang. But what was shocking was the lack of press attention.

Everyone at the Yard expected the case, with its links between high society, sex and drugs, to create a feeding frenzy on Fleet Street. Perhaps strings were pulled and palms were greased to protect the old family names, but as it turned out the press were more concerned that summer with the effects of the late-season heatwave in the capital which had claimed fifty lives and the unemployment figures which had reached new highs as the economic depression bit.

Mowbray, for one, was pleased not to see his name in the papers, although he still had on his office wall a clipping from his last major case. That was a likeness of him giving evidence at the Old Bailey, sketched by the courtroom artist.

This time, there were no pictures. Only the barest of facts were reported and the real identities of all involved except the murderer were concealed, as were the methods she had used and the reasons for her actions. *The Times* summarised it on page seven below the fold:

Celia Maxton-Forbes (21) of Grosvenor Square, Mayfair, was today found guilty at the Old Bailey of the murder and attempted murder of several West End women. All the victims were known to the police and Mrs Maxton-Forbes was said to have fully cooperated with the officers at Scotland Yard. Her motive, however, remains a mystery which she will take with her to the gallows.

Sergeant Baker was charged with archiving the files now that the cases were officially closed. As he was organising all the paperwork and crime scene photographs, there were a number of inevitable loose ends that still occupied his mind.

His main concern was the identity of the victims. For four of the women, they only had their working names. The very least the investigation could do was to assign the real names to these women who had met such tragic and anonymous ends.

He knew Mowbray would not sanction the use of police time to follow these up, so he undertook to do it on his own initiative and in his own spare time. The sergeant, however, quickly met a brick wall. There was no obvious way to put birth names to these women who led such clandestine lives.

Undaunted by the difficulty, Baker wracked his brain to find a way into the problem. What he needed was another head working on it. When he returned the Addicts' Index to Vine Street, he got chatting with the sergeant over there.

He learned that C Division had also been collecting similar files on the prostitutes in the area. As his opposite number got the files out of storage for Baker, he explained that they did not have much from the last five years or so, but the older files went back to well before the war. As the sergeant at Vine Street understood it, someone at the station had had an idea at one time of keeping track of all the working girls, and whenever they nicked them, they would take their details and their mugshots and then update the records if ever they saw them again. However, in more recent years the practice had rather fallen by the wayside.

When Baker opened one of the file volumes, he knew immediately they might be the key. As well as dates of arrest, the page listed known biographical details and, importantly, the prostitute's real name.

Also stuck to each page was a small photograph of each woman, taken at the time of her first arrest. The sergeant at Vine Street was more than happy for Baker to take the files back to the Yard to work on and remarked that it would probably be the first time they had been of any use.

*

After many hours' work on the countless pages, Baker made some progress, but he was still reticent about going to Mowbray with his findings. At several points during these recent murder investigations, Baker had found himself more allied to the pathologist than his own chief inspector. As such, he decided to share his findings with Dr Cuthbert in the first instance. He was sure, from what he knew about the doctor, that he would be interested, and he was also certain he would know how best to proceed.

Baker packed up the relevant pages and took them over to St Thomas's Hospital. When Cuthbert saw him, he wondered what had prompted the visit.

'It's always good to see you, sergeant, but I wasn't expecting you. Are you here to tell me I've forgotten something?'

'Not at all, Dr Cuthbert. I was hoping, once again, to get your opinion on a matter. A loose end, really, in the Maxton-Forbes case. The thing is, I've been trying to put some names to our victims.'

Baker told Cuthbert about his wish to give the victims of

Celia Maxton-Forbes their real names for the files, and how he had found out about the records that C Division had been keeping for years on the London prostitutes.

'They've got their photos and their dabs, as well as any details they could collect in what they call the Foreign Prostitutes and Associates Album. The records are likely to be incomplete and they mainly cover the years 1905 to 1925, but I thought I'd take a look, especially as all our victims were a bit older. If they'd been on the game for a while, they might have been recorded at some point in the last twenty years or so. We know their street names and we have their fingerprints, and we even have an idea of what they looked like at least in their later years, so I thought it might be as simple as going through all the files and cross-checking.'

Cuthbert was developing a profound respect for Sergeant Baker. He had worked with him now on several important murder cases, and he had watched him grow in ability and maturity into a thoughtful police officer. This was another example of his commitment.

Cuthbert himself had always been troubled every time he had sat through the duty-room case conferences, listening to these women being referred to by their street aliases. In Cuthbert's eyes, Baker's wish to give them back their real identities, even after they had died, spoke volumes about the man's character.

'And was it that simple, sergeant? Did you find any of them?'

'I've been going through the volumes from 1905 to 1910 and I've managed to find Dutch Edie and French Renée. Edie was just seventeen when she was first arrested in September 1909, and at that time she was calling herself French Fifi, but her real name was Edith Harwell, from Poplar. So she has her name back at least. French Renée was arrested for the first time in August 1910, and she would have only been sixteen. She was really Rose Atkins from Southend.'

'Good work, sergeant. What about Josie La Belle?'

'She turns up in the next volume and was first arrested in December 1917, when I reckon she was twenty-three. She had been a domestic servant in one of the big houses in Belgravia and had lost her position. Whatever happened, they never gave the girl any references, and like so many of them, she ended up on the streets. Her name was Josephine Caxton, and she was originally from Truro.'

'Have you had any luck with the woman we've been calling Jeanette X, sergeant?'

'I'm not sure you'd call it luck, sir, but I have come up with something.'

Baker looked grave, and Cuthbert was puzzled over what there might be in such historic files that could have upset him so.

'I think I have found her, sir. The fingerprints are a good match even though she looks very different. She was the first to be nicked, in June 1908, and there aren't many details because the arresting officer has made a note that she couldn't speak English. But we do have her real name, Claudette Martin. And she was originally from Paris, sir.'

Cuthbert could see where the sergeant might be going with this, but thought it was unlikely. After all, at the time, the London streets were full of French girls who had been trafficked across the Channel.

'I don't think that necessarily means what you think, sergeant.'

'Oh, there's more, sir. Take a look at her picture.'

Baker handed Cuthbert the yellowed pages and pointed out the small black-and-white photograph glued to the top of the page. The young girl bore no resemblance to the discoloured corpse Cuthbert had examined on his mortuary slab. She looked pale and frightened, but she stared from the page with eyes that both of the men had seen before.

'Good God, Baker, do you think it could be her?'

'I'm sure of it, sir.'

'We can't be certain though. Yes, she's French and she has her eyes, and the dates are right, but it could still be a coincidence.'

'No, sir. Didn't you see it? In the photograph, look closely.'

Cuthbert peered at the small image and saw what Baker had already recognised. The girl was wearing a necklace from which hung a letter 'C'.

'C for Claudette.'

'And C for Celia, sir. It's the one she always wore. She mentioned she'd had it gilded and the diamond added. It's the same one.'

Cuthbert sighed heavily and put the file down. It was clear to him now that Baker was right. Celia Maxton-Forbes had indeed found the mother she had looked so hard for on the streets of London, but for whatever reason she had failed to recognise her.

Perhaps Jeanette X, or Claudette Martin as she should now rightly be called, didn't give her the right answers to her questions. Perhaps she was wary of the cross-dressing stranger or the desire 'just to talk'. Perhaps she was the worse for drink at the time, and with her cataracts had failed to see the necklace clearly in the dim gaslight. Whatever the reasons, Celia had unwittingly murdered her own mother. And she had gone on to kill two more women and attack a third as she continued her desperate search.

'Dr Cuthbert, what do we do with this? Surely we have to tell her.'

Cuthbert looked again at the frightened young girl in the photograph. He double-checked the date of her arrest and calculated that the girl in the picture must have been three months pregnant with the daughter that she would later be forced to abandon in a Soho doorway.

The daughter who would later be raised in an East End orphanage and who would run away only to find the unimaginable brutality of the streets. The daughter who would be forced into a life of prostitution like her mother, but who unlike her would use her wits and drive to rise through society and escape. The daughter who would change her name and find respectability through marriage. The daughter who would hold on to the only remnants of her past that she possessed and who would spend her nights trying to recover the rest. The daughter who would search the back streets of Soho for the mother she never knew. The daughter who would tell her story to sad women in squalid rooms and when she found they were strangers would silence them. The daughter who would never recognise her mother even as she was looking into her eyes before smothering the life out of her.

'No, sergeant, we don't. Celia Maxton-Forbes will hang for her crimes, and there is no need to hang her twice.'

'But I'll need to tell Chief Inspector Mowbray.'

'No, sergeant, I don't think you do. I think you found the others in the files from Vine Street, but try as you might, you have been unable to put a name to the one we've called Jeanette X.'

With that, Cuthbert tore the page with Claudette Martin's details and photograph from the file, folded it in two and tucked it in his inside pocket. 'As you said, sergeant, the files are unfortunately incomplete, and it's a miracle you managed to find the real names for any of the others.'

'Yes, Dr Cuthbert, you win some, you lose some. It's a pity, but I suppose we'll just have to keep her on file as Jeanette X.'

'Good man.'

When Baker left his office, Cuthbert went out into the laboratory to look for his assistant, only to be told by the mortuary technician that Dr Morgenthal had gone for the day. Cuthbert consulted his pocket watch and frowned, not so much at the time but at the scuff mark he noticed on the toe cap of his boot. He forgot why he wanted to see Morgenthal and went back into his office to polish them.

His observance of the order and process was close to religious ritual. He knew only too well what had given him this obsession with having spotlessly clean boots. Although he had tried, he could never forget that night in the trenches – the mud, the rain, the fear and the horror of finding the rotting entrails of that dead German soldier clinging to his boot. Still it haunted him, and he could not remember it without his heart beginning to race, without choking on the stench, without experiencing the panic as his mouth filled with the taste of it.

He understood why it had started, but he did not understand why it persisted all these years later.

He opened the wooden box from his bottom desk drawer, arranged the tin of black polish and the rag on his desktop, adjusting them so they were exactly positioned, and then untied first his right then his left boot, for he never wavered from that order, and only then could he begin.

In small swirling movements, he worked the polish on the rag into the leather. As he felt it become gritty, he added his own spit and began again. He would spend as much as an hour to get the mirror-like shine he needed, and he would do it every day.

When he returned home, Madame Smith knew he was tired. It would never be anything he said, for his manners were unshakeable and his courtesy and respect for others would be the very last thing he would surrender to fatigue. But as she watched him come in, he was stooped and walking heavily. He hung up his coat and hat, and when he saw her, he brightened and greeted her warmly.

'Please, monsieur, go into your study and I will bring you some tea.'

'There's no need, madame. I'm aware you're already quite busy enough.'

She answered by taking his arm and leading him to the leather chair in his study. 'As you have learned by now, monsieur, it is usually best for us both if you simply do as I ask.'

He sat back and closed his eyes for a moment, only to jolt them open to escape the images that swam into his memory just before he fell asleep. It had been twelve years since the war ended, but like so many others who had been at the front, he was still reliving it in his thoughts and dreams. And this case had troubled him more than most by the memories it had stirred.

He thought of the prostitutes he had examined on his slab, and their countless clients. He knew what men were like, but he could never imagine himself to be one of them. Only he knew deep inside that he was exactly the same and just as guilty as all the others. He could fight his fatigue no longer, and he closed his eyes again . . .

*

It was his twenty-first birthday. They had been under bombardment for days and his sergeant had dragged him to a village near Ypres for 'some respite'. Cuthbert was the first of their squad in line.

As he was about to knock on the door, it opened and out walked a grinning, flushed youth adjusting his flies. He reached up and patted Cuthbert on the shoulder and winked. 'I've warmed her up good for you, mate.'

The room was tiny. The curtains were drawn to keep out

the light, but it crept around the edges and under the ragged hem. A single mattress sat on bare floorboards. As Cuthbert's eyes accustomed to the gloom, he saw the girl behind the door. She was bent over, washing between her legs with a cloth. Without looking up, she asked him to leave the money and pointed to a bowl where he could wash himself.

In silence, Cuthbert placed his two coins on the table and found the bowl of water and carbolic in the corner. Curly black hairs floated on the scummy surface. He began to wash his hands.

'Monsieur, not your hands.'

Without turning around, he unbuttoned his flies and tried to wash, but his hands were shaking. He did little more than splash the dirty water on himself, knowing that it was going to do little to protect either of them.

When he looked back, the girl was lying on the mattress and was spreading her legs. She could have been no more than 16. She wasn't frightened; she simply looked at him blankly to make her assessment of how long this was going to take. She sat up and leaned over, reaching into his unbuttoned trousers. 'Let me help you.' He was soft, and she sensed his reluctance, but she had a schedule to keep. She took him in her mouth.

He was startled at the sensation and the warmth of her tongue. He closed his eyes, trying to imagine he was anywhere but here. All sorts of pictures floated through his imagination, but he found one in particular that he held on to. He felt himself harden in her mouth and she pulled his hips towards her. Suddenly, he felt himself empty in her mouth, Then again. And again.

She slid her mouth from him and spat into a glass on the floor.

'Time to go, monsieur. Come back again and bring your friends.'

As he fumbled with his flies, trying to rearrange himself, he looked around the room and at the girl, and he was filled with the deepest sadness he had ever known. He had nothing to say. As he bolted from the room, another from his squad eagerly barged past him to get in.

Cuthbert pushed his way through the hallway full of men and out onto the street, where he turned up an alleyway, leant against the cold stone and wept.

*

Madame Smith could see he was becoming agitated in his sleep. She woke him up, poured his tea and handed him the cup.

'The case is over now, monsieur?'

'Yes, this one is over. The woman who did it will hang tomorrow, but there will still be prostitutes in the streets tonight, frightened young girls being abused by violent men who care nothing for them except their bodies. This city at night is a dreadful place, madame. But somehow the fact that it was a woman who did these terrible things makes it worse. Apparently, the prostitutes in Soho are used to selling themselves to women. Some even say they prefer it. And Sergeant Baker tells me there is a nightclub in the West End where women go. Women who want to meet other women, who wish to find love. It's called the Archways Club. I had never heard of such a thing.'

'It is in Chelsea.'

'Have you heard of it? How do you know?'

As he asked the question of Madame Smith, he immediately tried to bite his tongue. It had been a reflex, but he had just asked for an explanation to which he had no right. She could have ignored him, the way she often did to avoid his questions, but this time she felt it was the right moment to be honest with the man whose house she had kept for the last five years.

'I have been there, to the green door in the white wall. More than once. In fact, I would go as far as to say I am a regular – if that word can be used to describe me and those like me. Dr Cuthbert, I do not expect you to understand or to condone anything I do, nor, I must confess, do I need you to do so. As I have told you many times, what others think of me is no longer of any interest.'

Cuthbert asked for nothing else from her. His expression betrayed neither surprise nor acknowledgement, but in his silence, she found the space to say what she had never said to anyone.

'I am a woman, and I have the same desires as any other woman, but I have never found a man who cared enough to satisfy them. My husband was a brute who felt nothing for me as a person. He merely used me for his own pleasure – as all men use women.'

Cuthbert knew she was only speaking from her own experience, but he was still troubled to be included in such a generalisation. Then the image of a young girl in a shabby room in Belgium during the war floated across his mind, and he dropped his eyes.

He waited, but she said nothing else, leaving him to imagine what her life might have been like. Together, they sat in silence. Finally, he whispered, 'Marie, not all men are like that.' Whether the words were meant to comfort her or him was unclear.

She touched his arm and smiled to let him believe it might be so and told him dinner would be served at six.

*

The Morgenthal baby was born that same night. In the morning, when Simon arrived at the department bleary-eyed, Cuthbert could see he wasn't his usual self. He sat at the bench in the laboratory without removing his coat and stared into space.

Cuthbert watched him sit there for a good five minutes before he moved, and then it was only to glance around. The young man saw his mentor and immediately stood up and unbuttoned his overcoat and reached for his whites.

Cuthbert came out into the laboratory seeking an explanation. 'Is something amiss, Dr Morgenthal?'

'Not at all, sir. Everything is rather wonderful in fact. Last night, Sarah had our baby. He's seven pounds eight ounces and has everything you'd expect in all the right places. I counted his little fingers and toes, Dr Cuthbert, and they're all there. And he has such a head of dark hair.'

Cuthbert watched the young man swallow his emotion and fight back his tears of joy.

'Congratulations, Simon. You're a father. And there is nothing more creative you will ever do. Tell me, is Sarah well?'

'Oh, she's wonderful. I don't know how they do it, sir. But she has made the most beautiful baby I have ever seen. You know he actually held my finger. He can do that already and he's only a few hours old.'

'I'm sure he's going to be a very gifted child, just like his parents. Now, young man, you don't look as if you've had too much sleep. Why not take yourself home and come back in tomorrow when you're rested? The work will still be here.'

Morgenthal looked at Cuthbert and wanted to thank him for much more than the time off he was being granted. He wanted to tell him that his wisdom and guidance had been what had kept Sarah and him together these last months. And he wanted him to know that now he understood what his life was for.

'Get your coat on and get yourself home to bed. That's an order. And tell Sarah I couldn't be happier for her. I know she has not always been my biggest fan, but please do tell her I hope she'll introduce me to the latest addition to the family soon. I don't suppose you have a name for the young lad yet?'

'Oh yes, we do. It was Sarah's idea. We're calling him Jack, after someone we both admire enormously.'

Cuthbert tensed and swallowed hard to save himself from embarrassment. He nodded and smiled at Simon and ushered him away with a flap of his hand.

He went back into his office, closed the door and leaned back against it. He thought about the young man's rapture on becoming a father, he thought of the new mother, and he thought of the baby called Jack. He closed his eyes to imagine how he himself might feel if he had a son – someone to raise and mould, to protect and find pride in, to admire and ultimately to be in awe of. A babe, a child, a boy, and then a man to take his place when his life was over. He wrestled with the images, but the thoughts were futile.

The telephone on Cuthbert's desk rang loudly, wrenching him away from his dream. It was an outside call, and he sighed. What did the Yard have for him now? He let it ring for a moment longer than usual to recover some composure and then picked it up. The detective constable on the other end apologised as always for disturbing him but asked if he could come straight away.

Author's Note

This is a work of fiction, but I have tried to set it in a very real world that existed on the streets of London and Paris around a century ago. This is a world we can imagine, and it is one which we can revisit to some extent through the many testimonies left behind by those who lived in it. The work of remarkable contemporary historians also allows us to see that world through multiple lenses and different eyes.

I am indebted to many people whose work has made this novel possible, especially those who have written eloquently about Paris in *La Belle Époque*, the forensic analysis of drugs in the early twentieth century, the London drug scene in the early 1930s and the Metropolitan Police's approach to street prostitution in the interwar years.

Specifically, I would like to acknowledge the following:

John Glaister's 1915 3rd edition of his *A Text-book of Medical Jurisprudence and Toxicology*.

Charles C. Fulton & John B. Dalton's 1941 paper in the *Journal of Criminal Law and Criminology* which provided invaluable details of the micro-crystal identification tests for heroin, morphine and cocaine.

Virginia Berridge's 1988 article in *Medical History*: 'The Origins of the English Drug "Scene" 1890–1930'.

Christopher Hallam's 2016 thesis, 'Script Doctors and Vicious Addicts: Subcultures, Drugs, and Regulation under the "British System", c. 1917 to c. 1960'.

Stefan Slater's 2007 article in the *London Journal*: 'Pimps, police and *filles de joie*: foreign prostitution in interwar London'.

Stefan Slater's 2009 article in *Crime, History & Societies*: 'Prostitutes and popular history: notes on the "underworld", 1918–1939'.

Stefan Slater's 2010 article in the *Journal of British Studies*: 'Containment: managing street prostitution in London, 1918–1959'.

Stefan Slater's 2012 article in *Law, Crime and History*: 'Street disorder in the metropolis, 1905–1939'.

Jacqueline Banerjee, who has written about the history of the Foundling Hospital in Bloomsbury on the website Victorian Web – www.victorianweb.org.

THE DR JACK CUTHBERT MYSTERY SERIES

BOOK 1 *The Silent House of Sleep* (January 2025)

Death is a lonely business

No one who meets Dr Jack Cuthbert forgets him. Tall, urbane, brilliant but damaged, the Scottish pathologist is the best that D.C.I. Mowbray of Scotland Yard has seen. But Cuthbert is a man who lives with secrets, and he is still haunted by demons from the trenches in Ypres. When not one but two corpses are discovered in a London park in 1929, Cuthbert must use every tool at his disposal to solve the mystery of their deaths. In the end, the horrifying truth is more shocking than even he could have imagined.

BOOK 2 *The Moon's More Feeble Fire* (spring 2025)

She was someone's daughter

In 1930, the killing of a Soho prostitute is hardly a priority for Scotland Yard. But when a second, similar murder comes to light, and then a third, everything changes. Cuthbert and his team find themselves in a nightmarish world of people-trafficking, prostitution and drug use amongst the upper classes. Using all his forensic skills, Cuthbert sets out to solve one of the most baffling cases of his career. One final question remains unanswered until a faded photograph reveals its tragic secret.

BOOK 3 *To the Shades Descend* (summer 2025)

The dead all have stories to tell

A visit to Glasgow for a job interview in 1931 unexpectedly places Cuthbert at the centre of a devastating crime. Unwittingly, he finds himself working at the intersection between rising British fascism, anti-Semitism and the infamous Glasgow razor gangs. To solve the case, Cuthbert needs to rely on all the expertise he can gather from those around him. But who can he trust?

BOOK 4 *The Shadows and the Dust* (autumn 2025)

Sins never stay buried

Like all pathologists, Cuthbert finds dealing with dead children the hardest part of his job. However, when the body of a young boy is found in the grounds of a church orphanage, Cuthbert not only has to steel himself for the task ahead, he is also forced to revisit his own childhood grief. The boy in his shallow grave has been interred with some ritual, but just how did he die? And why was he killed? Working closely with his assistant and the team at Scotland Yard, Cuthbert slowly and painstakingly reveals the terrible truth.

Acknowledgements

Many people who read the first Dr Jack Cuthbert novel, *The Silent House of Sleep*, asked, 'What happens next?' And it is to them that I owe the publication of this second novel. Again, I must particularly thank my earliest readers, Anne, Ellen and Alec as well as Valerie, S.J. and Alex, all of whom gave me invaluable feedback on my first drafts. I would also like to acknowledge the editorial contributions made by Sharon Mail.

Once again, the team at my publisher, Polygon, have been both supportive and generous with their time. My amazing editor there, Alison Rae, has excelled herself once more to ensure that my telling of Jack Cuthbert's story is as clear as possible.

And finally, no acknowledgement would be complete with mention of the one person who makes my writing and my life possible: Moira.